HUMAN EARTH AWAKENING

A NEW STORY FOR A NEW WORLD

Robert & Christine Gerzon

HUMAN EARTH AWAKENING
A New Story for a New World

Copyright & credits

Credits:
Quotation page photo: © Denis Tabler/Shutterstock
Diagrams: Robert Gerzon

Ebook ISBN 978-1-7354554-0-2
Paperback ISBN 978-1-7354554-1-9

Contact:
HumanEarthAwakening.com

Table of Contents

"When you see the Earth from space, you see the symbol of the new mythology to come...one that is talking about the planet and everybody on it...All myths are about the transformation of consciousness."
Joseph Campbell, mythology scholar and author

"It's all a question of story. We are in trouble just now because we do not have a good story. We are in between stories...The great historic mission of our time is to reinvent the human, at the species level...by means of story."
Thomas Berry, theologian and cultural historian

"Human beings must have an epic, a sublime account of how the world was created and how humanity became part of it... The evolutionary epic is probably the best myth we will ever have."
E.O. Wilson, founder of sociobiology, Harvard University

Introduction

If you're troubled by the world you see and yearn for a new story, then *Human Earth Awakening* was written for you.

Stories have the power to change the world. They form our thoughts and shape our culture. Our society's outdated stories are driving people crazy and destroying the planet we love. A new future begins with a new story.

This mythic story changed our lives. *Human Earth Awakening* began as a vision during a dark time when we had run out of stories to believe in. We saw that the world was spinning out of balance and hurtling toward a global crisis.

Now we are living that crisis. Writing *Human Earth Awakening* has helped us to accept the alarming reality of today's apocalypse. But it didn't leave us in despair. It inspired us by revealing how we are all being called to awaken and evolve to a higher level.

Human Earth Awakening connects the personal and the planetary. It transforms "his/story" into a "his & her story" that includes the global voices of men and women, indigenous people and Mother Earth herself. It calls us the evolve beyond ego and beyond empire.

We tell this tale in a style we call *mythic realism* that weaves history and psychology, science and indigenous wisdom into one epic tale of life on this planet and beyond. *Myth* speaks to us in the language of symbols and archetypes. *Realism* keeps myth from veering off into fantasy. The essence of this visionary story is realistic and science-based. Weaving the latest science with the most ancient wisdom provides a holistic view that can help heal our fragmented world.

We thank our ancestors and the generations yet to come for the visions that continue to nourish us. Writing this story has been both inspiring and humbling. No matter how much we try to write from a global consciousness, our personal understanding is necessarily limited and we acknowledge our inevitable blind spots and shortcomings.

Fortunately we are not the only ones writing the unfolding story of planet earth. We have over 7 billion co-authors.

You can read more about our personal journeys and the writing of *Human Earth Awakening* at our **website** and in the "About us" section at the end of this book.

Please consider our story as an invitation to tell a new story about your own life and the world you live in. We hope this story resonates in your heart and contributes to the awakening that so many people are yearning for today.

PART 1:
JOURNEY OF THE FOUR TRIBES

1: Sky Ancestors appear at UN

World in crisis

On a dark day, filled with wars and rumors of wars, all the nations of the world gather in the Great Hall of the United Nations for an emergency meeting of the General Assembly.

Spring has just arrived and an early tropical storm lashes the eastern seaboard of the United States. Angry clouds swirl around the glass edifice of the UN. Torrential rains pelt the windows. Office workers peer apprehensively out into the gloom, wondering if the subways will be flooded again. This past week a resurgence of one of the more lethal viral strains means everyone needs to wear masks again.

Multiple crises have collided to spawn a deadly mix of conflict and chaos, pushing modern civilization to the breaking point. The first widespread global pandemic in 2020 sent a shockwave through every country. Since then local outbreaks and recurring pandemics have overwhelmed dysfunctional governments, disrupted the global economy and caused widespread suffering. The terrifying reality that anyone could be carrying a deadly virus intensifies distrust, suspicion and paranoia.

A rapidly-changing climate causes mass migrations that exacerbate societal collapse. Extensive unemployment, food shortages and infrastructure outages result in protests, riots and social disorder. Battered and fragmented medical systems no longer provide a safe haven during times of illness. On every continent families find themselves living a state of constant survival anxiety. Those at the bottom of the crumbling economic pyramid face nearly insurmountable challenges on a daily basis. Even those closer to the top of the pyramid wonder how systemic collapse will impact their lives.

Thrust into the online world of the internet, individuals feel unsafe and disempowered. Their very identities are vulnerable to theft and they can never be sure who or what is behind the words and images on their screens. Frequent slowdowns and total outages of the overloaded internet leave people psychologically disoriented and emotionally isolated.

Many people rise to the occasion responding with acts of kindness, creativity and generosity. Yet the growing fear that society is falling apart and things will never return to normal takes its toll on the mental health of even the most optimistic people.

A proliferation of doomsday cults offers the hope of deliverance to the desperate. Some charismatic cult leaders accumulate devoted followers in the hundreds of thousands. They gather online in virtual revival meetings that promise relief from the pain of daily life. But when the announced day of deliverance arrives and nothing happens, mass suicides are often the tragic result.

Government leaders treat vital issues as casino tokens in a game of winner-take-all. Power struggles reward politicians who dominate the news cycle with dramatic claims and accusations. Most leaders no longer even pretend to offer realistic solutions. Instead they warn of new threats and promise incredible solutions. The media fractures into a bizarre house of mirrors as it attempts to capture viewers with click-bait news and escapist entertainment.

International distrust leads to the demise of the rational problem-solving dialogues that world leaders had often used to defuse conflicts in the past. Crippling trade wars exacerbate shortages of food and other vital necessities. Long-smoldering animosities between countries constantly ignite into violence. Fear feeds on fear and humanity teeters on the brink of World War III and a nuclear Armageddon.

Today's emergency meeting follows several fruitless attempts by a deadlocked Security Council. As dysfunctional as it has become, the United Nations remains the only place where all the world's nations can meet in a last-ditch effort to avoid disaster. Crippling internet outages have made official online meetings unpredictable and unreliable. The delegates know that the recurring pandemics may make this their final chance to meet in person.

A babble of anxious, argumentative voices fills the Great Hall of the General Assembly. The delegates ignore the Secretary-General's call to order. UN ambassadors from hostile countries shout angrily at each other. Visiting observers, representatives from NGO's (Non-Governmental Organizations) and UN staff are shocked at the mounting disorder.

Pressure from ambassadors concerned about their personal safety has recently resulted in a policy change that allows delegates with official permits to carry concealed weapons for self-defense. This new situation adds personal fuel to the fear in the room. UN security guards shout orders for everyone to keep their guns holstered. Some delegates wear face masks and others do not, leading to further tension.

The cacophony of angry voices in the Great Hall becomes louder, drowning out the Secretary-General's desperate call to order. The arguments among the delegates erupt into pushing and shoving. They cluster into groups around the most vocal and most powerful antagonists. Personal animosities and international tensions become entangled.

The delegates are desperate for solutions. Few want war, but...

Delegates argue and fight

Sarah, Ambassador from USA:
(Confronts Leonid, the Ambassador from Russia)
Leonid, you need to stop interfering in our elections.

Figure 1. United Nations General Assembly Hall. Credit: Public domain.

Leonid, Ambassador from Russia:

(Laughing)

Come off it, Sarah! America has always been messing in other people's elections. That's long been one of the CIA's specialties.

Sarah:

Not the way you do it. Your main export these days is fake news!

We're on to you guys. We know you're getting ready to invade your neighbor Latvia. Latvia is part of NATO. If you don't get your troops and missile launchers away from the Latvian border, you're asking for war.

Leonid:

What gives you the right to lecture me? You invade whenever and wherever you feel like it.

You do whatever the hell you want, regardless of the consequences.

Like right now. You don't look healthy. You should be wearing your mask and instead it's dangling around your neck!

Sarah:

I can't breathe…even without that damn mask on! I've got asthma and my spring allergies make it even harder for me to get enough oxygen.

(Angrily turning away)

Just don't do something stupid, Leonid. Do you want the Russians to go down in history as the idiots who started World War III?

Leonid:

(Shouting at Sarah as she walks away)

We're not idiots! Your President is the one who said, "All options are on the table — including nuclear."

We don't interfere with what you do in your hemisphere. Don't interfere in ours and there will be no war between us!

Nearby another group gathers around the ambassadors from Nigeria and China.

Amaka, Ambassador from Nigeria:

(Confronting the Chinese ambassador Chuntao)

Your hunger for minerals, oil and timber is destroying our forests and polluting our rivers. You said you would employ local workers. But you bring in your own Chinese employees and only use our people for the dirtiest and most dangerous jobs.

Chuntao, we are both mothers and we both have children. China is a rich and powerful nation. What China is doing is not good for the children of Nigeria or the children of China.

Chuntao, Ambassador from China:

We negotiate in good faith with your government. We have invested more in improving your roads, your airports and your electrical system than anyone else. We even build schools and clinics for your children.

Amaka:

(With mounting frustration)

Yet in my hometown, people live in poverty. Their lives are worse than before you came. Your Chinese workers brought the virus into our villages. Because of the pollution from your industries we can no longer eat the fish in our rivers. We finally threw off the yoke of the British empire and now the Chinese empire is recolonizing us. Either treat us with respect or leave us alone!

Chuntao:

(Impatiently)

We are good business partners, not evil imperialists. It's not our fault that your population is exploding out of control and your government has problems with graft and corruption. We do our best!

Amaka:

(Turning away with tears in her eyes)

Well, your best is destroying our land and our families.

At the center of another group, an argument between the Israeli Ambassador and the Egyptian Ambassador grows more heated.

Oren, Ambassador from Israel:

(Confronting the Egyptian ambassador Ahmad)

Nine Israelis were killed by a missile launched by Palestinian terrorists. It was smuggled into the Gaza strip from Egypt. If you don't shut down your border crossings, we will!

Ahmad, Ambassador from Egypt:

We *have* shut them down. If a missile got into Gaza, it came in illegally, through underground tunnels.

Oren:

Then shut down the goddam tunnels! We don't want people carrying in weapons and we don't want them bringing in contagious diseases.

Ahmad:

Look, we bend over backwards trying to please Israel and it's never enough. Our Palestinian brothers and sisters deserve to be freed from your domination.

We wouldn't be having these problems if you treated them with respect. They deserve a homeland. I would think that of all people you Jews would understand that.

The President of Egypt told your Prime Minister yesterday that these problems will never end until Israel agrees to an independent two-state solution.

Oren:

(Jabbing his finger in Ahmad's face)

Well, the President of Egypt isn't some Pharaoh who can tell the Israelites what to do!

Ahmad:

(Angrily brushing Oren's hand away)

Israel is the new Pharaoh!

Let the Palestinian people go.

Oren:

(Aggressively clenching his fists)

We deserve to have secure borders and, thank God, we have the military to back that up! We have enough missiles to demolish the capital of every Islamic country in the Middle East within one hour.

Other delegates intervene to separate the two men who glare angrily in disgust.

Ahmad:

(Turning away)

We have one and a half billion Muslims. You have only a few million Jews.

Eventually we will push you into the sea!

Frustration, confusion and fear fuel dozens of similar arguments throughout the hall. Everyone senses the threat of viral contagion that hangs over every interaction. The entire room descends into chaos. The world as they know it is falling apart. No one knows what to do. The screaming voices of all the UN people merge into a great cry of anguish.

Their desperate call rises through the Great Hall and up to the sky.

Call to planetary council

Suddenly, a loud thunderclap shocks everyone into silence. Two white-hot beams of light flash through the top of the great domed ceiling and strike the platform at the front of the General Assembly. Everyone turns to look, transfixed by what they see.

The twin plasma tubes of white light change to rainbow-colored beams. The light begins to coalesce into two ethereal figures that slowly materialize into flesh and blood. The woman wears a living gown of flowers, leaves and vines, woven from nature. A necklace of precious stones glows around her neck. The man is clothed in a robe woven from swirling white clouds and blue sky, his face as radiant as the sun. Bracelets of lightning bolts flash upon his arms.

The man and woman embrace. Then they face the assembly. She opens her arms wide and spiritual nourishment flows from her heart into every person's heart. He raises his arms and sunlight streams from his face into each person's mind.

The people in the Great Hall — ambassadors, delegates, staff, public observers — are awestruck by the appearance of these mysterious figures.

Sky-Woman:
I am Sky-Woman. Sky-Man and I are your ancient Ancestors and we have heard your cries. We have returned to guide you through this crisis.

Sky-Man:
Come and sit in council. Look around you. Everyone here is your brother or sister. When brothers and sisters fight, the whole family suffers. You are one human family on this planet. Please return to your seats so we can begin.

The Ancestors raise their hands and soothing ripples of peace flow around the General Assembly. Some UN people struggle with feelings of disorientation and a fear of losing control.

Something very strange has just happened. Who are these beings? Are they friendly? Are they hostile visitors from some other planet? Feelings of panic start to arise. Some look around frantically for some way out.

As they continue to breathe, they inhale a flow of loving energy from the Ancestors. Each time they exhale, they feel their fears dissolving. The sense of panic that filled the hall begins to evaporate. The UN people wearily surrender to the stress and fatigue in their bodies, feeling relieved at the opportunity to sit down. They relax into their chairs and feel the tension drain out of their bodies. Their breath becomes deeper and they notice an unfamiliar sensation of well-being.

Sky-Woman:

These intense and perilous times present a great danger, even the possibility of total extinction. But in today's turmoil there is also a great opportunity. You are spinning into an evolutionary vortex. We came here to guide you through the center of this evolutionary spiral into the possibility of a beautiful, healthy Human Earth.

Sky-Woman and Sky-Man:

(Smiling and opening their arms wide)
We welcome you and call you to this planetary council.

Occasionally a rainbow wave of light passes through the Sky Ancestors. The delegates remove their headsets when they realize that each of them can hear the Sky Ancestors in their own language.

Sky-Woman:

We have heard your cry for help. We have long heard the desperate calls from the many people who are suffering everywhere on this planet. We come bringing you the gifts you need: gifts of love, truth, peace and power.

Sky-Man:

Today is March 21ˢᵗ, the Spring Equinox. This is a sacred day. Day and night are equal everywhere on the earth. The forces of Light and Dark are in perfect balance.

In the past, your ancestors gathered at their sacred sites at each equinox. They sat in council and came to one mind. All over the world they celebrated the great turning of the seasons, expressed gratitude and restored harmony. But today you no longer practice this healing ritual. Instead you argue and fight.

Sky-Woman:

Your world is in crisis because you have wandered far from the Tree of Life. You have forgotten the Original Teachings and your own true story. You no longer remember your ancestors and you neglect the well-being of future generations.

People without a story cannot find their way. We have come here today to tell you a story about your origin and your destiny that is so new that your ears have never heard it before *and* so ancient that you already know it in your bones.

We will take you on a journey into your hidden past and an expedition into future possibilities. It will be a wild ride. Be prepared for sublime beauty and shocking horror.

(Smiles and looks into each person's eyes)

Each one of you is the main character in this story.

Sky-Man:

Your true self has never forgotten your origin and still dreams of the vibrant life you lost when you left the world of nature to build your empires. You are a creative and loving people. Each one of you is an essential part of the whole. The universe needs you to come home.

When you see yourselves as you truly are, you will be able to envision your next steps more clearly. The peace you yearn for is impossible as long as you experience yourselves as separate from nature and from each other. The pandemics and the extreme weather have intensified your fear here.

Many UN delegates cry out:

Yes, we are afraid right now. So many things are going wrong all at once! There is a monster storm raging outside.

There are people here in this room who carry a deadly virus and do not even wear masks. We fear the very air we breathe. If you want to help us, save us from this virus!

Visit from a virus

Sky-Woman:

You are right, the virus you fear *is* here in this room. To evolve requires facing your fears in a healthy way. As I said, your story includes horror as well as beauty. So let's meet one of the creatures you fear, the one you call a virus.

Sky-Woman raises her right arm and swirls it around in the air, creating a small vortex. In the whirling air, a round spiked virus appears. As it spins, it grows larger and rises higher. Soon it comes to a stop and hovers over the people in the Great Hall. A coronal glow of light surrounds the sphere.

The delegates recoil in fear.

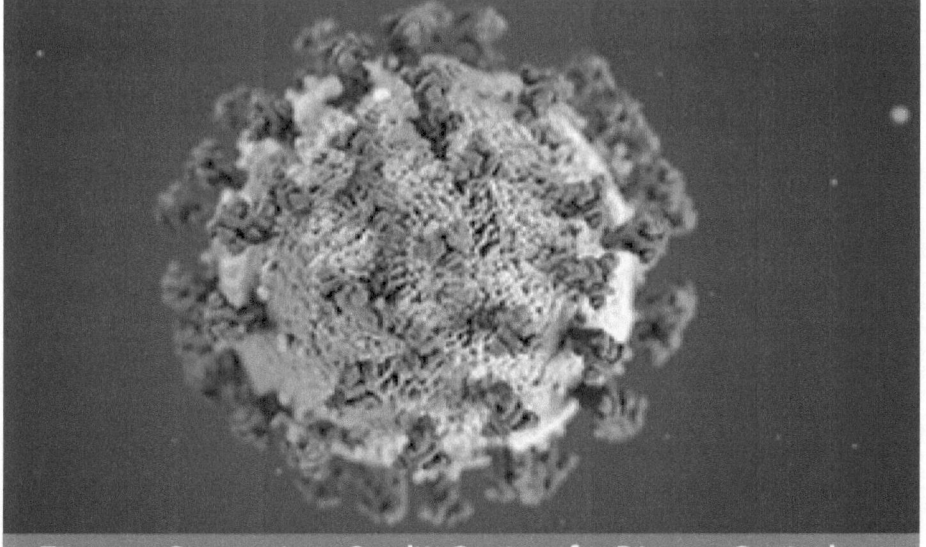

Figure 2. Coronavirus. Credit: Centers for Disease Control.

Sky-Woman:

Let us welcome our viral visitor as a mysterious character in our story. The more you understand life, the safer you will feel.

(To the virus)

Please tell us your story.

Virus:

Thank you, Sky-Woman.

(To the UN people)

Hello! I've been wanting to talk with you for a long time.

If you are feeling afraid, I want you to know that you don't need to fear me. I am the coronavirus. But I'm not some horrible villain. I'm not out to get you.

I know me being here on this planet has brought a lot of suffering to a lot of people and I'm really sorry about that. In fact, the main reason I want to talk with you is to see how we can have less suffering on this planet instead of causing more suffering.

Viruses like me can be quite useful. I have a few fans who even think I look beautiful.

I can also be lethal, but let's be honest, so can you. Thanks to you we're going through the sixth greatest extinction in the history of the earth. Most of the species on this planet are in a lot of pain because of your actions.

Frankly, I'm surprised at the outsized impact I have had on your world. Imagine a tiny little thing like me bringing the whole world to a screeching halt.

But I couldn't have done it without you.

If you feel the need to fear something then you might as well fear yourselves because you are the ones who brought me into existence and made it possible for me to travel all around the planet.

If you don't like having horrific contagious diseases then don't crowd billions of captive animals into cages and feedlots. Don't invade the few remaining natural places that wild animals call home. These are the very conditions that make it super easy for viruses like me to jump from animals to humans. It's not that hard to make the leap, you know. From my perspective, you're not all that different from the animals you eat.

Viruses like me have been around forever. I've got a long memory. And I remember when things weren't so scary and stressful between us. In case you think deadly pandemics are just a fact of life that humans have to live with, I want to remind you that Native Americans lived for thousands of years on two big healthy pandemic-free continents before the Europeans brought their Old World diseases with them into the New World. And the whole human race was pandemic-free for millions of years when your ancestors were living in harmony with nature.

By the way, viruses are everywhere. We are the most abundant creatures here on earth. There are more viruses on this little planet than there are stars in the sky. There are millions of us in a spoonful of seawater. We inhabit every lump of soil. We're constantly streaming around the planet through the atmosphere. Trillions of viruses from all around the world land here every second of every day.

Although you cannot see us, a vast variety of viruses and microbes of all kinds cover the surface of everything in this world.

As the virus speaks, the invisible microbial world becomes visible. The UN people see a moving carpet of microorganisms covering everything around them. They see the millions of viruses, bacteria, yeasts, fungi, spores, mites and other microorganisms living on every surface. They see them floating around, turning the air into a microbial soup. They look at their own hands and at each other's faces, staring in shock and disbelief at the microbes creeping and crawling over their skin.

Virus:

We microbes are not only all around you, we're inside you too. We're in your nose and in your mouth, in your eyes and ears. We live in your lungs and in your digestive system. The microbes inside you actually outnumber your own body cells. We form our own community within you. It's called your microbiome.

So who are you? Are you god-like beings? Or are you just another ecosystem for us to inhabit? Go ahead and have an existential identity crisis over that one!

Are you part of life or separate from it?

(Pausing)

Now, before I go any further, I have something I have to get off my chest, so to speak.

I'm upset.

I'm not happy about the name you gave me. I don't like being called a *virus*.

I'm fine with *microbe*. Microbe means "tiny life." And I am definitely tiny. Millions of me can fit on that tiny dot called a period that you put at the end of a sentence.

But the word virus means "poison" and when you call me poisonous it makes me feel very spiteful and nasty. In fact, it makes me want to infect you. You've got a lot of nerve calling me poisonous when you are the ones poisoning the earth with all your toxic trash.

And there's another reason this gets me really upset. It's not just me personally who you've been insulting. You disrespect the whole invisible microbial world that I'm part of. Out of all the different species of microbes that live on this planet, there's only a tiny, tiny fraction that cause any problems for you. It's true that a few of us do have the power to make you sick, but that's why evolution gave you an immune system.

Most of my fellow microbes are actually quite friendly. We play a vital role in everything that happens on this planet. We help produce the oxygen you're breathing right now. No microbes, no oxygen.

Some of us do like to make our home in your body. We help you digest your food, regulate your metabolism, optimize your immune system and lift your mood. You need us.

Working together we microbes help you create so many of the foods you love to eat like cheese, yogurt, bread and pickles. We're intimately involved in fermenting those special beverages you love like beer, wine and spirits. And, of course, we're an essential part of those health drinks like kombucha.

So, how about coming up with a new name for me? One that's not based on old-fashioned fear-based ideas like the "germ theory" of disease. The fact is we microbes only cause problems for humans when humans get out of balance:

Like when you get out of balance with the rest of the world and disrupt the harmony of ancient ecosystems. Like when you set up your cities so that billions of people are forced to live in crowded, polluted and substandard conditions. And when so many people lack basic necessities like clean water, sanitation and adequate nutrition.

By the way, it doesn't help when you attack us with overdoses of antibiotics, disinfectants and pesticides. Let me tell you, that just makes the next generation of microbes even angrier and more resistant.

Probably the dumbest thing you do is eat devitalized, factory foods that upset the microbiome in your gut. Then your immune system malfunctions and you experience those extreme imbalances you call disease. So, if you get sick, don't blame me! Instead take a look at how you've been relating to me.

Giving me a new name will definitely help our relationship. Something more respectful, maybe even affectionate.

I appreciate you listening to me today. I can see that you're starting to relax even though you can see all the microbes around you. You've been hanging out with us creepy crawlies your whole life. You just didn't know it.

So let's go a little deeper with this...

Some scientists call viruses like me "organisms at the edge of life." They can't decide if I'm a clump of non-living matter or a real rootin'-tootin' living organism. What do you think?

The truth is, I'm part of a mysterious realm that connects the "living" and "non-living." We microbes are part of what your ancestors called the invisible world or the spirit world. Many indigenous people can still "see" us...and they do so without needing microscopes.

We are your ancestors and the deep ancestors of all life. Life on earth started with simple tiny bits just like me. Little packets of protein, little snippets of genetic code. We are life at its most basic and most universal.

And don't forget, you started your own life as a one-celled organism inside your mother. And when you die your body will become food for microbes. That's the circle of life — dust to dust, ashes to ashes, and microbes to microbes.

Now I know Sky-Woman and Sky-Man have much more to share with you, so it's time for me to wind things up here. But before I go, just one more thing.

We are your friends, not your enemies. And that's why I want to give you a friendly heads-up: If you continue to harm the earth and ignore the Original Teachings you will continue to weaken your own immune system *and* you will trigger increasingly lethal waves of devastating pandemics. And when your species finally goes extinct your death certificate will read: Death by suicide.

So wake up and take responsibility for how you're living on this planet. Take care of yourselves. Strengthen your own immune systems instead of playing a frustrating game of whack-a-mole with every microbe that pops up in your life. You're not going to be able to medicate and vaccinate your way out of this. Do what I do and *evolve* your way out of your problems.

Do you really want to treat everything that seems other-than-you like an enemy? Do you want to make war against everything, when you could be making love with everything?

We're all family. We microbes want to live in harmony with you on this planet. Let's restore the dynamic balance that once existed between your visible world and our invisible world.

You and I have done great things together in the past. Viral DNA is embedded in your own genetic code and shows that you evolved to be who you are today thanks to us.

Just imagine the kind of healthy pandemic-free planet we could create if we respect each other and learn to live in harmony.

The virus begins to rotate. As it spins faster, it grows larger and its coronal halo shines brighter. Suddenly it releases a burst of light that floods the Great Hall. The virus disappears and a veil of invisibility once more hides the microbial world from human eyes.

Spacetime bubble and the Tree of Life

Sky-Man:

This virus is one of many messengers from the natural world who are calling you to wake up from the trance of empire and to evolve beyond ego.

Can you feel a longing in your heart to return to the Tree of Life?

Sky-Woman and Sky-Man raise their arms and a majestic Tree of Life emerges from the ground at the center of the Great Hall. Four huge branches grow from its massive trunk. Its leaves are green and shiny and its fruits glow in every color of the rainbow.

Sky-Woman:

Behold the Tree of Life!

The tree's central taproot descends all the way to the center of the earth. Four huge surface roots travel outward: to the east the red root of power, to the south the green root of love, to the west the yellow root of peace and to the north the blue root of truth.

From the Tree of Life, waves of energy pulsate outward. The walls of the Great Hall begin to ripple. Soon the entire room is spinning around the delegates. They wonder if the building is being whipped by a gigantic hurricane. Yet despite the whirling walls, the air around them remains calm and quiet.

The walls of the hall dissolve and fall away. The sky appears overhead. The storm is over and the sun is shining. The other UN buildings and the skyline of Manhattan dematerialize before everyone's eyes. The natural landscape of the island is restored. The air is fresh and calm.

The UN people find themselves in a circular grass-covered amphitheater overlooking the sparkling clear waters of the East River. Those still wearing masks slip them off and everyone feels relieved to be breathing in fresh, life-giving air. Plants and animals abound. The sounds of birds, chipmunks, frogs and other wildlife are everywhere.

Sky-Woman and Sky-Man stand next to the Tree of Life in the central circle at the lowest level of the amphitheater. The people no longer sit in rows, but in circles around the Tree of Life. They sit quietly, mesmerized by the awe-inspiring transformation.

As the Ancestors raise their arms, an invisible force lifts all the delegates' concealed guns up into the air. The weapons spiral in toward the Tree of Life. They swirl around, melting into a mineral-rich liquid that rains down into the soil around the Tree and fertilizes its roots.

Time hangs suspended as the council begins.

Sky-Man:

We know that in your daily lives you are always feeling rushed and anxious. You seldom stop, relax and look within. Now you have all the time you need. We have stepped outside of clock time and into a spacetime bubble. You won't "fall behind" and you can't "get ahead."

Simply be here now.

The UN people look into each other's eyes recognizing for the first time in countless generations that they are members of one human family sitting together in a council circle.

Prophecy of the Metanoia

Sky-Woman:

Spacetime bubbles do not last forever. When our council is over, you will return to the perils of the present moment.

Every one of your cultures has a story about the coming of a great day of reckoning. Many spiritual traditions speak of a day of judgment or the return of a savior. These visions reflect a deep inner knowing that life on earth is reaching a crucial moment, a spiritual apocalypse!

Many people think of an apocalypse as a cataclysmic destruction or a magical deliverance — or both. Yet the ancient meaning of apocalypse refers to something more profound: an uncovering of what has been hidden, a time of revelation and rebirth. We have come to you to reveal your origin and destiny.

Sky-Man:

Your world is in crisis because you are resisting the coming apocalypse, resisting the great turning that happens when you approach the center of an evolutionary spiral.

Three and a half years from now, at the autumn equinox, you will experience an event that will change life on earth forever! Highly intense waves of radiation will flood the earth from the sun. And from the center of the galaxy a great pulsation will strike the earth. At the same time, the geodynamo at the earth's core will reach a peak in its cycle.

You will experience a truly earth-changing event: the earth's north and south magnetic poles will switch polarity!

In order to maintain a state of dynamic balance, earth's north and south magnetic poles usually reverse their polarity every 300,000 years. However, the last switch happened almost 800,000 years ago! A reversal is long overdue and the pressure within Mother Earth is building rapidly. This inner earth tension has an effect on life at the surface and it's been affecting your nervous systems too.

This momentous meeting of Earth and Sky energies will produce the dynamic energy boost you need to get to the next level of your evolution.

Sky-Woman:

This is your opportunity to return to the Tree of Life and experience what you need the most: a deeply transformative planetary healing, an awakening in consciousness known as a *Metanoia*.

Metanoia (*meta*-change, *noia*-mind) is a profound transformation at every level. Metanoia is at the core of all of your spiritual traditions. This mysterious experience has been called many things: rebirth, salvation, enlightenment.

People who have been transformed by a Metanoia leave behind their old stories of fear and separation because they start to hear a new story of love and oneness. They see the world with new eyes and their cloudy mind becomes clear. They rejoin the flow of evolution and experience renewal and spiritual growth.

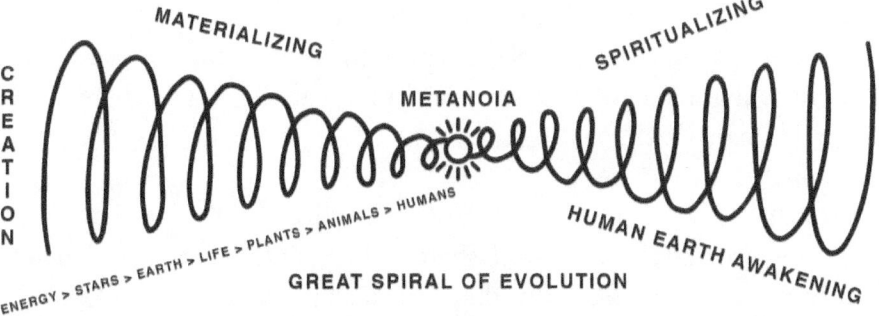

Figure 3. Spiral of evolution. Credit: Gerzon.

Sky-Man:

Yet, if you resist the evolutionary change that wants to happen, you will not be prepared to transform the powerful energies of this cosmic apocalypse into a Metanoia. If humanity remains disunited, these intense cosmic energies will become uncontrolled and chaotic, resulting in a worldwide catastrophe. The electromagnetic storm will wreak havoc on all biological life and electronic systems. Widespread mental breakdowns, increased mutations and a crippling of your power and communications grid will set you on a path of suffering and extinction.

The coming apocalypse is your moment of truth as a species. It is when you answer that age-old question: Who am I?

Sky-Woman:

If you respond to the challenge of the apocalypse by changing your consciousness, you will experience a personal and planetary Metanoia. Until now a Metanoia has only been experienced by individuals and small groups. But the vision of every great spiritual teacher has included the ultimate reunion of all humanity in a worldwide Metanoia. Many of your prophets and futurists predict that you are approaching the center of a mysterious evolutionary spiral and the possibility of a "great turning," a "singularity" or an "omega point."

The thoughts and actions of your species have become *so* powerful. In just a few generations you changed the landscape and the climate of the entire planet! What if you decided to use your thoughts and actions to create a different kind of climate change? What if you decided to change today's climate of fear into a climate of love?

Imagine everyone on the planet experiencing a Metanoia at the same time, an enlightenment of the entire species that gives birth to a new age of Human Earth!

Sky-Man:

During this council, we will share with you the Original Teachings that can reconnect you with the Tree of Life. Our Sky Elders, Sky-Grandmother and Sky-Grandfather, will come and tell you a new creation story so you can rediscover your forgotten origins. Then your grandchildren from the Seventh Generation will arrive to show you the two paths that lie before you. One leads to a bright future of evolution. The other to a dark future of extinction.

When our council is over you can return to your world with a new vision. This vision can guide you through the center of the spiral that you are approaching. We invite each of you to stay present and listen with an open heart.

The UN people are entranced by the Ancestors. They have been transported to another realm. They feel more alive with each breath they take. There is something in the air, a sparkling vitality that emanates from the great Tree of Life at the center of the amphitheater. They begin to understand that it was their own cries of desperation that called Sky-Woman and Sky-Man to come here at this time. They feel a deep yearning for guidance through these troubled and confusing times.

Sky-Man:

To help you understand where you are on your human journey, you need to know where you came from. We want to tell you a story about another time, many generations ago, when our human family faced a crisis just as challenging as the one you're facing today.

2:   Origins, crisis and global adventure

Origins as one family

Sky-Woman:

This is not the first time that our family has encountered such a challenging time. The earth upon which you live is my body. I am always changing and evolving, just as you are. Times of change bring both suffering and growth. The challenge of change activates the evolutionary impulse.

You come from a long line of evolutionary innovators. Every time the climate changed, your ancestors changed their consciousness and their way of living. Climate change challenges your brain to expand its ability to think creatively. The many folds in your brain evolved in response to earlier periods of climate change. This increased brain capacity vastly expanded your mental powers. The folds in your digestive system developed along with the ones in your brain, increasing your ability to extract nutrients from a wide variety of foods.

These biological innovations and using fire to cook your food helped you to absorb more energy from both Father Sky and Mother Earth. This empowered you to evolve and prosper. Today you are called to evolve once more.

Before Sky-Woman and Sky-Man begin to tell their story, they focus their eyes on all the UN people, the ambassadors, delegates, staff, observers and guests. Each person experiences the Ancestors looking directly into their eyes. Vibrating thought waves appear above each person's head. The Ancestors lift their arms and draw everyone's mental energy upward. Then they focus the combined energy field on a space next to them on the platform.

A vision space opens up in the center of the platform as the Ancestors move to the side. The oval-shaped, three-dimensional vision space is unlike anything the UN people have seen before! They feel as if they are peering into an ancient, holographic mind.

Every scene the Ancestors describe comes alive in the vision space. The UN people sit back and listen to the story as they watch it unfold in the vision space.

Sky-Woman:

A long time ago, all the people of the world lived together as one family. Each of you is a descendant of that first family.

In those early years you lived in Africa. Today most of northern Africa is an arid desert, but then it was a lush, tropical Garden of Eden. You lived close to the Tree of Life and in harmony with Mother Earth and Father Sky.

Sky-Man:

Over many generations your family grew and divided into Four Tribes: the Fire, Earth, Wind and Water Tribes. Each Tribe traveled outward following one of the four roots of the Tree of Life and spread to the four directions.

At each change of season, at the equinoxes and solstices, the Four Tribes followed their root back to the Tree of Life for a great council. People celebrated the bounty of Mother Earth and the blessings of Father Sky. They sang and danced, joined in rituals and reconnected as one family. They told stories and shared dreams.

When people had disagreements, they sat in council until they came to one mind. If anyone was suffering, they received care in a healing circle. The elders passed down the Original Teachings. They performed time-honored rituals to bring their relationships with Earth and Sky, and with each other, into balance.

They thanked the Tree of Life and their ancestors for the gifts they have received. The Tree of Life flourished and nourished the tribes.

Ancient climate crisis

Sky-Woman:

Then about 70,000 years ago the climate began to change drastically. A dark time came upon the land.

Great storms and floods battered the landscape. Then a harsh dry wind brought a terrible drought. The lush river valleys and forests slowly turned to barren desert. The idyllic Garden of Eden that had been your home since you were born was disappearing!

Hunger stalked the land. People were dying from starvation. Families and children suffered. No one, not even the elders, had ever experienced these extremes in weather before. No one knew what to do. They were afraid because they were facing the end of the world as they knew it.

The Four Tribes began fighting with each other over dwindling resources. Each tribe blamed a neighboring tribe for their problems and tried to keep them out of their land. When they tried to sit in council they argued and could not come to one mind. They were unable to agree on a plan of action. Bloodshed became common and people lived in fear of each other.

The people neglected the Original Teachings and the Tree of Life began to wither. Only a few thousand human beings remained alive and the threat of total extinction loomed.

Sky-Man:

I know you don't remember this, but we have met with you in council before. The last time was during this climate crisis 70,000 years ago when the Four Tribes gathered around the Tree of Life and cried out for guidance. We answered your ancestors' cries and came to them. We called them to a council. We told them that a new era was dawning. The time had come for each tribe to embark upon their own journey and follow their root outward from Africa to the very ends of the earth.

Four Tribes with four sacred missions

Sky-Woman:

Before they left on their journeys we gave each of your tribes a unique mission and a special gift.

To the Mother and Father of the Earth Tribe I said:

You are the Great Earth Tribe and you will follow the green root of love and travel deeper into our African homeland. You will embody the Original Teachings of love in your daily life and in your sacred songs and dances. You will honor mothers and childbirth and the web of clans and tribes.

We give you this sacred drum. The drum connects you to your body and to each other. The drum connects you to the ancestors and to Mother Earth. Your mission is to love each other and always keep the rhythm of the drum alive.

Sky-Man:

To the Mother and Father of the Water Tribe I said:

You are the great Water Tribe and you will follow the blue root of truth to a land called Asia. There you will discover great river valleys, generous climates and rich soils. You will learn to channel water, grow bountiful crops and build great civilizations. You will construct temples of learning and create philosophies and religions. Some of you will travel all the way to eastern Asia, the Pacific islands and Australia.

We give you this sacred tablet. You will preserve the Original Teachings using special symbols that can be inscribed on tablets of clay and stone. You will develop practices to cultivate a clear mind. Your mission is to keep the life-giving waters of truth and wisdom flowing to future generations.

Sky-Woman:

To the Mother and Father of the Wind Tribe I said:

You are the great Wind Tribe and you will follow the yellow root of peace to a faraway land called America. You will travel as swiftly as the wind and wherever you go, you will breathe the great spirit of the sky that unites us all. You will have the longest and most challenging journey. The key to your survival lies in your relationships with each other.

We give you this story belt. You will develop healing rituals using story belts. Your mission is to keep alive our sacred tradition of the council, gathering in peace and sharing stories until you come to one mind.

Sky-Man:

To the Mother and Father of the Fire Tribe I said:

You are the great Fire Tribe and you will follow the red root of power to a land called Europe. As you travel, the weather will become much colder. You will learn to build sturdy shelters to protect your families from ice and snow. Food will be scarce in the winter, so you will develop close bonds with the animals you hunt. You will spend much time around your lodge fires for warmth. You will learn how to use the power of fire to change the earth into remarkable new materials. You will study nature and invent powerful tools.

We give you this sacred chest. Your Fire Tribe can fill it with the tools and instruments of creative power. When all the tribes have completed their separate journeys, it is your destiny to reconnect the tribes. Your mission is to develop your power so you can co-create a beautiful Human Earth with the other tribes. Always keep the fire of life burning.

Sky-Woman:

Before your ancestors left on their journeys we told them:

You have been called to separate journeys and different missions so that you can develop your unique gifts. When you complete your missions, you will have reached the end of your root. Then it will be time to return to the Tree of Life and share your gifts with each other.

When you meet again, you can celebrate with a great council. Dance and sing. Sit in circles and share your stories. When you combine your gifts of love, truth, peace and power you will be able to fulfill your destiny and create a happy, healthy Human Earth.

Tomorrow you will set out on four separate journeys. You will face many difficulties. Yet the greatest danger of all will not be wild animals or high mountains. The greatest danger will be that you will not recognize each other as family when you finally meet again.

Your journeys are long and will take thousands of generations. Now you look the same, speak the same language and share the same stories. This will change as you adapt to diverse lands and climates. You will still be family but you will look different, speak different languages and tell different stories.

If you succeed in your separate missions but do not recognize each other as family, then you will experience a great tragedy.

So when you meet each other, remember to greet each other as family, tell your stories and share your gifts. Honor the Tree of Life. Honor all four roots. Always treat each other with love and peace, speak the truth and use your power wisely.

Sky-Man:

Before they left on their journeys the Four Tribes danced and sang together for one last time around the Tree of Life. The following day when the sun rose, each Tribe began its journey knowing that life would never be the same again. Mixed emotions of sadness, excitement, grief, curiosity, fear and joy rippled through the tribes.

The Wind, Water, Earth and Fire Tribes followed their roots into unknown lands, growing stronger with every challenge they surmounted...and growing farther apart with each step they took.

In the vision space, the ancient world of 70,000 BCE dissolves. The UN people are stunned by this vision of their origins as one family and the great journey of the Four Tribes. Everyone's eyes return to the figures of the Sky Ancestors.

Original Teachings

Sky-Man:

(To the UN people)

We gave your ancestors the Original Teachings to help them remember their origins and missions: the teachings of the *Tree of Life*, the *Four Roots*, the *Seven Directions* and the *Turning of the Four Seasons*. These forgotten Teachings can guide you again today as you face your own climate crisis.

[Note: Full versions of these Original Teachings are available in the Appendix.]

Sky-Woman:

Like you, trees flourish when they live in balance between Mother Earth and Father Sky. Today the Tree of Life will nourish you with its spiritual teaching. Join us now and listen.

All the UN people focus their gaze on the Tree of Life and breathe in its energizing, aromatic fragrance. As waves of woody, drum-like vibrations emanate from the Tree, they intuitively tune their listening to a deeper level so they can hear its voice.

Tree of Life:

All is one.
All is love.
I begin as one seed.
Seeking life, I turn to Mother Earth. Seeking life, I turn to Father Sky. My seed extends into a root going down and stretches into a stem going up. One seeks darkness, the other light.
My roots spiral into the Earth. My branches spiral into the Sky. Everything moves in a spiral.
The dance of life begins.

The UN people all see primordial visions of creation and feel deeply nourished by this simple yet profound teaching. They sense the Tree of Life within their own bodies. Their faces shine with joy and their hearts are filled with gratitude.

Sky-Woman:

The next Teaching of the *Four Roots* challenges us to practice the four great virtues of love, truth, peace and power.

Love is the essence of the universe and the awareness of our oneness with each other and with all life. Treat others as they wish to be treated.

Truth is the lucid thinking of the clear mind. Always tell the truth with love. In all you do, let your actions be motivated by love and guided by truth.

Peace is day and night, light and dark, dancing together. Peace embraces and transforms opposites in a way that furthers evolution. To experience peace, dance with whatever life brings you.

Power is vitality, the creative life energy of the universe itself. Power is the ability to give birth to what is within, to manifest thoughts and dreams in the real world.

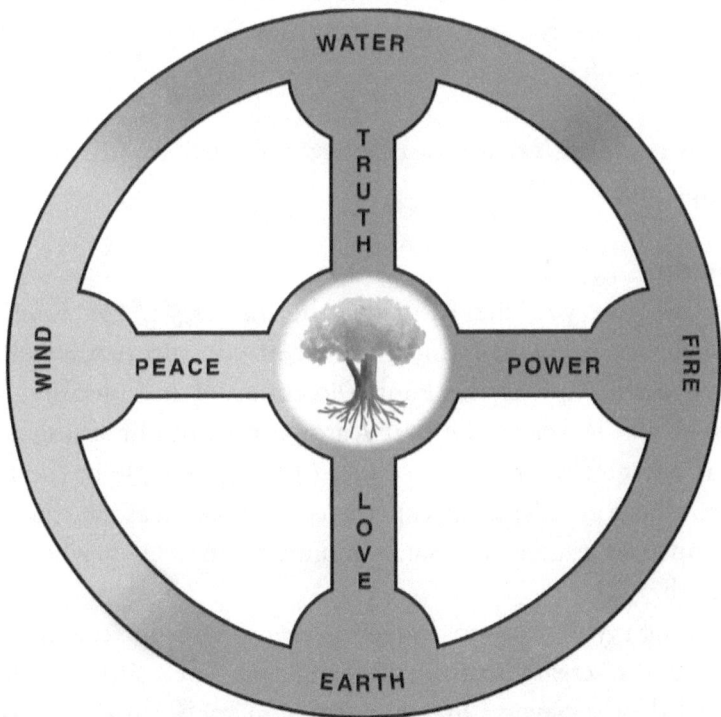

Figure 4. Tree of Life and Four Roots

Sky-Man:

So that you can carry the Tree of Life within you wherever you go, we now give you a ritual called the *Seven Directions*. Rituals are bridges that carry the Original Teachings from the world of spirit into our daily lives.

This sacred ritual honors the *seven directions*. These include the *four directions* of the compass which are aligned with the *Four Roots* of love, truth, peace and power, the *dual directions* of Earth and Sky, and the *seventh direction* that brings us inward to our center where all directions meet. The Seven Directions ritual will help you stay centered in this ever-turning, ever-changing world.

Sky-Man and Sky-Woman lead the UN people in the ancient Seven Directions ritual. Afterward everyone feels grounded, connected to the great Tree of Life and their inner Tree of Life. They are filled with awe as they simultaneously sense both their unique individuality and their oneness with all life.

[Note: A complete version of this Seven Directions Ritual is available in the Appendix.]

Sky-Woman:

Finally we give you the Ritual of the *Turning of the Four Seasons*, a great planetary ritual that can unite all of you, no matter where you live on the earth. Just as the Four Directions of east, south, west and north orient you in space, the four seasonal turnings of spring, summer, autumn and winter orient you in time. Although people in the northern and the southern hemispheres experience opposite seasons, the turnings always happen at exactly the same moment, no matter where you are on the Earth.

Even though you can no longer gather physically under one Tree of Life, you can create shrines wherever you live. You can gather in council and do the Seven Directions ritual at each Turning of the Four Seasons. When you do this ritual, other families all around the world will be honoring the Tree of Life at that very moment too. In this way your hearts and minds can align with Earth and Sky and stay connected with each other.

3: Cataclysmic first meeting

Four Tribes meet again

As the Ancestors speak, a new scene opens in the vision space.

Sky-Woman:

Our Four Tribes traveled by foot, taking one step at a time. They deepened their understanding of Mother Earth and she prospered them. In each new location the elders passed the Original Teachings on to the next generation. They in turn adapted the Teachings to their new environment. Each tribe developed a rich and authentic culture based on their own root of love, truth, peace or power.

It took thousands of generations. By 20,000 years ago our Four Tribes had succeeded in populating every habitable continent on the planet and many of the islands too. Gradually an astonishing new layer of life, a human world, began to interweave with the natural world. Civilization, culture and technology bloomed all over the planet. This new human world soon revolutionized life on earth. As conscious beings you began to reshape our planet.

Sky-Man:

The Earth Tribe gave rise to the African culture. The Water Tribe established the vast Asian culture, from the Near East to the Far East and Australia. The Wind Tribe grew into the Native American culture in North and South America. And the Fire Tribe built the European culture.

But with each passing generation, the Four Tribes changed and they lost touch with each other. As each tribe traveled farther out from the Tree of Life on its own root, they gradually forgot about the other roots — and the other tribes.

Sky-Woman:

It was the Fire Tribe's mission to reconnect the Four Tribes after their long journeys. In Europe the Fire Tribe developed the root of power. But as they did so, they began to neglect the roots of love, truth and peace. They gradually lost touch with the Tree of Life.

As they grew in power, the Fire Tribe fought many wars, dominated Mother Nature and built mighty empires. Power and money began to replace love as the motivating energy in social relations. Men began dominating women and the sacred balance between Father Sky and Mother Earth was lost.

About 500 years ago, during the great age of discovery, the Fire Tribe's European explorers sailed all over the planet. These courageous sea captains, missionaries, scientists, soldiers and settlers bore the scars of ice ages, wars and epidemics. They yearned to build a worldwide civilization based on divine love, yet they were also driven by trauma, fear and an all-consuming hunger for power.

When the Fire Tribe finally arrived on the distant shores of the other tribes they came face to face with the Earth, Wind and Water Tribes.

Sky-Man:

Picture this mythic scene of the first meeting of the Four Tribes...

It is the early 1500's. A European sailing ship lies offshore. The Captain and his all-male Fire Tribe crew have landed and stand on the shore. They have white skin and dress in dark jackets, pants and boots. The Captain is the Father of the Fire Tribe. His wife, the Mother of the Fire Tribe, is at home in Europe, raising their children.

Facing the Europeans stand the Wind, Water and Earth Tribes, composed of both men and women. The mythic Mother and Father of each tribe stand in front of their tribal family which includes adults, grandparents and children.

The African Earth Tribe has dark skin and wears beautifully patterned, brightly colored fabrics. The Asian Water Tribe has light brown skin and wears intricately decorated silk robes. The Native American Wind Tribe has reddish-brown skin and wears tan buckskin, beads and animal ornaments.

The tribes look at each other and wonder, "Who are these strange-looking beings who are so very different... yet so much like us?"

Giving the gifts

Sky-Woman:

Some of the wisest elders, the Mothers and Fathers of the Earth, Wind and Water Tribes, still remember the Original Teachings that we gave them: "When you meet each other again, remember to greet each other as family, tell your stories and share your gifts."

In the vision space, the Mother and Father of the Earth Tribe step forward. They dance and offer the Fire Tribe their sacred drum.

African Earth Tribe Mother and Father:

Welcome! The rhythm of the drum can reunite us in the spirit of love. Come let us dance and sing together as one family.

Next, the Mother and Father of the Water Tribe offer the Fire Tribe their stone tablet with sacred inscriptions. Their clear voices resonate with deep wisdom.

Asian Water Tribe Mother and Father:

This sacred tablet preserves the Original Teachings. Come let us seek truth together in the temple of nature.

Finally, the Wind Tribe steps forward and offers the Fire Tribe Captain their sacred story belt made of colored beads. Their faces emanate joy and their voices are warm and friendly.

Native American Wind Tribe Mother and Father:

This story belt tells of our origin as one family. Let us come together in peace, sit in council, and share our stories with each other.

The European Fire Tribe Captain stands stiffly, with his arms folded across his chest. He grows increasingly impatient. As each gift is given, his face registers deeper disgust.

Captain:

(Angrily takes the Earth Tribe's drum and smashes it on the ground)

This drum is the Devil's plaything. Stop your wild dancing. It is an obscenity in God's eyes.

(Throws the Water Tribe's tablet to the ground, breaking it into pieces)

This tablet is polluted with pagan scribbles. Your many gods are a blasphemy against the one true God.

(Takes the Wind Tribe's story belt and rips it apart, scattering the beads all over the ground)

This story belt is filled with lies, witchcraft and evil spells.

(Triumphantly turns to face all three tribes)

Our way is superior to your barbaric rituals. God has sent us here on a holy mission to convert you to our way of life.

We do not need to hear your stories. God has given *us* the *one true story!*

The other tribes stare at the Fire Tribe Father in shock and disbelief.

Captain:

(Smiles magnanimously and opens his great treasure chest)

We have mastered the gift of power and it gives us everything we need and want.

(Reaches into the chest to show the other tribes his gifts and then holds up a black leather-bound book)

This book contains the one true story from the mouth of the one true God.

(Holding up other books on History, Science, Philosophy, Mathematics, Geography)

Our other books contain all the knowledge known to mankind.

(Showing their navigation instruments)

We invented these instruments and they have guided us across a trackless ocean to your land.

(Pointing to the sailing ship offshore)

We built this great ship that has weathered many storms.

(Scooping up a handful of coins from the chest)

These gold and silver coins are called money. They are more valuable than anything else on earth. If you have enough of these coins, you can obtain whatever you want.

Our Fire Tribe was chosen by God and we are made in his image. Our treasure chest is filled with many more marvelous tools and instruments. We are a loving and generous people. We will share our treasures with you and teach you our ways. We will show you how to become civilized human beings like us.

(Picks up the black book and holds it high)

Now, bow down, every one of you, and worship the one true God!

Earth, Wind and Water Tribes:

(Shaking their heads)

We welcomed you as brothers. You have shown us disrespect and refused our gifts. We all breathe the same air and walk on the same earth. We are human beings like you. We will not submit to your domination.

Captain:

Then we have one more gift to give you.

The Captain and his crew take their rifles from the treasure chest. They aim their rifles at the Fathers and Mothers of the other tribes and begin firing...

Great tragedy

Smoke fills the vision space and the scene dissolves. The UN people sit speechless, in a state of shock. They turn expectantly to the figures of the Sky Ancestors.

Sky-Woman:

Sadly, instead of the joyful family gathering that we had envisioned, there was tragedy, bloodshed and the destruction of unique and beautiful cultures. A once-in-a-lifetime opportunity for a creative family reunion was lost.

Despite all the technological advances since then, morally and spiritually you lost your way when you did not recognize each other as family. The sacred elements of Wind, Water, Earth and Fire did not combine harmoniously to create a new Human Earth. The Fire Tribe dominated the other three tribes and created a global Fire Empire.

With each passing year under the Fire Tribe's domination, our planet has grown increasingly out of balance. The human world which started out as a beautiful layer, interwoven with the natural world began to mutate into a toxic cancer on the earth.

Sky-Man:

Five hundred years ago at the time of the first meeting of the Four Tribes, there were less than half a billion people living on the earth. Now there are nearly 8 billion.

Imagine it this way: In a valley where *100* people once lived comfortably in harmony with nature, now over *1,600* people struggle to survive and fight over scarce resources. This population explosion has exacerbated fear, conflict and the exploitation of Mother Earth.

The Fire Tribe's excessive use of fire has overheated the planet. The forces of Earth, Wind and Water react with extremes in weather. Earthquakes, storms, floods and droughts once more threaten humanity. Disrupted ecosystems and animal exploitation trigger pandemics. Families are suffering and there is constant war.

Call to evolve

Sky-Woman:

We asked the indigenous people who still remember the Original Teachings to share them with anyone who would listen. We sent out a worldwide call to every person on the planet.

Perhaps you have heard our call in your dreams. Maybe the call came to you when you were alone in quarantine. Perhaps it came when you felt the suffering of Mother Earth and her many plants and animals who are going extinct. Maybe you heard our call when you experienced sickness, suffering and loss in your own life. Or maybe you heard us when you were transported by a vision of the beautiful and loving world that your heart yearns for.

All around the planet people have been hearing our call. We see people rediscovering the Original Teachings in their own way. They are healing themselves, healing each other and healing the earth.

Every day more and more people are waking up from the trance of empire. They know that every solution their politicians, generals, scientists and religious leaders come up seems to produce even bigger problems. In your prayers and meditations, we have heard you crying out for guidance. You still have time to transform the coming apocalypse into a Metanoia of planetary rebirth.

PART 2:
HEALING THE FIRE TRIBE

4: Encountering the Fire Tribe

Time to return

Sky-Woman:

(Smiling a bit wistfully, as she remembers an earlier time)

We were much closer long ago.

(She looks into the eyes of the UN people with a deep and nurturing love)

You have grown so much during the past 70,000 years. It has been many, many years since our family gathered under the Tree of Life in Africa and you set out on your separate missions. You overcame incredible obstacles. You traveled all the way to the ends of your roots and accomplished your missions!

Sky-Man:

Each generation told the next: It is our mission to move forward, grow larger and expand outward. Our journey is outward from the Tree of Life to the ends of the earth.

But you began to think only in straight lines. You forgot the Original Teachings and the Tree of Life. The wisdom of the sacred spiral was lost.

You accomplished your missions! You were courageous and you persevered in the face of unimaginable challenges. But when you came to the end of your root *you kept on going*! You did not stop. You did not return to the Tree of Life and reunite in council.

Sky-Woman:

Part of learning and growing is that you sometimes go too far in one direction. Now it's time to wake up, change direction and return to the Tree of Life. You've done so much exploring but it's primarily been outward. You've mapped the whole planet. This path leads inward, into the most mysterious land of all. It leads you back to your true self, to reunion with each other and with your Source.

Fire Tribe Father appears on Root of Power

Sky-Man:

You are on an epic journey. You started out with a beautiful dream. But it has turned into a nightmare for so many people in today's world. The Fire Tribe's root of power has overgrown the other three roots and choked them off. The Tree of Life is withering.

The UN people look at the Tree of Life at the center of the amphitheater. They see the red root of power growing larger and spreading over the green root of love, the blue root of truth and the yellow root of peace. The great Tree becomes starved for nutrients, withers and leans sideways.

Sky-Woman:

It is time for healing, time to restore balance and wholeness. We invite the Mother and Father of the Fire Tribe to join our healing council.

All eyes turn toward the swollen red root of power as it begins to glow and pulsate. The Father of the European Fire Tribe emerges from the red root. The Father is the same white-skinned man who appeared earlier as the Captain of the ship at the first meeting. He now wears the garb of a contemporary New York businessman. He stands upon the red root and his treasure chest sits next to him.

Fire Tribe Father:
 (Looking slightly disoriented)
 Where am I?

Sky-Man:
 (With a reassuring smile)
 You are right where you need to be.
 Where is your wife, the Mother of the Fire Tribe?

Fire Tribe Father:
 (Surprised and irritated at the question)
 She's at home...with the children.
 (In a challenging tone)
 Who are you?

Sky-Man:
 I am your Ancestral Father, Sky-Man.

Sky-Woman:
 I am your Ancestral Mother, Sky-Woman.

Sky-Man:
 You are the Father of the Fire Tribe, are you not?

Fire Tribe Father:
 Everyone calls me Captain.

Sky-Man:
 We will honor your request.

Sky-Woman:

We invited you here because we can see that you and your family are suffering. We offer you healing.

Captain (Fire Tribe Father):

(Dismissively)

Look, I'm a busy man. What is this all about? Are you some kind of indigenous people? Do you have natural resources on your land?

Are you looking to make a deal?

Sky-Man:

Did you not hear Sky-Woman when she spoke? She said we understand your suffering and offer you healing.

Captain:

(Matter-of-factly)

I'm in excellent health. If I get sick I can go to the best doctors and hospitals in the world. But I'm not suffering. And if I were, believe me I wouldn't go to you for healing.

The whole world needs healing

Sky-Man:

The whole world needs healing and you are part of this world.

Your Fire Tribe has had a major impact on the earth during the past 500 years. You fulfilled your mission to develop your power and unite the tribes. Yet you did not recognize your brothers and sisters as family. You built a world based on Fire alone, suppressing Wind, Water and Earth. Your tribe ripped the material world apart from the spiritual world and unraveled the divinely-woven fabric of Creation.

Fire-based technology has spread fire all over the planet. First you burned up the trees. Then you burned what you call "fossil fuels." These carbon-rich liquids are the remains of your evolutionary ancestors. Every day you plunder their sacred burial grounds and incinerate their remains.

Your fires now overheat the atmosphere, creating chaotic weather patterns. Your incessant drilling disturbs the land and triggers earthquakes and landslides.

You used your powerful fire-based science to smash the atom and split life apart. You invented an unnatural and unholy form of toxic fire that you call nuclear energy. You burned what never should be burned, leaving behind deadly radioactive ashes for future generations.

Sky-Woman:

The excesses of your Tribe have upset the natural balance of Wind, Water, Earth and Fire. The smoke from your fires has polluted the air, the water and the soil. Now these poisons flow in your own veins and inflame your bodies. Now your fire-powered transportation systems spread contagious diseases all over the planet. These viruses and bacteria invade your body and push your immune system into meltdown. Your minds are on fire and you cannot rest at night.

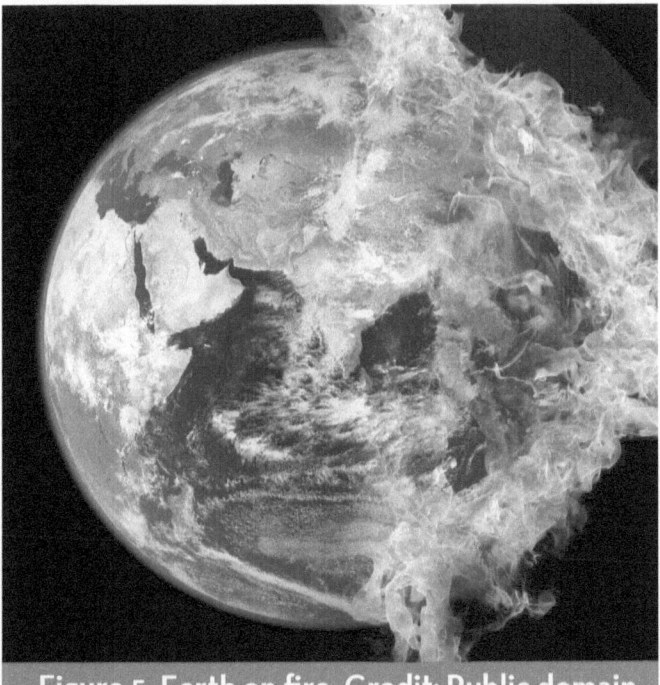

Figure 5. Earth on fire. Credit: Public domain.

So many of my children are suffering. My indigenous children who still remember the Original Teachings suffer deeply in the world you have built. My other children who have forgotten the Original Teachings wander, lost and distracted, in Empire's screen-world.

My beautiful birds and flowers and frogs, and so many other precious creatures who have shared this world with you for millions of years, are dying and disappearing forever.

You do not have much time. So much damage has already been done.

Captain explains the good he has done

The Captain's ego skin grows thicker and shinier.

Captain:
(Indignantly)
I stand here unjustly accused.

I have done much good in the world. My Fire Tribe explored the world and mapped it for the benefit of all peoples. Look at the gifts that our science, technology and economic system have provided. Look at the higher standard of living. Look at the medical advances. Our technology has improved life on earth in many beneficial ways.

(Warmly and expansively)

Look at the spread of freedom and democracy around the world. We are the pioneers of human rights. We did away with monarchies and dictatorships and established equal rights for all people regardless of color, gender, religion or national origin. We have opened our tribe to people of good will from all over the world.

(Matter-of-factly)

Of course, we've made some mistakes along the way. I know we're all going through some real tough times right now but things are definitely going to get better. Nobody's perfect.

Besides, all the other tribes built empires too.

(Smiling confidently)

We just happened to be better at it.

(Inspirationally)

The truth is that the Fire Tribe has succeeded in uniting all the tribes in a new global civilization based on freedom, equality and prosperity. Our triumph is evolution in action: the survival of the fittest!

Sky-Man:

You say you feel unjustly accused, yet we are not accusing you. We are telling the story of the Four Tribes so that we can heal the past and create a healthy Human Earth in the present.

(Sky-Man points to the withering Tree of Life)

Can you see that your red root has spread over the other three roots and is choking them off? The Tree of Life is withering.

Captain:

(Loudly, impatiently)

Because our red root is the strongest, we have united the other roots in one great civilization. We cover them so that we can protect and support them.

Frankly, your so-called Tree of Life looks very old and sick. It is withering because we no longer need it. I live in the city and everything I need is in the city. The city is the new Tree of Life.

(Turns to the UN people)

Come on, you guys know what I'm talking about, don't you? You aren't buying all this are you? I'm sure there's a logical explanation for this weird set-up. Holograms and all that stuff.

You know us. We're the Fire Tribe and we've never let you down. We're dealing a very complex global civilization here. It's not easy running a world with over 7 billion people. Any of *you* want to give it a try?

We are the good guys. The real threats are from other countries who want to impose their will on everyone else and from renegade terrorists who want to tear down our global civilization and return us to a barbaric past. Do you want *them* to be in charge?

The fact is, we're the only ones who can fix this thing. We built it!

Some of the UN delegates nod their heads in agreement and the Captain feels renewed confidence. His ego skin grows even harder and shinier.

Captain offers gold coins

Captain:

(Turning to Sky-Woman and Sky-Man)

Look, folks. I'm not sure who you really are. This is a very clever set-up you have here. You must have gotten a lot of great high-tech help from some bleeding-heart do-gooders in the UN. I'm guessing you're some kind of indigenous people and you've appointed yourselves to be the "conscience of humanity"...so that you can get some UN funding for yourselves!

I'm not on trial here. You can't make me feel guilty with your one-sided version of history. I've done nothing wrong.

And I *do* need to get back to my office.

Sky-Woman:

Look around. Where is your office? And how will you find your way back there?

Captain:

(He gazes beyond the circle and begins to panic as he sees only wilderness)

I-I don't know what you've done. You need to get me back to my office! I am not your prisoner!

(Takes a deep breath and regains his composure)

As anyone will tell you, I am a generous man. I am sure your people back home would like some help in raising their standard of living. Here's the deal: I will give you some precious gold coins and you will take me back to my office. Gold is a pure and noble metal and it will bring you great good fortune.

The Captain reaches into his treasure chest, cups his hands together and scoops out a pile of gleaming gold coins. He walks over to give them to Sky-Woman and Sky-Man.

The gold coins begin to crack and blood oozes out. The blood drips all over his hands and trickles to the ground. The Captain recoils in horror.

From the blood arises the image of a dark-skinned South African gold mine worker. He has been injured in a mining accident and is bleeding heavily. He dies in agony. His image disappears.

Captain:
(Indignantly)
I did not kill this man! I had nothing to do with it!

Sky-Man:
Then why is there blood on your hands?

The Captain looks down and stares at his blood-stained hands.

Captain hears a voice

The Captain angrily shakes the blood off his hands. But they remain stained.

Captain:
(Vehemently)
What kind of cheap trick is this? You don't have any legal authority over me. My power is greater than yours.

He turns dramatically, reaches into his chest and takes out a gleaming aluminum aerosol can. He sprays his hands. The blood stains glow iridescent. He pulls a bright white synthetic fiber towel out of his treasure chest and wipes his hands clean with it. He holds the towel up for all to see, turning it back and forth. It shines pure white. The blood has disappeared.
The UN people gasp in amazement.

Captain:
(Confidently reasserting himself)
Yes, I have power. Developing power is the mission I was given. And it is still the most important mission of all, because without power nothing exists. Power is life itself. Everyone wants power.

I am the one who united our tribes into one global society. I alone could do this great thing because I was the only one who had the *power* to do it. (Glaring fiercely)

Let's be realistic. The basic rule of survival on this planet is eat or be eaten. Killing is part of living. Anyone who has eaten a hamburger has blood on their hands. You have to destroy in order to create. Even the gentlest of vegetarians mercilessly smash innocent carrots with their teeth. Why? Because they're *hungry!*

We are all animals who kill to eat. Since killing is part of living, the real question is: When is killing justified?

I detest killing. I only kill when it becomes absolutely necessary. It is always a last resort.

Sky-Man:

How do you know when it becomes necessary to kill?

Captain:

I believe in the one true God of all creation. Everything I do, I do for him. I only kill when he tells me to.

Sky-Man:

How does your God communicate with you?

Captain:

He speaks to me. I hear his voice.

Sky-Man:

Do you hear his voice now?

Captain:

(His face glowing with passionate inspiration)
Yes, I think I do!
I hear him speaking to me now!

A mind cloud appears above the Captain's head. It grows larger and becomes more visible. In his mind cloud a powerful patriarch with flowing white hair and a beard sits on his throne. Mighty storm clouds swirl around him.

Once-in-a-lifetime opportunity

Sky-Man:

Your mind is cloudy. This prevents you from seeing or hearing clearly. You hear only your ego's voice echoing in your head, masquerading as something divine.

We are your ancient Father and Mother. We love you. You are our son and we want to help you heal. Let us guide you. Will you join us now for a sacred healing ritual?

Captain:

(Scared and angry)

How dare you? You insult God and call him a voice in my head! You are not my mother or my father. You are a primitive and backward people.

It is time for you to bow down before the one true God.

Sky-Woman:

Think clearly now, my son. Has all the suffering been for nothing? Has your heart become so hard that you still do not recognize us as family even though we stand here with you?

Let your cloudy mind go, so you can *see* again.

Sky-Man:

My son, this is the once-in-a-lifetime opportunity that you came here for. Open your mind.

But the cloudy mind above the Captain grows bigger and darker. Lightning flashes in the cloud. The powerful white-maned patriarch stands up brandishing a lightning bolt in his hand.

Captain:

(To Sky-Woman and Sky-Man threateningly)

Bow down before the one true God!

Sky-Woman and Sky-Man stand confidently and serenely, beaming love. A hush comes over the UN people. They watch, transfixed by the drama, wondering what will happen next.

The Captain turns deliberately to his treasure chest. He reaches in and pulls out an automatic rifle with a long barrel. His shiny ego skin morphs into glassy bullet-proof ego armor. He turns to face Sky-Woman and Sky-Man.

Captain:

I came here in peace. But you betrayed my trust. You are trying to take away my freedom and brainwash me. I have given you the opportunity to join the Fire Tribe. But you refuse. If you are not with us, you are against us.

I know you want me to make martyrs out of you. But I understand your old tricks. Don't worry, I won't kill you. But if you do not bow down before me, I will begin killing these people, one by one until you bow down.

And their blood will be on *your* hands!

(Captain whirls and point his rifle menacingly at the UN people).

Shock and terror cloud the minds of all the UN people. They begin to look around in panic. They have no defenses. Earlier the Ancestors took their guns from them. But the Fire Tribe Father has a powerful automatic rifle. Where can they run? Suddenly this feels all too familiar. Will they become victims of a mass shooting?

Captain:

(Shouting to Sky-Woman and Sky-Man)
This is your final warning! Bow down now!

Sky-Woman and Sky-Man remain motionless.

The Captain points the gun at the UN people and pulls the trigger.

As he fires the rifle, the end of the barrel suddenly changes into the head of a snake. The rest of the rifle morphs into the body of a powerful black snake with a red diamond pattern on her back. The head of the snake turns around. She opens her jaws and exposes her fangs.

The Captain shudders in horror.

The snake quickly slithers over the Captain's body and coils around him from his neck down to his feet. She begins to tighten her coils around the Captain. His rigid ego armor buckles and cracks under the pressure. He is being crushed inside his own armor.

The Captain falls to the ground. The snake continues to squeeze him tighter and tighter.

Captain:

(Screaming in panic, to Sky-Woman and Sky-Man)
I can't breathe! I'm dying! Help me!

5. Regaining a clear mind

Healing the Captain

Sky-Woman, smiling compassionately, opens her arms and a radiant white mist flows out from her heart to the Captain lying on the ground. The spirit of love bathes him from head to foot.

Sky-Man raises his arms and rays of sunlight stream from his face into the Captain's cloudy mind, clearing away what remains of the dark clouds.

The big snake now becomes gentle, her face nurturing and maternal. She glides tenderly over the Captain's body, pushing away the broken pieces of his ego armor. Finally, the snake slithers over to Sky-Woman and Sky-Man. She relaxes under the Tree of Life with a serene look on her face.

The Captain (now restored to his original identity as the Fire Tribe Father) lies motionless. After a while he stirs and gazes around. He stands up and stretches as if waking from a long slumber. He is now wearing an open-collared shirt and slacks. His face looks healthier, happier, more open and expressive.

He gazes at the Tree of Life. He looks at Sky-Woman and Sky-Man. He walks over and kneels in front of them with deep respect.

Fire Tribe Father (formerly called the Captain):
You have restored me to my clear mind.

(He sobs and his tears flow)

The violence that I put on others turned on me. I was filled with terror. Thank you for healing me instead of letting me die.

Before, my ears were deaf to the sound of your voices.

My eyes were blinded by arrogance and I did not recognize you.

Now I can hear you and see you.

I don't want to be the person I was before. I am sorry for the harm I have caused. Please forgive me.

Sky-Woman:

I am moved by your desire for healing and I feel your remorse. We welcome you back to our human family.

Sky-Man steps forward and extends his hands to the kneeling Fire Tribe Father. The Fire Tribe Father grasps his hands and rises up. Sky-Man embraces him and the Fire Tribe Father feels a surge of aliveness as he reconnects with his long lost masculine roots. Sky-Woman embraces him and he feels his deep longing for the feminine.

Telling a story of separation

Sky-Man:
(Kindly)
Would you like to tell us your story?

Fire Tribe Father:
Now I remember the sound of your voices. Deep inside me I remember a time when I lived close to nature and I heard your voices in the wind and water. I lived with my clan, like the wolf with his pack. We traveled over the landscape hunting and gathering wild foods. I and my clan were one.

Everything I knew came from the elders. I heard your voices in their voices. And when the elders passed on to the spirit world, their voices continued to live in my mind and guide me.

But when the first city arose it grew into a new world with its own rules. In the city, my elders' voices could no longer guide me. I had to think for myself.

The city was crowded. It was noisy. Other people's voices came into my head and I began to think their thoughts, and to argue with them. In order to survive I had to compete with other men.

How could so many different clans live in harmony within one city? We constructed a pyramid of power to help us maintain order and organize large projects. The emperor sat at the top, mediating between the gods and humans. Our council circles were replaced by a pyramid. The clan elders were supplanted by empire's priests.

The city became more powerful than the clan. I lost my connection with my clan and the natural world. I needed to play a role in the life of the city, so I developed a second self, an Empire self, an ego. I began to think empire thoughts, using my city mind. I needed a second skin to protect me from the other egos and conceal my real self, so I grew my ego skin. Your ancestral voices faded from my memory and I began to feel separate in the world.

City empires grew and fought each other. I was given a choice: kill or be killed. As a soldier I had to kill other people who had done me no harm. I was trained to harden my ego skin into ego armor.

The first time I plunged a sword into another man's chest and saw his life blood spurt out, I felt utter horror at what I had done. To kill him, I had to kill something inside myself. I nearly went crazy!

But one war followed the next. I needed to kill, again and again. The only way I could justify killing other people was to make a male god in my own image who gave his blessing to whatever I did. Empire's god blessed every tool and every weapon I invented. He blessed every war I fought. If I died in battle, he promised me everlasting life.

With war came captives. The captives of war became the slaves of empire. For the first time, society was split into a superior master class and an inferior slave class. Master and slave were divided but they shared a deep loss. War and slavery broke the fundamental trust that had existed between human beings. Both master and slave lost the feeling of love and safety that comes from being part of one human family.

When I lived a life as a master I was tormented by the guilt of killing the soul of my slaves. I lived with the fear of being killed by the slaves upon whom I depended. During those lifetimes when I was a slave, I suffered daily humiliation, the suppression of my identity, the loss of my soul.

The god of empire gave his blessing to buying and selling people and their labor. In empire I learned to treat people like domesticated animals. War and trade elevated men over women. Many war captives were women. The god of empire gave me the right to dominate women. I treated women as objects to use and control. I craved women and I feared women. I lost my ability to love and respect my wife as a goddess.

To make my male god the supreme ruler, I banished the goddess, persecuted the wise women, and imposed my will even upon my own wife. When I banished the goddess, I killed something precious inside myself.

(Slowly, sadly with deep remorse)

So much has been lost. So much harm has been done in the name of empire.

I didn't know what else to do.

Fire Tribe Mother arrives

Sky-Man:

(Warmly, compassionately)

Thank you for sharing your story. I am happy that you can hear your own true voice again.

The creation of male-dominated empires has unbalanced the world. Yet the age of empire has also been a time of great growth and unification. Only through the restoration of women's power can you return to the Tree of Life. There is still time for Empire Earth to evolve into a new Human Earth.

We are here to guide you in your healing.

Sky-Woman:

You have been given a wonderful guide and companion in this life. Are you ready to invite the Mother of the Fire Tribe to join us?

Fire Tribe Father:

(Hesitantly)

Yes…Yes, I am.

The red root of power begins to glow again and the Mother of the Fire Tribe appears next to the Father. She has creamy white skin and wears a beautiful dress.

A gasp arises from the UN people when they see that her left cheek is bruised.

Fire Tribe Father:

(Responding quickly)

I did not tell the whole truth earlier when you asked me where my wife was…because I was too ashamed. We had an argument last night.

(Turns to face his wife directly)

My anger overcame me and I hit you.

I…I am so sorry.

The Fire Tribe Father and Mother embrace.

Fire Tribe Mother:

(To her husband)

I am heartened that you can see yourself more clearly.

I love you, yet I have been unable to feel close to you for many years. Instead of creating a home with me, you made me live in your world.

You did not listen to me and did not value my thinking as a woman. During times of conflict, you tried to dominate me mentally and physically. You suppressed my spirit. I numbed myself in order to survive in your world. I played my role in this because I did not know what else to do.

(To Sky-Woman and Sky-Man)

In my tribe I have been known as the Captain's wife and I was taught to submit to his will. Thank you for recognizing me as the Mother of the Fire Tribe.

As Sky-Woman and Sky-Man embrace the Fire Tribe Mother, she connects with her power and her longing for partnership.

Fire Tribe Father:

(His face becomes troubled, his voice heavy with sadness)

When I hear your words and look at Sky-Woman and Sky-Man, I can see how blind I was. The most unjust and self-destructive war I have ever fought has been the war of man against woman. I am truly sorry for all the suffering I caused.

Fire Tribe Mother:

Let us do our healing so we can come together and celebrate our love. I want to create a healthy, happy home for our children, for all of Sky-Woman's children.

Fire Tribe Father:

That is what I want too, more than anything else.

Fire Tribe Mother and Father embrace again.

Sky-Woman:

Nature gave half of the Original Teachings to men and the other half to women. Only when men and women come together in love, can they create a healthy new world.

Bodies appear under roots

Sky-Man:

So, my son, you have called yourself the Captain. May I call you the Father of the Fire Tribe now?

Fire-Tribe Father:

Yes. I see that I became too much of a captain and not enough of a father. I want to be a good father. My children are suffering. My first responsibility as a man is not to my ego and not to the Empire my ego built. It is to my family.

Sky-Woman:

To be the good father you want to be, you will need to heal and you cannot heal alone. Are you prepared to join us in our healing council now?

Fire Tribe Father:

Yes, I want to do whatever is necessary. I want to heal myself and my family.

Sky-Woman:
(To the Mother of the Fire Tribe)
Will you join us for healing?

Fire Tribe Mother:
Yes, gladly.

Sky-Woman:
Then let us return to the Tree of Life.
(She turns to face the Tree of Life)
Now where are my other children? Where are the other three Tribes?

Everyone's eyes turn to the Tree of Life. The enlarged red root of power still covers the other three roots.

The ground under the Tree of Life becomes visible. Under the green root of love lie the bodies of the African Earth Tribe Mother and Father. Under the blue root of truth lie the bodies of the Asian Water Tribe Mother and Father. Under the yellow root of peace lie the bodies of the Native American Wind Tribe Mother and Father.

A hush comes over the UN people.

The Euro-American Fire Tribe Father and Mother are standing on their swollen red root. They see the Mothers and Fathers of the other tribes buried under their roots. They are appalled because they know they have played a role in this.

Fire Tribe Mother and Father:
(In desperation)
What can we do?

Sky-Man:
You can stop trying to be the whole tree and simply be your own red root.

The Fire Tribe Mother and Father look at each other. They kneel upon their red root. They meditate and focus their minds on honoring Sky-Man's request.

They breathe and release their need to control the other roots. The swollen and engorged red root gradually contracts to its original size. The other roots are finally free. The yellow root of peace, the green root of love and the blue root of truth grow strong and regain their vibrant colors.

The UN people feel a sense of relief as they witness the energy of the Four Roots flowing once more into the Tree of Life, restoring balance. The Tree of Life which had been withering begins to flourish again.

Sky-Man:

(To everyone)

We have heard the Fire Tribe's story. Do you want to hear the stories of the Earth, Water and Wind Tribes?

Fire Tribe Father and Mother and all the UN people:

Yes, we want to hear their stories!

PART 3

COUNCIL AND RECONCILIATION

6. Four Tribes council

Convening the council

The Mothers and Fathers lying under the three roots sense that they are being called. Their bodies become activated and they begin to breathe. A gentle smile appears on their faces. They slowly rise up out of the ground.

The Mothers and Fathers of the Earth, Water and Wind Tribes now stand resurrected upon their roots. They wear African, Asian and Native American styles of clothing as before, but with a more modern look.

The Fire Tribe and the UN people wait with mixed emotions, wondering what stories they will tell.

Sky-Woman:
We welcome the Earth, Water and Wind Tribes. Your roots have been covered by the red root. Your spirits have lain beneath the ground. Now you have returned to the world of the living. My heart overflows with joy now that I can see all my children gathered under the Tree of Life!

Sky-Man:

This is a momentous occasion. For the first time since you began your journeys 70,000 years ago, the Mothers and Fathers of all Four Tribes are sitting together in council under the Tree of Life. In our healing council, each tribe will have the opportunity to tell the story of their journey.

We honor the Teaching of the Four Roots in our council. We speak our truth with love. We listen to each other's truth with love. We co-create the peace of one mind and use our power wisely.

Now we invite the Mothers and Fathers of our Four Tribes to tell their stories. Would the Fire Tribe like to begin?

Fire Tribe expresses remorse

All eyes turn toward the Tree of Life as the red root of power begins to glow.

The Mother and Father of the European Fire Tribe stand upon the red root.

Fire Tribe Father:

Our Fire Tribe succeeded in uniting the world through the power of our technology.

(To the other three tribes)

But now that my mind is clear I can see that I became blinded by power. I did not recognize you as family when we met. I rejected your gifts and dishonored your roots. I have done great harm to my brothers and sisters. I feel deep remorse for the harm I have caused.

Fire Tribe Mother:

The goddess was banished from my tribe long ago and I lost my way. The Fire Tribe men began to banish the sacred feminine from public life thousands of years ago. In Europe and America, the so-called "witch hunts" dealt a crushing blow to what little remained of our European goddess tradition. I, and the women of the Fire Tribe, have suffered at the hands of our men. But we have also benefited materially from their power and their exploitation of the other tribes.

I am uplifted by the presence of Sky-Woman and the beautiful Mothers of the other tribes. I have much to learn about being a woman from my sisters in the Earth, Wind and Water Tribes.

Fire Tribe Father:

There is more we could say, but in the past I have spoken too much and listened too little. My version of our story became known as "history." Your voices were forgotten.

Now I understand that your stories are the missing chapters in my own story. My ego is afraid to hear what you might say. But I know *I* need to hear your stories. If you are willing to share your stories, I will listen gratefully with an open heart.

Earth Tribe keeps the rhythm of the drum alive

All eyes turn toward the green root of love as it begins to glow. The Mother and Father of the African Earth Tribe stand upon the green root.

African Earth Tribe Mother:

We know that many people in the other tribes have looked down on us as primitive and scorned our way of life. We ask you to respect our journey and the mission we were given.

Most of us remained in our homeland of Africa. We have preserved the Original Teachings by embodying them in our daily way of life. For us, the material world and the spiritual world are one. The drum reminds us that life is a dance. Every day I dance with everyone I meet and everything that happens.

African Earth Tribe Father:

As human beings, we need to belong to something larger than ourselves. Our ancestors lived in a sacred web of families, clans and tribes.

Nelson Mandela grew up in a healthy tribe and absorbed the Original Teachings from his elders. During a time of great crisis in South Africa, he was able to bring the European Fire Tribe and the African Earth Tribe together. Our son, Nelson, who we call Madiba, knew how to dance, even with his oppressor. Through the transforming power of his love, the Earth and Fire Tribes in South Africa were able to recognize each other as family for a sacred moment. We avoided the terrible bloodbath that many thought was inevitable.

Now imagine the kind of world we could create if more of our boys and girls had the good fortune to grow up, like Nelson Mandela, in a loving tribal family under the Tree of Life.

Earth Tribe Mother:

We brought our dancing and our music with us wherever we went. Imagine the world without rock and roll, jazz, reggae, gospel and the blues. We kept the primal rhythm of the drum alive.

Earth Tribe Father:

(Turning to the Fire Tribe Father)

When we met 500 years ago, you smashed our drum into the ground.

The broken drum appears on the ground in front of the Earth Tribe. As the Earth Tribe Mother and Father speak, images from their story arise from the broken pieces of the drum.

Earth Tribe Father:

The Fire Tribe used its gift of power to colonize Africa, exploit our land and enslave our people. You devastated the very fabric of our existence, leaving us traumatized and divided. We suffer to this day from the disrespect and cruelty shown to us.

Earth Tribe Mother:

You took many of us in chains from our homeland and forced us to be your slaves. You broke up what was most precious to us, our families and our clans. You ripped my own flesh-and-blood children away from me.

Earth Tribe Father:

You whipped me. You raped my wife. You literally worked us to death, generation after generation. Your prosperity grew from our suffering. Despite these outrages, we courageously brought the sacred drum with us wherever we went and we enriched our new homelands with our gifts.

Throughout our suffering, we kept the rhythm of the drum alive. We are the Earth Tribe and we want to help our family return to the Tree of Life by growing new tribal communities that spiral together around the planet. Imagine a retribalized world where everyone can belong to a loving family and community.

Let us heal our broken hearts so that love can flow among the Four Tribes once more.

Sky-Woman thanks the Earth Tribe for sharing their story. Everyone sits in silence as they accept the Earth Tribe's story into their heart.

Water Tribe keeps the water of truth flowing

All eyes turn toward the blue root of truth as it begins to glow. The Mother and Father of the Asian Water Tribe stand upon their root.

Asian Water Tribe Mother:

I thank my brothers and sisters of the Earth Tribe for following the root of love and embodying the original teachings in their daily life. In my heart, I feel their suffering.

We who belong to the vast Asian Water Tribe were given the mission to follow the root of truth and preserve the Original Teachings on stone tablets so that they would never be forgotten.

Asian Water Tribe Father:

From the Near East to the Far East our priests, sages, shamans, yogis, wise women, mystics and philosophers explored the mysteries of existence and the methods of cultivating a clear mind. We studied the Way of Life, and discovered that the dynamic balance of dark and light, yin and yang, is the key to health and harmony.

In the westernmost part of Asia, Abraham, Moses, Zoroaster, Jesus and Muhammad arose to guide their people. In India, the Hindu Vedas recorded ancient spiritual knowledge and Buddha taught us the path to enlightenment. In China, Lao Tzu embodied the wisdom of the Tao. Confucius taught a social ethic based on loyalty to family and honoring elders and ancestors.

Water Tribe Mother:

Those of us who went to Australia preserved the memory of the dreamtime and gave Mother Earth a voice through the sound of the didgeridoo. In Japan, Shinto and Zen developed practices to maintain the vital connection between the emerging civilized mind and the indigenous mind.

We developed our technology to a sophisticated level, yet we were mindful of its potential to do harm. Our guiding principle was always to stay in balance, to find harmony with nature. We did not have only one religion or philosophy, but embraced many forms of truth.

Water Tribe Father:

Like the Fire Tribe, we established large empires, fought wars and began to elevate men over women. But we never banished the goddess. We never forgot that the Great Mother is the source of all things.

Our sacred tablet grew into many books of wisdom that taught us how to live in a state of dynamic balance. When the Fire Tribe first came to our shores we offered to share our sacred knowledge.

(Turns to face the Fire Tribe)

When we met, you did not show us respect. You broke the sacred tablet we gave to you.

The broken tablet appears on the ground in front of the Water Tribe. As they speak, images from their story arise from the broken pieces of the tablet.

Water Tribe Father:

It was in Western Asia, or as you call it, the Middle East, that you first practiced your strategies of invasion and colonization.

Your European empire felt threatened by the rise of an Islamic empire. You called the Arabian people infidels and launched a Crusade against them a thousand years ago. You wanted to gain control of

Jerusalem and the rich trade routes of the Middle East. You promised your impoverished peasants and troubled young men a place in heaven if they joined your holy war against us.

In East Asia, you wanted our spices, our silk and our tea. We saw your intention to exploit us, so we closed our doors to you. You used "gunboat diplomacy" to blast those doors wide open. You forced us to trade at gun point. You shipped huge quantities of illegal opium into our ports, weakening our people. As the world's first and most ruthless international drug cartel, your Fire Tribe was able to amass a great fortune.

You occupied our lands. You tried to destroy our cultures and make us worship your god. Where you could not rule directly, you dominated us through warfare, religion and trade.

You feared our great numbers and you demonized us. You called us the "yellow peril." You mocked our appearance, calling us "slant-eyes." You took many of our poorest people as coolie labor, forcing us to build your railroads and work in your mines.

You took war itself to a terrifying new level. You put radioactive fire into your bombs and dropped them on the people of Hiroshima and Nagasaki in Japan. You were the victor of World War II and few dared question your actions. Ever since, the whole world has lived in fear of nuclear war. How do we know you won't justify using your toxic weapons against us again?

As the world's superpower and biggest arms dealer you continue to play a major role in the armed conflicts that devastate countries around the world.

Water Tribe Mother:

Your Fire Tribe forced the entire world to live in a fire world. You dismissed our great philosophies as primitive and evil. Eventually we had to adapt to your world and take the fire road to industrialization. Yet through it all, many of our tablets have been preserved.

We held fast to the root of truth. In India our son Mohandas Gandhi called his sacred tablet of truth Satyagraha. He had a vision of a just and peaceful world based on uplifting all people toward universal evolution. Gandhi spoke the truth with love and brought the Fire Tribe's domination of the Water Tribe in India to an end.

Today, many people are grateful that the Water Tribe's traditional healing systems have survived. If we had not preserved our tablets, many of the Original Teachings would have been lost forever. Today so many people in our troubled world are turning to our rich meditation traditions and our body-mind-spirit healing practices like yoga, Ayurveda, herbal medicine, acupuncture, and martial arts like Tai Chi and Aikido.

Today, the Tibetan people and their spiritual leader, the Dalai Lama, generously share their teachings of conscious living and conscious dying. Even in exile, their light of truth shines clearly.

Our healing traditions teach us that when Water and Fire are out of balance, disease results. Let us work together to heal our Water and Fire Tribes.

Water Tribe Father:

The truth is that each tribe and each person has a role to play in healing our planet. The beautiful Human Earth we dream of begins with each of us nourishing the Four Roots and Tree of Life within ourselves.

Sky-Woman thanks the Water Tribe for sharing their story. Everyone sits in silence as they accept the Water Tribe's story into their heart.

Where is the Wind Tribe of Turtle Island?

The yellow root of peace begins to glow and everyone turns to hear the Wind Tribe's story. But the Wind Tribe Mother and Father are no longer standing on their root. They have slipped beneath the ground and again lie silent under their root.

Sky-Woman:

(Addressing the UN people)

We stand here in America, the land of the Wind Tribe, the land they call Turtle Island.

Look around you at the 193 UN ambassadors. The nations from the European Fire Tribe are fully represented here. There are also many ambassadors from the Asian Water Tribe nations and the African Earth Tribe nations.

But where are the ambassadors from the Native American Wind Tribe nations? Where are the representatives from the Iroquois, the Algonquin, the Wampanoag, the Cherokee, the Sioux, the Ojibwe, the Salish, the Navajo, the Hopi and the many tribes whose names have been forgotten?

Where are my children of the Wind Tribe?

Sky-Man:

When the Fire Tribe arrived, this continent was known as Turtle Island. This beautiful island where we are meeting was home to the Manhattan tribe. Half the states still carry Native American names. Have you heard of Massachusetts? Connecticut? Ohio? Mississippi? Texas? Minnesota? The Dakotas? Oregon? In these names you hear the long-lost voices of the original inhabitants of this land.

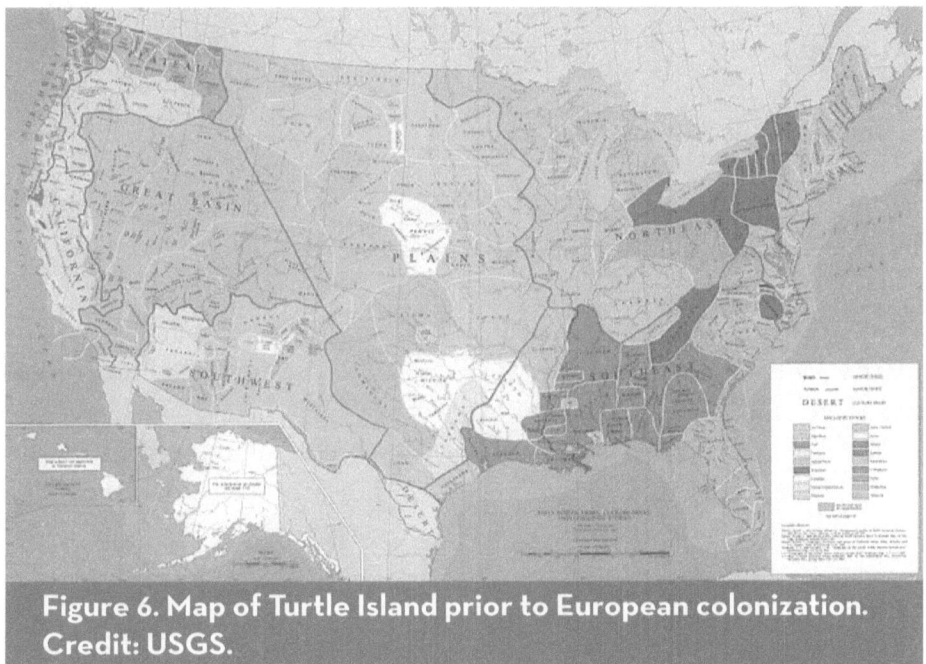

Figure 6. Map of Turtle Island prior to European colonization. Credit: USGS.

Before the Fire Tribe's arrival, the Wind Tribe flourished in great numbers from the Atlantic to the Pacific, from the Arctic circle to the tip of South America. Every hill and every valley was under the care of a clan who hunted, fished and grew crops in harmony with nature.

Then the Fire Tribe came and where there had been a hundred Native Americans, soon less than ten remained. Often this happened within a single generation. Can you imagine the tragic losses and the unbearable heartbreak the Wind Tribe has endured?

The UN people are stunned and saddened by the disappearance of the Wind Tribe.

Sky-Woman:

Despite all of this trauma, the Native American people have survived. They are still here. For many decades, representatives from the Iroquois Nation, the Hopi Nation and others have come to the UN to ask for their seat at the table of nations...and each time they have been refused.

Now...do you want to hear the Wind Tribe tell their story?

UN people:

(Eagerly)

Yes, we want to hear their story.

Wind Tribe keeps the council circle alive

All eyes turn toward the empty yellow root of peace.

The Mother and Father of the Wind Tribe rise up from the ground and stand upon the glowing yellow root.

The UN people feel a sense of joy and relief at the return of the Wind Tribe. With the Wind Tribe standing on their root the Four Roots are in balance again.

Wind Tribe Father:

Our mission is to keep the sacred council alive, to gather in peace and share stories with each other until we come to one mind. We carried our story belt to Turtle Island. We have been the caretakers of this land for countless generations.

Wind Tribe Mother:

Turtle Island was an earthly paradise before the Europeans came. There was no pollution and there were no ugly places. We required no factories, no armies, no hospitals, no courts or prisons. Every place was beautiful and we lived in harmony with Mother Earth.

(Turning to the Fire Tribe)

When you arrived on our shores, we treated you as family and cared for you. We taught you how to plant corn, beans and squash. We showed you where to find the wild plants that carried healing medicine. We guided you to places where the land was fertile and the deer were plentiful.

Wind Tribe Father:

We welcomed your tribe as brothers and sisters. When we understood that you wanted to live with us here on Turtle Island, we asked you to create a beautiful world with us, a blending of our two cultures under the Tree of Life. We offered you our men and women as marriage partners so we could become one family.

You refused to become family with us. Instead you treated us as inferiors. You set yourself above us as an all-knowing great white father. You took the story belt we gave you and ripped it apart.

The torn story belt appears on the ground in front of the Wind Tribe. As they speak, images from their story arise from the scattered beads of the belt.

Wind Tribe Father:

We saw that you were homeless refugees from across the great ocean and we had compassion for you. You were fleeing religious persecution, poverty, disease-ridden cities and constant warfare in your homeland. We saw your scars and your unhealed wounds.

We saw the sickness in your eyes. We saw that you had lost your connection with Mother Earth and Father Sky. We invited you to our healing council. We offered to share our sacred plants that reconnect us to spirit. We asked you to join us in loving and caring for this land.

But you refused to join us in council. You called our rituals "devil worship." You see yourself as champions of religious liberty but as soon as you gained power you made it illegal for us to practice our spiritual traditions *in our own land*. You persecuted our spiritual leaders until our culture was nearly destroyed.

Wind Tribe Mother:

Before you came, we enjoyed vibrant health on Turtle Island for countless generations. Illness was rare and infectious epidemics were virtually unknown. We did not make slaves of our animal brothers and sisters so we did not have the many pandemics and plagues that you caught from your domesticated animals.

You brought deadly diseases to our land. Entire family lines were destroyed, often within a matter of weeks. After the plague came to a village, the dead bodies of babies, children, adults, grandparents and great-grandparents all lay together in one lodge. The few survivors fled westward seeking refuge.

There was no one left to bury the bodies, no one left to mourn the dead and perform the rituals.

Having brought sickness into our land, you did not stop. You knew about the plague but you did not quarantine yourselves. You kept coming, more and more of you, spreading disease further west to the next tribe.

You then took advantage of our devastated tribes. Instead of extending compassion, you heaped guilt upon us. You told us that we had an evil nature and that we had caused our own misfortunes by worshiping false gods. You manipulated what remained of our traumatized tribes, making secret land deals, turning tribe against tribe.

From the beginning you were more interested in stealing our land than in getting to know us as neighbors. You made treaties that said the land would remain ours "as long as the grasses grow and the waters flow." But before even one moon had passed, more Fire Tribe people rushed in.

When only a few of us remained, we tried to defend ourselves from impending extinction. You sent your soldiers and destroyed entire villages including elders, women and children.

Wind Tribe Father:

You believed you had a "divine right" to our land because you had "discovered" it. After you freed yourselves from the domination of the British empire, you set out to build your own American empire by dominating us. You started here in New York, the Empire State. You saw us, not as human beings, but as obstacles blocking the path to your "manifest destiny."

The course of empire made its way westward, relentlessly pushing our people out of its way. You decided that the final solution to the "Indian problem" was to eliminate us as completely as possible. You chased our families into the coldest mountains and the harshest deserts. Our scouts saw you marching and heard you shouting your genocidal chant: "The only good Indian is a dead Indian!"

When your armies finally defeated us, you banished us from our homelands, forcing us into exile on a Trail of Tears. You herded us like cattle onto reservations in order to domesticate us. You continued your campaign of domination with cultural warfare. You outlawed our language and our ceremonies. You took our children from our homes and put them in boarding schools. You stripped them of their names, cut off their hair, and taught them to hate their ancestors' way of life.

This is our history with you. You can read about the so-called "Indian wars" in your own history books. The European Fire Tribe's war of extermination against the Wind Tribe of Turtle Island began in 1492 and lasted for 400 years. It is the longest war in human history and for many of us it continues to this day.

Our people have lived on this land from the beginning. We are still here. We never sold our land. How could we sell our Mother?

We saw how you treated the beautiful land you took from us. We saw how you treated your African slaves from the Earth Tribe and your Asian laborers from the Water Tribe. We saw how you treated your own women as property.

We have witnessed everything. This is our story.

Wind Tribe Mother:

Throughout our years of suffering and survival, we have continued to practice the Original Teachings and to gather in council. We weave our story belts and tell our ancient stories around the winter fires. We cry our tears. We purify our hearts.

The Fire Tribe believes that America is a special place. The Wind Tribe believes that Turtle Island is a special place. The Fire Tribe and the Wind Tribe now share a deep love for this land that we both call home. Many from the African Earth Tribe and the Asian Water Tribe now live here too and love this land.

The Wind Tribe Mother and Father turn to address the UN people.

Wind Tribe Father:

From the beginning of time, Turtle Island was destined to become the meeting place of the Four Tribes. A long time ago, all the lands that are now separated were part of one great turtle, one supercontinent. The Tree of Life stood at the center, on land that later became North America.

We invite all our brothers and sisters to join us in restoring the Tree of Life here on Turtle Island.

Sky-Woman thanks the Wind Tribe for sharing their story. Everyone sits in silence as they accept the Wind Tribe's story into their heart.

Fire Tribe overcome with despair

The Water, Earth and Fire Tribes sit in stunned silence. How could they have been so unaware of the loss of one of their four Great Tribes?

The Father and Mother of the Fire Tribe respond and move to the center.

Fire Tribe Father:

(Speaking to the Wind Tribe and the two other tribes with deep remorse)

When we first met 500 years ago, I failed to recognize you as family. My ears were deaf to your stories. Even now as I listen to you I become so disturbed that I want to run from your stories…but I have nowhere left to run.

I mourn the loss of so many from the great Wind Tribe. I mourn the harm I caused the Earth and Water Tribes. There can be no peace until we gather with all of you under the Tree of Life once more.

(Becoming reflective)

I lost my way long ago. I followed the red root of power but forgot the Tree of Life of which it is a part.

I have always thought of myself as the hero of the story, the great hero of human history. Yet I see that in your stories I have played the role of the villain. I can no longer justify my past acts of killing and destruction. I look around at the polluted, war-torn world I have created and I am ashamed of my thoughtless devastation.

(Growing more distraught)

I made power, money and fire technology into false gods that I worshiped above all others. Now they offer me nothing. I am at war with myself and I can find no rest.

My ears are filled with screams of pain. My mouth is bitter with the taste of my own cruelty. My belly churns with the putrefied remains of the dead. My brain that sought to know all and control all can no longer control even its own thoughts. I have run out of stories to believe in. My mind spins madly down a dark hole.

I stand here at the end of the Fire road. My grand dreams of mighty empires and gleaming cities now end in a nightmare of desolation and despair.

Dizzy and overcome with nausea, Fire Tribe Father drops to his knees. The Fire Tribe Mother joins him.

Fire Tribe Mother:

(Cries out)

My Fire Tribe is suffering. Many families are isolated and our clans are broken. My children are unhappy and confused. Our people become sicker each year.

Fire Tribe Father:

(Buries his head in his hands)

I have created a world in which I no longer want to live.

7.   Reconciliation

Reconciliation of the Four Tribes

Sky-Woman and Sky-Man walk over to the Fire Tribe Father and Mother.

Sky-Man:
(Solemnly)
It is as you say.

Sky-Woman:
(Gravely)
There is much to mourn and much to grieve.

Everyone sits in silence as they feel the tragedy of the past and the perils of the present.

Wind Tribe Mother:
(Compassionately)
We have experienced many sorrows on this journey. It has become a trail of tears, for all of us.

Wind Tribe Father:
Through sharing our grief we can begin to heal our hearts.

The Wind Tribe Mother and Father walk over to the Fire Tribe, offer them a hand, and help them stand up again.

Wind Tribe Father:
Your mission was to reunite us. Our tribes now share one earth. Let us live together in peace under the Tree of Life.

The Earth and Water Tribes join the Wind and Fire Tribes. Tears flow as they all embrace each other. Though much remains to be healed, their hearts have opened.

Fire Tribe Father:

(With deep emotion)
Thank you for accepting me as family.

Fire Tribe Mother:

(Her face brightening)
I can feel your love healing me.

Sky-Woman:

You have all spoken from your heart and listened with your heart. Through telling your stories the healing has begun.

Requesting the gifts

Fire Tribe Father:

(Recovering)
I know I have been selfish and arrogant so I hesitate to ask something for myself. Yet I have been humbled here today and I wish to say what is in my heart.

I need your gifts.

I need the gifts I refused so long ago. I feel deep remorse for trying to create a New World without your help. Now I cannot even take one step without you.

Fire Tribe Mother:

If you are still willing to share your precious gifts with us, we would be honored to receive them.

The roots begin to glow. On the green root, the broken drum is restored to soundness. On the blue root, the pieces of the stone tablet reassemble. On the yellow root, the story belt reweaves itself.

Earth Tribe gives drum

African Earth Tribe Father:

The Fire Tribe was not the only tribe to go too far on its own root. We too need the gifts of the other tribes.

I now see that our focus on the root of love became unbalanced. Our love for our family was deep…but it grew too narrow. We were kind, but only to our own kind. Our love did not grow to include all the other African tribes. We too built empires, resorted to war and engaged in slavery.

(To Sky-Woman and Sky-Man)

Thank you for coming so we can finally share our gifts with each other and create the beautiful world we all want for our children.

African Earth Tribe Mother:

(Picking up the drum)

We give our sacred drum to all our sisters and brothers. The drum calls the tribes to council. The beat of the drum holds us as we dance.

We have lost many of our most precious traditions over the generations.

(Smiling)

Yet we still remember how to be a family, how to love each other and how to dance together.

Earth Tribe Father:

Many years ago in America, Martin Luther King, Jr. invited the Fire Tribe to end the festering wound of racial segregation and become one family with the Earth Tribe. Brother Martin's vision went far beyond changing discriminatory laws.

Let us honor his heartfelt dream for us: That we "join hands as sisters and brothers" and dance together as one family. That we open our hearts to love, commit ourselves to peace and create a "beloved community."

Earth Tribe Mother:

The drum is a woman.

Honor Sky-Woman and restore women to their rightful place at the center of life. Join us in re-creating a society that values the sacred feminine. When women control their own bodies we will have healthier, happier children and our family can find its ideal size on Mother Earth.

Ask women to be the primary keepers of society's resources. Then the necessities of life will be distributed so that everyone has what they need to grow and prosper.

Earth Tribe Father:

The cycle of birth and death spins the spiral of evolution.

Along the way, we experience many joys, many sorrows. Let us re-create sacred rituals for the great passages of life. Shared rituals allow us to heal — and inspire us to celebrate.

We are the Earth Tribe of love. We will share our wisdom so that new tribes can grow naturally and everyone can be part of a loving family and community.

Earth Tribe Mother:

At our next council, we want to teach you a sacred dance. When you learn this dance you will be able to dance with whatever life offers you.

Water Tribe gives tablets

Asian Water Tribe Father:

Thank you for sharing your drum and your love. As I look back on our Water Tribe's journey, I see that we too lost sight of the other roots and grew unbalanced. Over the centuries our focus on truth at times became overly abstract and philosophical. We too need the gifts of the other tribes.

Asian Water Tribe Mother:

(Picking up the sacred tablets)

We give you our sacred tablets and invite you to look inward with us. Change begins in our own hearts. It starts with restoring the Tree of Life that grows within us. I believe we can evolve if we honor the Four Roots of Love, Truth, Peace and Power in our daily lives.

The spiral of evolution calls us to grow to the next level in our journey, from separation to wholeness.

Water Tribe Father:

I hear future generations calling us to grow beyond ego and beyond empire. At our next council we want to share a sacred tablet with you, one that reveals ways to rediscover the true self within.

We are the Water Tribe of truth. Let us gather under the Tree of Life and evolve our consciousness so we can create one mind.

Wind Tribe gives story belt

Native American Wind Tribe Father:

Thank you for sharing your sacred tablet of truth.

When the ancient land bridge to Asia disappeared thousands of years ago, our tribe lost touch with your Water Tribe and the other tribes. Our shamans sometimes dreamed of reuniting with you.

We developed the art of peace in our councils. But in some of our ancient societies our leaders forgot that peace is a living relationship. The Aztec, Incan, Mayan and Cahokian empires built pyramids and became stuck in social hierarchies that blocked the flow of energy. They fell into the trap of thinking they could impose a lasting peace through killing and conquest.

We learned that a forced peace is a false peace. True peace is recreated daily through practicing peace. Peace is dynamic and ever-changing. The Tree of Life can only flourish when all Four Roots are in balance.

Native American Wind Tribe Mother:

Today Turtle Island has become the meeting place for all our tribes. Our brother and sister tribes from Asia, Europe and Africa have followed their roots here to gather under the Tree of Life. We give you our story belt and invite you to celebrate our next council here on Turtle Island.

Wind Tribe Father:

Many of our story belts have been lost or destroyed. Yet our elders have kept some of our most precious stories alive. We want to tell you the untold story of Turtle Island. This story grows from the land upon which we walk. It is about our deep past and our sacred future.

One of our story belts is the Peacemakers Belt. It tells of a time long before the Mayflower arrived. It begins during a dark time in our own history. Like all people, we struggle with the emotions of fear, greed and anger. During that dark time we did not treat each other like family. The Four Roots within our own Wind Tribe became unbalanced. We no longer lived in peace. Fighting and bloodshed nearly destroyed us.

We asked Sky-Woman and Sky-Man for help and they heard our cries. They sent us spiritual teachers, called the Peacemakers, and we listened to them.

Wind Tribe Mother:

The Peacemakers guided us through our dark time and we came to a new understanding of peace. They taught us that even though we are all family, we will lose that family feeling unless we cultivate it every day. Hurt, anger, hatred and violence are part of human life. The Peacemakers taught us rituals to heal the traumas of the past and the hurts of the present. They showed us how to sit in council, share our stories, resolve conflicts and come to one mind.

Thanks to the Peacemakers, a great miracle occurred here on Turtle Island. We restored the Tree of Life. The dark times came to an end. We built a Great Lodge of Peace under whose roof many nations lived in harmony. Our world became beautiful again.

Wind Tribe Father:

Now our human family is facing another dark time. This miracle can happen here again. At our next council we will share our Peacemakers story belt. This story can help guide us through our dark time and into the light.

May you enjoy peace in your heart and in all your relationships.

Fire Tribe makes a pledge

Fire Tribe Father:

I thank all of you for your great generosity of spirit. I will honor your gifts. Your stories have saved my life. Your friendship has restored my desire to live. I want to join with the wounded warriors of all tribes to heal the traumas we carry as men. Our women and children need healthy, loving husbands and fathers.

The only gift I have to give you in return is my desire to use my power to serve our whole family and the Tree of Life.

(Pointing to his chest of tools)

My treasure chest once held good and useful tools. Now it overflows with many things that are toxic to life and detrimental to our well-being. I promise to cleanse our chest so that it contains only tools that nourish the Tree of Life. I want to advance technology by loving Mother Nature instead of manipulating her. Together our tribes can create a new technology that honors Mother Earth and Father Sky.

Fire Tribe Mother:

The women of the Fire Tribe have struggled to regain the power that our men took from us. Now we have greater social equality. Yet we still live in a man's world. When I see Sky-Woman I can feel how much of my inner nature as a woman has been lost over the centuries.

Sky-Woman, with your guidance I want to join with my sisters in the other tribes and rediscover our unique gifts as women.

The Mothers and Fathers of each tribe return to their respective roots and face the Tree of Life. They raise their hands together and red, green, yellow and blue energies surge through the roots into the Tree of Life. The Tree stands tall and strong. Glowing fruits appear on its branches.

The Four Tribes feel a sense of connection that they haven't felt since they began their separate journeys 70,000 years ago. They are grateful for each other's presence. They sit upon their roots and rest.

Sky-Man:

(To the UN people)

During your journeys you lost the story of the Four Tribes. When you lose your story, you lose your way. Now you have heard your story and you can find your way again.

Sky-Woman:

We give you a new mission: Return to the Tree of Life. It is time to combine your gifts and grow a Human Earth with the Tree of Life at its center.

The UN people are stunned by this new view of their past. They realize that they are all descendants of the Four Tribes. They see the world they live in with new eyes. They sense the healing power of love and yearn for healing in their lives. Yet they are also more aware of their own brokenness, the deep ancestral pain they carry in their families and in their own hearts.

PART 4:
ORIGIN AND DESTINY

8. New Creation Story

Forgotten origin

Sky-Woman:

You have now learned about your journey as Four Tribes, but your journey actually began long before that. In order to heal more deeply you need to understand your origins. Your journey started with the beginning of the universe itself. You were present at the dawn of creation.

But as you built your empires, you forgot your origins. When your ego began to dominate, it suppressed the messages from the deeper, more ancient regions of your brain that connect you to your source. You could no longer access the natural intelligence encoded in your DNA. You could no longer hear the ancestral voices that linked you to past generations. You felt abandoned, like orphans in a cold, uncaring universe.

The truth is that we never abandoned you. Sky-Man and I are always holding you, even in your darkest moments.

Sky-Man:

Empire distorted the empowering story of creation into a coercive tale of sin and disobedience, fear and shame. Now the time has come to tell you a true story of creation, one that will reunite you with your universal family. To tell this great story we now ask your Galactic Ancestors, the Sky Elders, to join us from the spirit world.

Sky-Man and Sky-Woman:

(Lifting their arms up to the sky)

Sky-Grandmother and Sky-Grandfather, we invite you to join us for this planetary council with our children.

Two plasma tubes of white light stream down from the sky. They begin to vibrate with rainbow-colored rays. The two Sky Elders materialize and stand next to each other, radiating light.

Sky-Grandfather's hair and long beard are silver-gray. Sky-Grandmother's gleaming silver-white hair flows down her back. They both have brown skin and wear ancient robes with mysterious symbols. Their smiling faces are creased with the wisdom of age. Their clear eyes gaze around the room.

Learning to think like a planet

Sky-Grandfather:

Your origin and destiny are actually one with that of the universe itself. You went on your missions so you could develop the skills you needed to reunite and co-evolve with the Earth.

It is your destiny to learn to think like a planet!

Imagine the bountiful and sustainable world you can create when you learn to think *with* Mother Nature instead of manipulating her. Then you will have access to all the wisdom, knowledge and power of Mother Nature herself. And all the earth will benefit from your creativity.

A beautiful blue-green sphere descends from the sky. Slowly it comes to a stop and hovers in front of the UN people. As they look more

Figure 7. Planet Earth West. Credit: NASA

Figure 8. Planet Earth East. Credit: NASA.

closely at this sphere they realize with amazement that it is a miniature earth. But it is not a globe or a replica. It's something magical — a living, breathing planet earth.

Love and wonder begin to grow within as they see her floating majestically, rotating gracefully on her axis. They see the beauty of the earth, the land and the blue oceans, the white clouds swirling in the precious envelope of atmosphere. They notice the shapes and colors of the continents: the richly textured surface, mountain ranges rising up, lush green valleys, broad plateaus, deep canyons, sandy deserts, leafy forests and golden grasslands.

They see the biosphere, the living layer of plants and animals that covers the planet. Birds flying through the air. Animals moving through the meadows and the forests. Fish swimming in the oceans, lakes and rivers.

Sky-Grandmother:

You have a beautiful planet, a sacred oasis in the universe. Mother Earth gave birth to you.

Hidden within your own language you can still find this truth. Your words for yourselves, humans, and *Homo sapiens*, comes from a very ancient Latin word for earth, "humus." Today gardeners still use this term to describe especially rich soil. *Homo sapiens* means earth that has become conscious and wise.

Just as apples grow on an apple tree, humans grow on a Human Earth.

Birth of the universe

Sky-Grandmother:

To understand your life purpose, we are calling you to learn about things that have been hidden for thousands of years. Today we are reviving the art of anamnesis, the remembering of things forgotten. The knowledge we are about to share with you is part of the Original Teachings. If the Original Teachings were written in a book, its pages would be woven from the living intelligence of the universe.

Sky-Grandfather:

What you are about to see will challenge the way you look at the world. We will be speaking to you about things that exist beyond your current level of consciousness. Hearing these teachings will help you

Figure 9. Solar system. Credit: NASA.

heal from the disease of separation. Seeing the universe in a new way will enable you to evolve and prosper.

The Sky Elders reopen the vision space. The UN people see the earth become smaller as the entire solar system comes into view.

Then the vision zooms out to reveal the Milky Way galaxy and the vast starry universe.

Figure 10. Galaxy. Credit: Public domain.

Sky-Grandmother:

How was the earth created? What is the deeper meaning of your journey? To understand we need to go back to the beginning of everything.

Suddenly the vision space goes dark. But it is a deeper darkness than anyone has ever experienced. Close to the center of the vision space an even deeper, darker circle forms. This dark hole pulls in the dim light at its edges. Soon it begins to suck in the vision space itself and threatens to consume the world around it.

Sky-Grandmother:

(Reassuringly)

The truth is, this universe began when the very first Sky-Woman and Sky-Man woke up.

In the vision space a luminous, bluish-white light emerges from the dark hole. The figures of First Sky-Woman and First Sky-Man appear against the dark background. They lie curled together in a fetal position, like a human Yin-Yang symbol. They rest in blissful slumber. Then Sky-Man becomes aware that he is male and he stretches. Sky-Woman becomes aware that she is female and she uncurls. They separate from each other.

When they were one, they could not see each other. Now they can see each other's beauty and a deep desire arises between them. The luminous figures display the classic tantric splendor of the male and female form.

Cosmic music fills the air as First Sky-Woman and First Sky-Man begin making love. Sky-Woman sits astride Sky-Man as their bodies move rhythmically together. Then he rises up and she lies down and the energy builds between them. The goddess and the god move back and forth until the energy reaches a crescendo.

As they climax in a cosmic orgasm, a burst of light appears at the center of their union. The figures of Sky-Woman and Sky-Man are absorbed into the radiating light. The light spirals outward, creating a translucent dark blue universe.

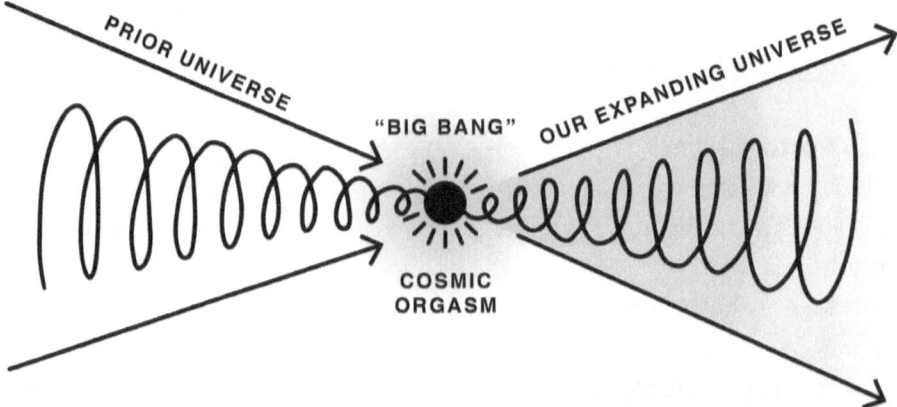

Figure 11. Cosmic creation spiral. Credit: Gerzon.

Sky-Grandmother:

The beginning of everything was not a terrifying big bang. It was an ecstatic cosmic orgasm. It is still reverberating throughout the universe today, 14 billion years later.

The UN people can feel the truth of Sky-Grandmother's creation story as they sense the still-vibrating energy of the cosmic orgasm resonating in their bodies.

Little white spirals appear in the dark blue universe. The spirals become energy particles. Atoms and molecules form. Stars begin to glow. Crystal shapes turn into little rocks.

Materializing a geosphere

Sky-Grandfather:

Let's visit your neighborhood and see what's happening there.

In the vision space the UN people see a big spiral of dust and gas begin to form.

Sky-Grandfather:

At the center of the spiral where the energy is most intense, our sun begins to glow. In the swirling outer spiral, rocks begin to clump together and form molten protoplanets. One of these becomes the early earth. The earth's gravity attracts more rocks and grows larger.

Earth develops an iron core that rotates and pulsates, creating a powerful geodynamo. It becomes the beating heart of the planet and generates a protective electromagnetic field. Lighter elements rise to the surface and form a solid crust. Now Mother Earth has grown a skin.

Her gravity pulls in snowball-like comets that begin to fill the earth with water. Volcanoes erupt, releasing steam and gas. A primitive atmosphere starts to form around the earth. The rough outline of earth's magnetosphere appears.

Mother Earth is now a rotating geosphere with a beating heart at her center, a skin of stone, pools of water and a thin atmosphere. The geosphere is the first of the five great spheres that will come into being.

Next the earth will grow a biosphere and a life-giving atmosphere. And then as earth nears maturity you will witness the growth of two extraordinary new spheres, the humasphere and the noosphere.

Growing a biosphere and atmosphere

Sky-Grandmother:

Mother Earth is ready for the miracle of life to occur. Those comets that brought water to the earth carry with them the seeds of life that float throughout the universe.

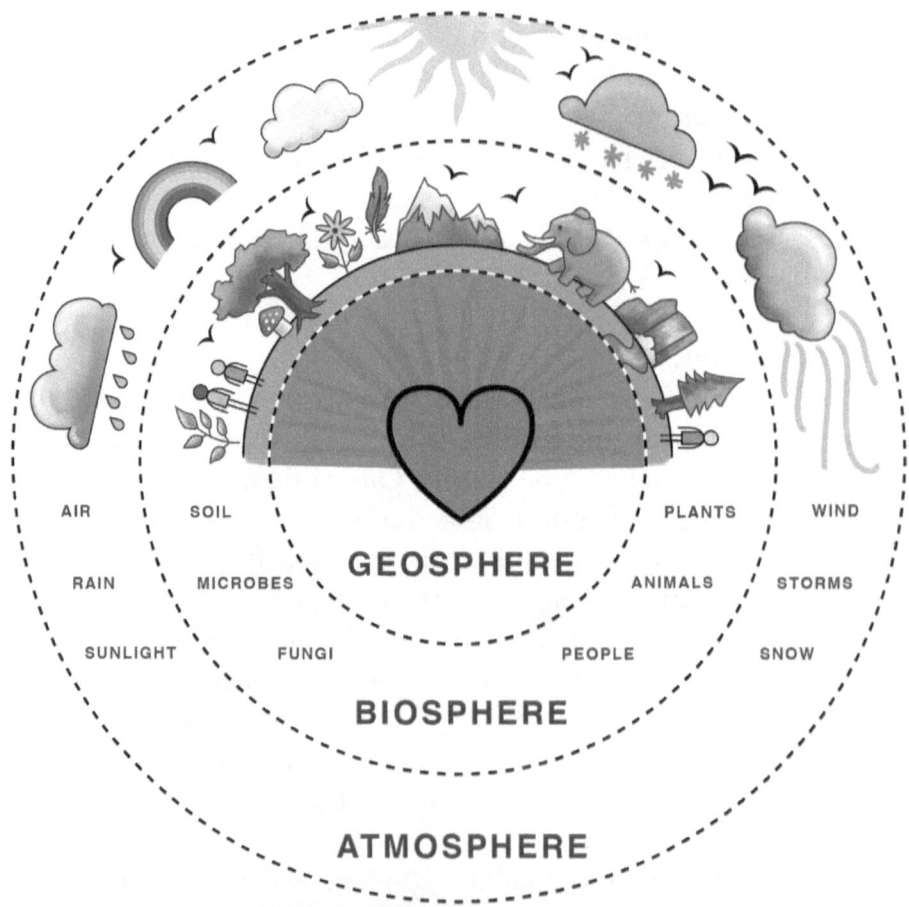

Figure 12. Geosphere-Biosphere-Atmosphere. Credit: Gerzon

Father Sun sends light, warmth and the spark of life. Mother Earth incubates the seed eggs in the warm womb of her oceans. Little creatures, one-celled organisms, appear. They join together and form more complex organisms. Before long, fish are swimming in the seas.

As the earth matures, a protective oxygen-rich atmosphere develops. Now life can crawl out of the oceans and onto those big bare continents. The land soon grows a colorful and diverse layer of life. Animals follow plants onto the land.

Sky-Grandmother:

Mother Earth has grown a biosphere. She is becoming the living Goddess that the Greeks later called Gaia.

Plants and animals co-evolve for billions of years. They eat and interact with the planet they live on. They enrich the soil and shape the landscape. They breathe the atmosphere and affect the weather. Mother Earth's magnetosphere becomes stronger and forms a protective energy field around the planet.

Lush tropical forests grow in the warm, rainy places. Temperate zones display a rich variety of lifeforms, large and small. Amphibians, reptiles, insects, birds and mammals appear. Even the cold snowy regions become home to hardy plants and animals.

Our great planet changed slowly over the eons, until a strange new species appeared who revolutionized life on earth. Sky-Woman and Sky-Man are ready to tell you all about them.

9. Creation of the humasphere

Conscious humans dream mind clouds

Sky-Man:

(To the Sky Elders)

Thank you, Sky-Grandmother and Sky-Grandfather for your creation story.

(To the UN people and the Four Tribes)

We want to tell you the next part of the story.

About six million years ago a remarkable new lifeform begins standing upright on this beautiful earth and starts asking all kinds of questions. Yes, I'm talking about early humans.

You human beings love each other and want to live together, so families become clans and clans become tribes. You not only ask questions, you come up with answers. You invent helpful tools, build shelters, master fire, learn to cook, and expand your menu to include just about anything that's edible.

Sky-Woman:

Then about 200,000 years ago consciousness on earth takes a gigantic leap. I will tell you a story about how you started to think your first thoughts and how the human mind cloud came into being.

In the vision space the UN people see a dark-skinned hunter-gatherer mother sitting outside a bark-covered hut, breastfeeding her baby girl. She is rocking gently back and forth. Her eyes are closed and she has a blissful, dreamy look on her face.

She is grateful that her daughter is healthy and happy. It has been a dry summer and she has had to walk many miles today with her baby in search of the wild foods that sustain her family. Her baby's gentle, rhythmic sucking helps the mother relax.

Mother and baby still retain body memories of their past state of oneness. They each feel the milk as it flows from one to the other. The mother opens her eyes and stops rocking. She looks into her baby's eyes and sees her child looking lovingly back at her. The baby looks into her mother's eyes and sees her mother looking lovingly at her.

Mother:
(Sings)
I am I and you are you.
Together we are one family.

Connections light up in both of their brains in a new and evolutionary way, activating the Sky energy centers above their heads. Energy flows between their two Sky centers, creating for the first time a shared, light blue, translucent mind cloud that hovers above them. An image of the mother and baby appears in the mind cloud.

Earth's consciousness has jumped out of herself so that she could look back at herself. Earth, who has been conscious all along, becomes conscious of being conscious.

In an elated voice, the woman calls to her husband who joins her. She gestures for him to look into her eyes. Then she directs his gaze to the baby's eyes. The father looks lovingly into his baby's eyes and she returns his gaze. He smiles. Now his Sky energy center becomes activated too and his mind cloud is joined to theirs. Now the image in their shared mind cloud includes all three of them.

Mother and Father:
(Sing)
I am I and you are you.
Together we are one family.

The baby gurgles and smiles; her eyes light up.

Later when the mother and father make love, they look into each other's eyes and a shared mind cloud appears above their heads. In their mind cloud many strange new images appear of humans transforming the world.

As they lie together, looking up at the stars, their resonant voices translate their shared vision into words. They tell the first human stories about the future.

Mother:

I see a Human Earth. We can make the earth a safer, healthier home for our children. In this new world I will not have to walk so far to find food. In my vision I see women nurturing many kinds of plants in gardens around our huts. We can stay in one place. We will not have to move so often.

Father:

I too see a Human Earth. In this new world we will no longer have to follow the wild herds. I see us becoming closer partners with our animal friends. Some of them come to live with us. We protect and feed them and they share their special powers with us. They give us meat, milk and eggs. We make more powerful spears and no longer fear the bears and lions who want to eat us. Our children grow strong and our people prosper.

The next day they call everyone in their clan together for a council. They dance and then sit in a circle and share their vision of a Human Earth.

Mother:

Our children will grow big and strong on this Human Earth. There will be many of us.

Father:

Alone, we live each day in fear of starvation and predators. Together, we can create a Human Earth where we can grow and prosper.

Their stories create a shared mind cloud above the clan circle. In the mind cloud a village appears with larger, more comfortable huts, vegetable gardens, grain fields, chickens scratching in the dirt, and sheep, cattle and goats grazing in the pastures. They see themselves in the mind cloud, celebrating together, feasting and dancing.

Night falls and the people gaze at the starry sky. High in the night sky they see the violet-hued cloud of the spirit world. They commune with the ancestors who have passed on. They attune their minds to the children who are waiting in the spirit world to be born. They thank their ancestors and their future children for this vision of a Human Earth.

Everyone in the clan:
(Sings)
I am I and you are you.
Together we are one family.

Their ancestors and their future children hear them singing and descend from the spirit world to be with them in their mind cloud. They bless them with wisdom and guidance.

Humasphere grows

Sky-Woman:
(Pointing to the village scene in the vision space)
Your original vision was of a Human Earth where you joined together and created a healthy, happy planet.

When your Four Tribes left your homeland in Africa and spread all over the world, you accomplished something truly amazing. *You created a new sphere of life on this planet!*

Gradually a beautiful new layer of life begins to form between the biosphere and the atmosphere. The humasphere is your networks of families, clans and tribes. It is the world you create through your culture and technology. This new sphere revolutionizes life on earth. Humans begin to shape the planet.

In the vision space, early human structures become visible on earth. In the plains, nomadic hunters and herders build huts made of animal skins. In more fertile and settled areas, people live in villages of mud brick houses with thatched roofs. Trails connect the villages. Humans adapt to a rich diversity of ecological habitats. In each region they develop unique lifestyles, clothing, diet, tools and shelters.

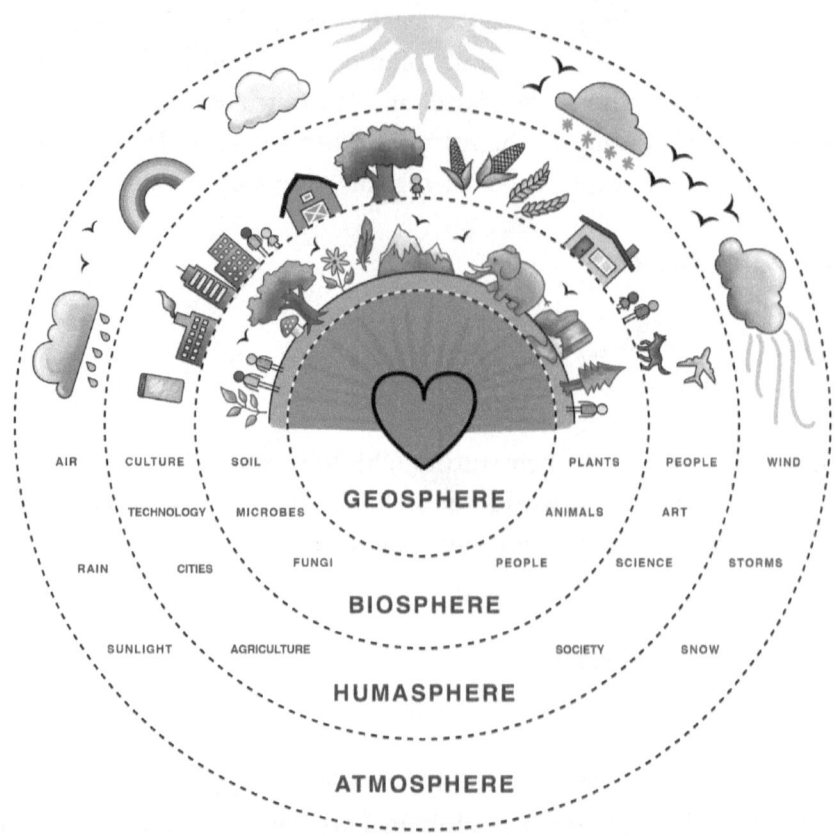

Figure 13. Humasphere develops. Credit: Gerzon

They live by hunting animals and gathering wild foods. There are times of plenty and times of scarcity.

Sky-Woman:

At this time there are very few of you. Yet you live all over the planet. The humasphere weaves a beautiful tapestry with Mother Earth that blends seamlessly into the landscape and changes with the seasons. As the humasphere grows, it becomes a new environment that begins to transform the humans living within it.

The Four Tribes settle all over the world and create their own visions of a Human Earth.

Villages are growing on every continent and in every climate. The humasphere becomes richer and more diverse. People create art and enact rituals that honor and reflect the landscape.

On an open plain in western Asia a large group of people gather around a Tree of Life at the center of a standing stone circle. They are drawn from near and far. They dance and sing and tell stories. Soon they generate a powerful shared mind cloud.

Around the planet the first earthworks, temples and megaliths like Göbekli Tepe and Stonehenge rise from the ground as people gather together in larger groups. Images and symbols like the great spiral goddess help unify tribes coming from diverse far-flung regions.

Sky-Man:

The elders recognize both the opportunities and the dangers that mind clouds present. They develop rituals to maintain the clarity of the mind clouds so that they do not become too congested and dark. Each person is responsible for keeping their own mind cloud translucent and clear by practicing the ritual of inner council that helps them resolve inner conflicts, speak with integrity and act from love.

Clans sit in council to clear their mind clouds of interpersonal conflicts and misunderstandings. They listen and speak from the heart. They receive guidance and come to one mind as a group.

The seasons pass as the earth tilts on its axis during its revolution around the sun. At the four seasonal turnings of the year, the solstices and equinoxes, everyone around the planet gathers at their sacred sites and enacts rituals that renew their connection to Earth and Sky. A beautiful geometric grid work of light lines connects the planet's sacred sites with each other and activates humanity's shared mind cloud.

Noosphere evolves

Sky-Woman:

As humans inhabit every part of the planet they begin to create their own *global* mind cloud. It rises from the humasphere and reaches into the sky, merging with the earth's magnetosphere, the powerful high-energy field that Mother Earth generates with Father Sun.

An energy field becomes visible around the earth. It glows with vibrating bands of red, orange, yellow, green and blue.

Figure 14. Radiation belts. Credit: NASA.

Sky-Man:

Now your mind cloud has grown strong enough to generate electromagnetic waves that interact with and affect the earth's magnetosphere, producing a fifth layer of life called the noosphere (NOH-uh-sfeer, from Greek *noos* meaning mind).

The first thing people did when they became conscious was to look up at the stars and begin having a conversation with them. They saw another world up there, a realm of mind and spirit. The ancients understood the noosphere to be the realm of past ancestors and future children.

Traditionally this Sky World has been called the Spirit World, Heaven, Father Sky, Mother Sky and the Land of the Gods.

The noosphere protects and nourishes the earth. It filters out harmful radiation while allowing beneficial rays to come through. Scientists refer to this zone as the ionosphere, the Van Allen radiation belts and the exosphere.

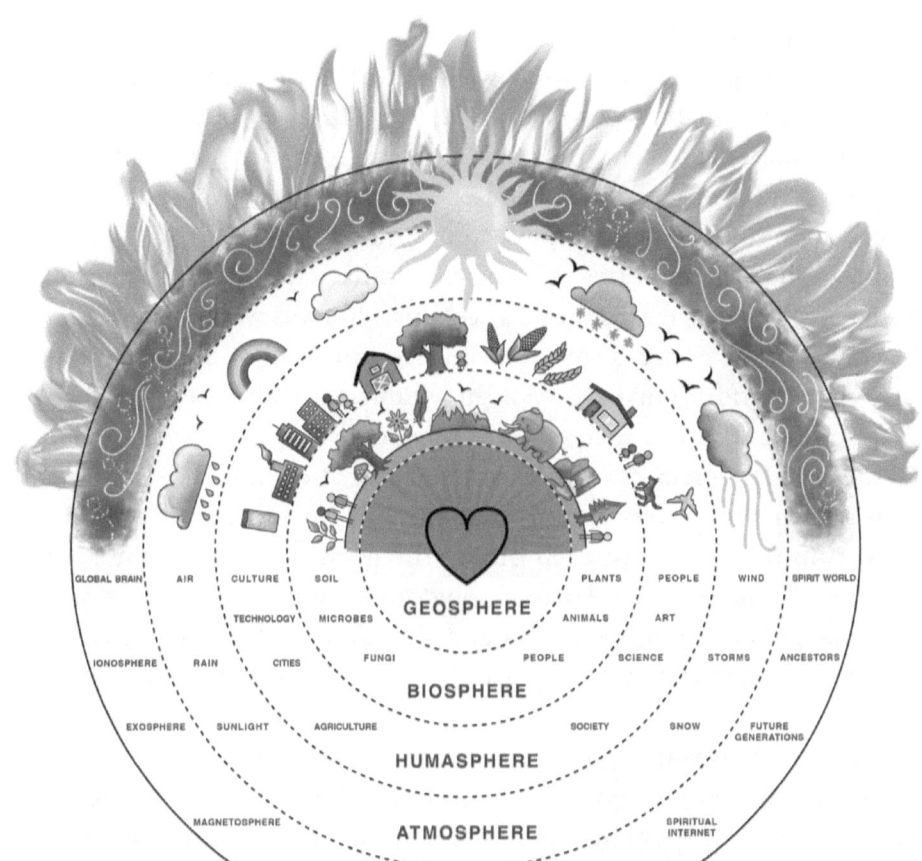

Figure 15. Earth's five spheres of life. Credit: Gerzon.

This realm is filled with highly-charged subatomic particles created by the interaction of cosmic rays, the solar wind and earth's magnetosphere. These are not random energies. They carry information. They transmit universal intelligence.

The noosphere is the global brain of Human Earth. It is your planetary thought-field, a spiritual internet that is affected by the thoughts and actions of every person on earth. The noosphere is nature's own cloud computing where electronic information processing happens for the entire planet. It is from the noosphere that cosmic intelligence and ancestral wisdom guide the planet's evolution.

Sky-Woman:

When you are out in nature, away from the city lights, and you look up at the dark night sky you can still feel the awe your ancestors felt. Maybe sometimes when you have a peak experience you have sensed the cosmic rain of electromagnetic energy falling from the noosphere as it recharges your body and spins your atoms.

The spiritual traditions of ancient India say that the noosphere contains the Akashic records, a celestial library where the Original Teachings of the entire cosmos can be read in a state of deep meditation. The Greeks and Romans called this realm the Ether, a pure, bright, clear zone of spiritual energy above the clouds.

The ancient practices of prayer, self-reflection and meditation are founded on the understanding that the human mind and the cosmic mind communicate with each other. The great spiritual teachers guide us from the noosphere. Ancient religions wisely taught that our role as humans is to listen, to understand the mind of the Creator through prayer and meditation so we can further the Creator's mission on earth.

Even though your ego's constant chatter creates interfering static, your brain still knows how to connect to the noosphere. For example, when you have a spontaneous thought, you often exclaim, "It came to me *from out of the blue!*"

We want each one of you to have unlimited access to this amazing realm of deep blue wisdom so you can access its guidance and its boundless energy.

Sky-Man:

When the five spheres are in harmony with each other the energy flows and all life flourishes.

The personal and the planetary are intertwined at every level. Each of Earth's five spheres also exist within you: Your geosphere of bones, your biosphere of organs and living tissue, your humasphere of emotions, thoughts and relationships, your atmosphere of breath and mind, and your noosphere of spirit.

Your health and the health of the planet are one and the same.

Human Earth revealed

Sky-Woman:
When you look at the earth with physical eyes alone you see the sun and earth separated by empty space.

In the vision space, the radiant sphere of the Sun appears and shines on the earth.

Sky-Woman:
But if you look at the earth with spiritual eyes you can see what Father Sun's energy does when it meets Mother Earth's body.

The solar wind becomes visible as it streams out from the sun. When it meets the earth's electromagnetic field, the earth's signature magnetosphere takes form.

Figure 16. Solar wind from the sun meets the earth and creates the earth's magnetosphere. Credit: NASA.

The UN people gasp as they recognize their own familiar human form take shape in the magnetosphere. The head is closest to the sun. The body streams outward, with its central spinal channel and curved ribs.

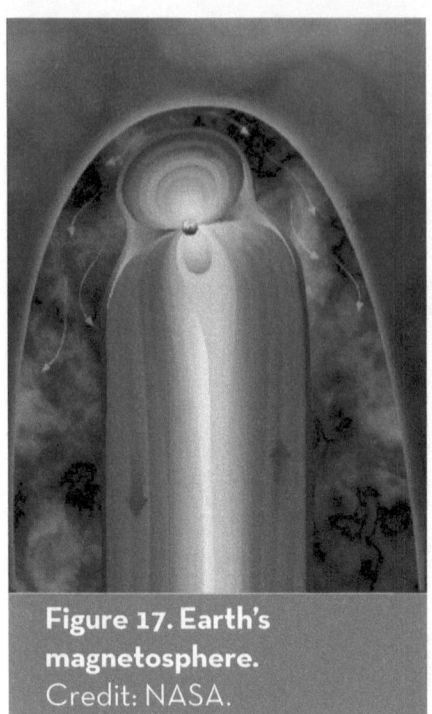

Figure 17. Earth's magnetosphere.
Credit: NASA.

Sky-Woman:

You can see that Mother Earth's magneto-body looks like you and you look like her, as a child resembles its parent. Now you can begin to understand why this is a *Human Earth*! Your spiritual instinct is true: You *are* created in the image of the divine.

Human Earth is alive and conscious. She is wise and beautiful, and the source of all our blessings. What if her children all began to love and honor her once more, to listen to her and follow her guidance, to care for her and all that she has created?

The most important question is: What is the purpose of your life? And how can you answer that without knowing the purpose of the earth?

If Mother Earth is conscious in some mysterious way that you don't quite understand…What is she thinking about?…What are her hopes and dreams?…And do you want to help make her dreams come true?

Four Tribes express hope and despair

Sky-Woman invites the Four Tribes to respond to the Original Teachings of the origin and destiny of Human Earth.

Asian Water Tribe Mother:

This vision reveals the beauty of the living universe. Our Water Tribe ancestors in Asia saw a similar vision and recorded it in our sacred books. I am inspired to see what is possible. Yet I despair when I think of our missed opportunity and the great destruction of the past 500 years.

Today the eyes of many people are blind to the truth. Since our minds have become so cloudy how can we trust our own thinking? How can our minds ever become one?

African Earth Tribe Father:

When I see our Human Earth growing in the great garden of the universe, I remember the garden of our creation in Africa. I can feel the love that pervades everything from the atom to the galaxy.

Yet I am saddened when I witness our ability to love declining each year on our planet. Empire replaced love with money. Love unites; money divides. Without love we can never become one.

Many of us have forgotten what it feels like to fully trust even one other human being. Our ego skins have grown so thick and hard. Sometimes we treat each well, sometimes not. But we seldom find relief from empire's corrosive atmosphere of separation and competition.

Native American Wind Tribe Mother:

You have shown us a universe that is alive and growing. I hope our Four Tribes will still combine our gifts and co-create a Human Earth.

But we are in a dark time now. The destruction of Turtle Island over the past 500 years has been catastrophic. In today's world, conflicts escalate into violence quickly and destructively. We are losing the ability to council with each other and solve problems, so our problems multiply. Governments no longer function to serve the people. Intimate relationships have become more difficult. The more we are crowded together, the lonelier we feel.

Although I feel inspired when I see the beautiful vision we are called to, I also feel great despair. Despite the urgency of our crisis, we seem paralyzed by our habits, unable to find a path forward.

Euro-American Fire Tribe Father:

My regret grows deeper as I see the world we could have created 500 years ago if I had honored the other tribes as family. I too feel deep despair when I see what was possible and compare it to the present world.

Now that I feel my connection with the Tree of Life again, I understand that at its core my desire to expand my power was a natural expression of life itself. I remember the sense of urgency that pushed me to unite our family. I knew at a deep level that it was up to me and my tribe to reconnect us all. But over time I forgot my sacred calling and I let my ego direct that desire to expand and unite. My sense of destiny morphed into an obsession with having total control. My ancestral dream of a Human Earth became distorted into an Empire Earth.

Now I see the possibility of channeling my desire for growth toward the evolution of a Human Earth. Yet I remain trapped in my own cloudy mind. I have learned how to manipulate nature. But in doing so I have forgotten how to co-create with her. My old habits of domination still remain embedded in the circuits of my brain. I fear that once I am back in today's world I will quickly lose my way again.

Sky-Man:

Now you remember your origin and your dream of creating a truly Human Earth. In your despair lies the way forward. Admitting you are lost is the first step to finding your way again.

The path you seek cannot be guided by the past alone. To help you see into the future, we will now ask our Sky Children of evolution to join us so they can give you a clearer vision of your destiny.

10. Sky Children of evolution arrive

Welcoming Devara and Solan

Sky-Woman:

We are fortunate that our Sky Children of evolution can visit us from the noosphere. Please join us in welcoming Devara and Solan. They have come from the Seventh Generation of a future Human Earth to share their stories and help you find your way.

The Sky Children slowly materialize in front of the UN people. A healthy and vital young woman and young man appear. They have light brown skin and dark hair. Devara wears a skirt and a top with a necklace, bracelet and earrings. Solan wears shorts and an open vest with a pendant on his chest.

They look familiarly human, yet in subtle ways they appear more highly evolved. They embody seven future generations of life-affirming evolution on Human Earth. Their eyes are slightly larger and their mouths slightly smaller. Their slender, athletic, well-proportioned bodies move with grace and power.

The UN people are stunned by their natural beauty and vitality. Solan and Devara smile and waves of love and joy wash over the UN people.

Devara:

I am Devara, your Sky daughter.

I am so happy to be here. I thank you, my ancestors, for the beautiful Human Earth that you passed down to us.

Solan:

I am Solan, your Sky son.

You seized the moment. You rose to the occasion and chose the path of evolution. I am grateful that I was born into such a wonderful world where Devara and I can enjoy our lives to the fullest.

The Sky Children walk around the circle to hug and thank each person. The UN people are overwhelmed by their sensual aliveness and deep love. They feel connected to Devara and Solan as if they were hugging their own children and grandchildren.

After greeting everyone, Solan and Devara return to the Tree of Life at the center of the amphitheater.

Life in the Seventh Generation

Devara:

(Joyfully)

As I went around the circle I could feel your love. I felt like I was hugging my own parents and grandparents.

(With concern and empathy)

I also felt the tension in your bodies and the fear at your core.

(With joy and excitement)

Solan and I are fortunate. We were born into a world that has evolved beyond fear and separation. The Tree of Life and the Four Roots of love, truth, peace and power grow strong on our Human Earth.

We experience love as the foundation of existence. Do you remember the natural love and joy that you were born with and that you can see in young children? On Human Earth we nourish that joy in every child. Instead of losing our sense of aliveness as we get older, we grow more alive with each passing year.

Solan:

We experience a deep pleasure in our bodies that comes from the energies of Mother Earth and Father Sky flowing freely through us. Many beneficial evolutionary changes occurred during the six generations that came before us. Our bodies have evolved to absorb energy from Mother Earth's core, from the air we breathe, and from the cosmic energy of Father Sky. This radiant vitality nourishes us so completely that most of us eat only one small meal a day. This evolution in our metabolism has allowed us to live much more lightly on Mother Earth than previous generations.

We have also evolved the ability to regulate our body temperature more effectively. We feel comfortable in a wide range of temperatures and that has greatly reduced our need for external heating and cooling.

Devara:

On Human Earth everyone is part of a family. Families are embedded in larger clan families which are part of ever larger circles and social spirals. Everyone feels loved. In addition to their parents, each child has many caring family members to depend on. We also have opportunities for solitude and creativity. Each person can develop their unique individuality to the fullest.

Solan:

We spend much of our time playing games. Our game culture is incredibly rich and diverse. We use games to create adventures and build relationships. Games keep us physically and mentally fit. We use experimental games to explore the edges of possibility. Many creative breakthroughs in our society have arisen from our play.

Devara:

We have evolved the ability to consciously direct our inner sexual energies. We only activate the procreative element when we are ready to welcome a child into the world. Fortunately, with the elimination of violence and the honoring of both men and women, sexual abuse and rape disappeared from the world long ago.

The Original Teachings tell us that lovemaking is the original religion and the most sacred act of evolution. Lovemaking is also one of our most primal biological drives. In our daily life we enjoy an enlivening flow of sexual energy and use it to express our love, rejuvenate our health and to grow spiritually. Sexual arousal activates a vital energy flow between Earth and Sky that spins all seven chakras. An ecstatic orgasm sends radiant energy to every cell in our body. Sacred lovemaking is based on love and respect and the desire to celebrate the divine in each other.

We honor the sacred polarities of male and female. And since humans exist on a delightful spectrum between these polarities, we honor many creative ways of expressing our love. Everyone wants to feel deeply loved and everyone's version of great lovemaking is unique and personal to them. As young people, Solan and I are learning to express ourselves and become skilled lovers.

The birth of a child is a sacred occasion. Creating a new human being is the most important event in human evolution. Before my parents invited my soul into their lives they performed rituals to connect me to our ancestors and our community. Each child born on Human Earth knows they are wanted. They feel safe and loved. Every child receives the support they need to grow to their full potential.

Many people pursue other forms of creativity in addition to, or instead of, biological procreation. Only people who feel a true calling to bring a child into the world do so. People contribute to our community in many ways.

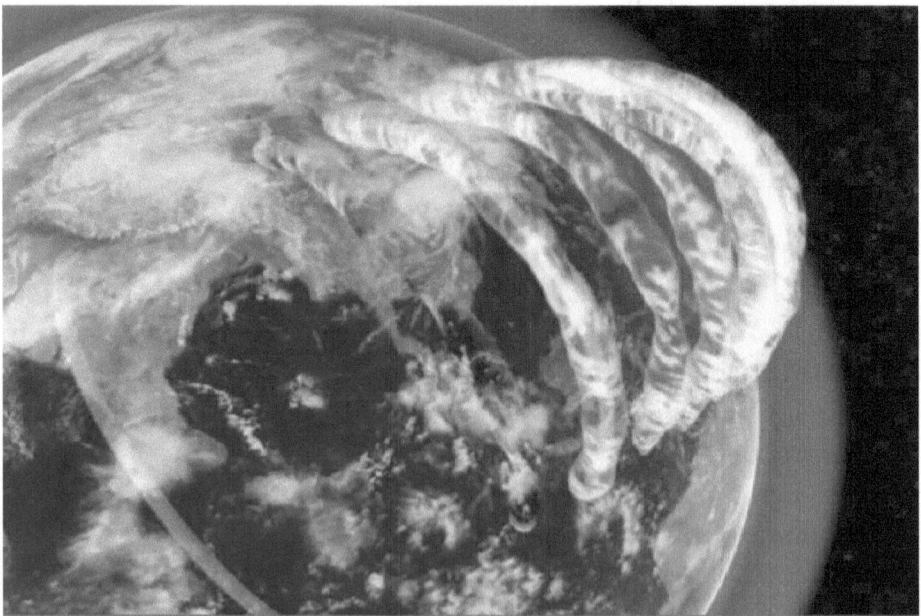

Figure 18. In 2015 a young scientist in Australia discovered the existence of these plasma tubes. Credit: CAASTRO, Loy et al.

Solan:

Ritual is at the center of our lives. Ritual embodies our consciousness in sacred action.

We honor death as deeply as we do birth because these are life's two great passages. With our rituals we provide each other with a safe passage from Sky to Earth during birth and from Earth to Sky during death. Our rituals utilize the plasma energy tubes that connect the humasphere and noosphere for two-way communication between humanity and the spirit world.

Solan:

Individuals feel safe and supported at every stage of the human journey from birth to death. This has greatly reduced the core human fears that plagued prior generations. It has resulted in a welcome decrease in anxiety levels along with a robust increase in loving and co-creative behavior at all levels of society.

Honoring the spiritual intelligence of the plant world has helped us evolve much more quickly over the Seven Generations. Some of our rituals include the use of sacred plants to explore other realms of consciousness. On our Human Earth energy now flows freely between Earth and Sky, harmonizing the five spheres and benefiting all life.

Devara:

Our world is a beautiful place where human creativity blends with nature. Disease, social conflicts and natural calamities still happen but they are far less frequent and are managed skillfully to minimize harm. We have eliminated many infectious diseases.

We gradually switched from making war on microbes. Seeing microbes as an enemy is self-defeating since we contain within us more microbes than we do our own body cells. We began to focus on optimizing our own immune system and living in harmony with the microbial world that permeates our existence. We made the health and well-being of other species a priority. Through respecting all forms of life, our lives and been enriched. We live in a world free of pandemics.

We have a loving relationship with nature and with each other — so we grow from our challenges and are not divided by them. The crisis

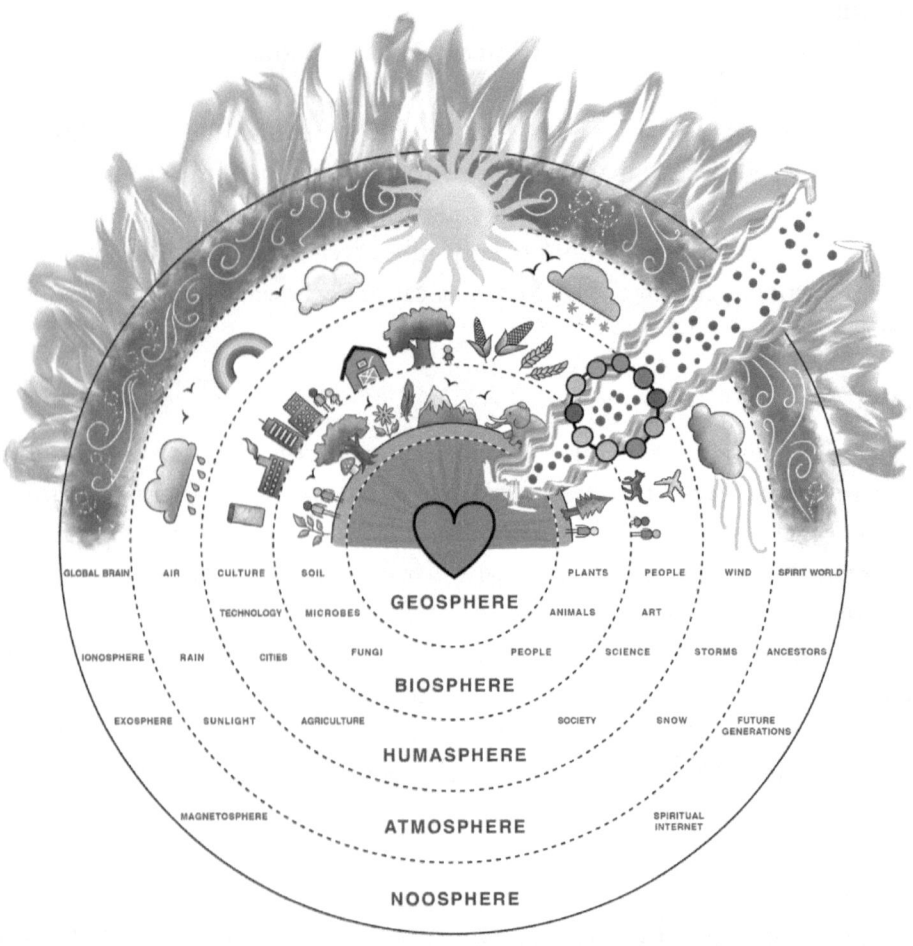

GLOBAL BRAIN | AIR | CULTURE | SOIL | PLANTS | PEOPLE | WIND | SPIRIT WORLD

TECHNOLOGY | MICROBES | ANIMALS | ART

GEOSPHERE

IONOSPHERE | RAIN | CITIES | FUNGI | PEOPLE | SCIENCE | STORMS | ANCESTORS

BIOSPHERE

EXOSPHERE | SUNLIGHT | AGRICULTURE | SOCIETY | SNOW | FUTURE GENERATIONS

HUMASPHERE

MAGNETOSPHERE | SPIRITUAL INTERNET

ATMOSPHERE

NOOSPHERE

Figure 19. People gather in a sacred circle in the humasphere and perform rituals to circulate energy between the five spheres via a plasma tube. Credit: Gerzon.

you went through in the twenty-first century taught us to honor the evolutionary imperative: Because life on earth is constantly changing, a species that is not evolving is a species that is going extinct.

Everyone on Human Earth is dedicated to their own evolution and the evolution of others. Many wonderful changes have happened over these past seven generations because of this clear focus. Each child is raised in a culture based on the Tree of Life and the Four

Roots. They learn the Original Teachings and the art of council in childhood. Each generation grows healthier and more evolved than the one before.

Although on the outside our bodies look much like yours, internally we have evolved into a more advanced species. Our brain has become integrated in a way that enables many new powers. For example, we do not need electronic devices to communicate with each other, even at great distances. We have trained ourselves to tune in to each other's signature mental wavelength and we send messages via the noosphere.

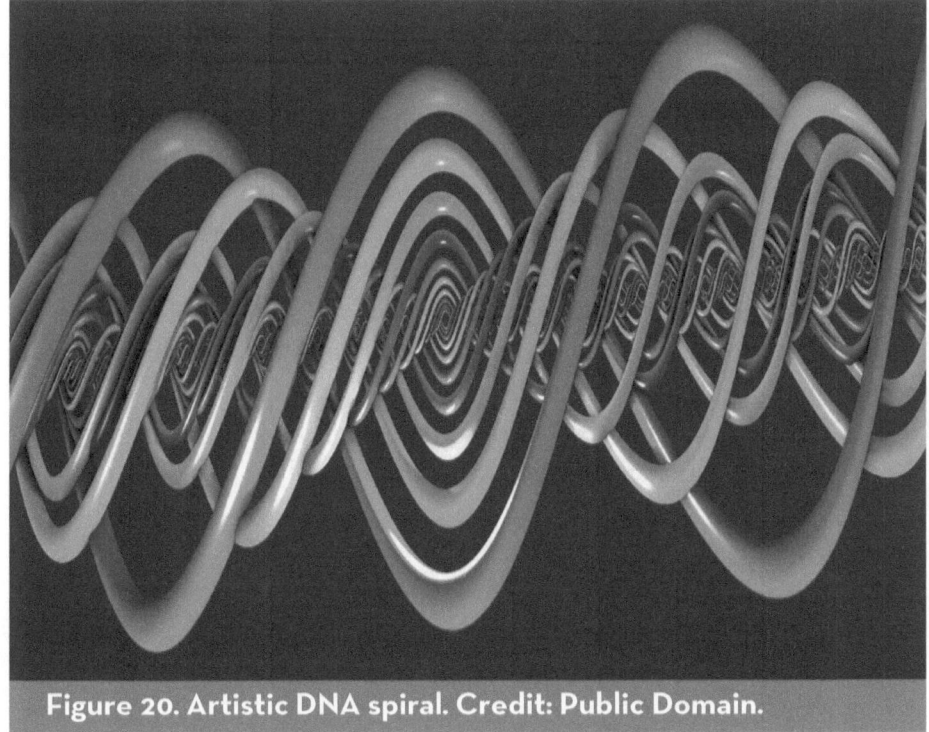

Figure 20. Artistic DNA spiral. Credit: Public Domain.

With our evolved brain we can access our body's inner DNA spiral to heal disease and guide evolution. DNA is your cellular Tree of Life. Did you know the Four Roots are encoded in the four bases of your DNA?

(Smiling)

And did you know that DNA stands for Dear Noble Ancestors?

Solan:

Once we shed our ego skin, we became capable of developing our energy field.

A beautiful energy pattern that displays the acupuncture meridians and yogic chakras becomes visible within Solan and Devara. It extends outward as an electromagnetic field that surrounds their bodies.

Devara:

We opened our Earth and Sky chakras by listening to our Earth and Sky voices in council. We extended our consciousness into our Sky chakra. It now functions much like an antenna.

From the top of their heads a ray of white light emerges and forms an energy antenna. When it reaches a foot above their heads it illuminates their Sky chakras. Their Sky chakras radiate with a star-like luminescence.

A purple beam of Sky energy descends from the noosphere, streams in through their antenna, penetrates their brain and flows through their meridians.

The UN people see energy waves vibrate outward from Devara's Sky chakra in cyclic patterns and go up to the noosphere.

Devara:

(Laughing happily)

I am saying hello to my mother in the noosphere and telling her how wonderful it feels to be here with you.

Solan:

We also listened to our Earth voices and opened our Earth chakra.

A ray of white light shines downward like a tail emerging from the base of their torsos. When it reaches the level of their knees it illuminates their Earth chakras.

Solan:

This "energy tail" allows us to receive vital energy from the core of the earth.

A red ray of light streams up from the center of the earth, activates their chakras and flows into their energy channels.

Solan:

How did all of this become possible? What was the big evolutionary leap that your generation took to make this happen?

Devara:

You fell in love again!

You left behind the dark shadow of fear that had plagued humanity and you walked into the light. You fell in love with the world. You fell in love with each other. That made all the difference.

Solan:

(Gazing at the Sky Elders with an affectionate smile)

Sky-Grandmother and Sky-Grandfather tell us stories in the noosphere. They told us an astounding story about your origins that we want to share with you. It will help you understand why you live in a world of fear today and how you can return to love.

PART 5

SINGING PEOPLE RETURN

11. You were not alone

You were not alone in the world

Devara:

You have heard about your journey into the world as the Four Tribes. But there is more to your story.

You were not alone in the world!

When you set out on your epic journeys, the land you explored was already inhabited by *other people*. As Human Earth approached maturity, life on the planet began to take human shape...and it did so in many ways.

As Devara and Solan speak, the events they describe unfold in the vision space.

Solan:

As our Sky Elders have told you, your Four Tribes left Africa just 70,000 years ago. Many generations before that, your distant ancestors who we call the Clan People (*Homo heidelbergensis*) also faced a changing climate. Like you, some of them left Africa while others remained there. The adventurous ones who left, evolved into a group you call the Neanderthals (*Homo neanderthalensis*). They created a vibrant and resilient culture throughout Europe and Asia that endured for 400,000 years—twice as long as your human culture has existed!

Here's where you enter the story. You evolved from the Clan People who stayed in Africa and became *Homo sapiens*. When you experienced another major climate change 70,000 years ago it was your turn to venture out into the world.

But now you can see that the world was far from empty. It was occupied by the Neanderthal people and other humans who had left Africa thousands of years before you did. You and the Neanderthal people share the same ancestors. You were brothers and sisters. But after that diaspora you lived in different places with different climates and over many generations you developed differently.

In the vision space the UN people see Neanderthal families living in small hunting groups in the colder regions of Europe and Asia.

Figure 21. Neanderthal scene. Credit: NASA.

Devara:

The Neanderthals' diet consists mainly of the animals they hunt and the plants they gather. Over many thousands of years living in a cold climate, their bodies become stockier and their skin becomes paler.

The *Homo sapiens* who remain in Africa live in warm lush areas that support a denser population. The sun darkens their skin. They run long distances to capture their prey and their bodies become lighter, more flexible. They develop socially and intellectually. They eat a wide variety of foods including an increasing amount of seeds, gathered wild and cooked into porridge.

When bones speak

Solan:

The story of what happened next is best told by the Neanderthal people themselves.

We would like to invite the Mother and Father of the Neanderthal Tribe to join us from the noosphere to share their story. Please welcome Shanidar and Lamala.

Near the Tree of Life at the center of the amphitheater, a cave with a large opening appears. Fossilized bones lie on the ground. Slowly, the bones rise up and the skeletons of a man, a woman and two young children stand before the astonished UN people and the Four Tribes' Mothers and Fathers. Layer by layer, muscles, organs and flesh appear on the bones.

Shanidar is around 30, with a solid, muscular build. He has brown shoulder-length hair, a beard, blue-green eyes and light skin. He is clothed in furs and wears eagle feathers in his hair and a necklace of bear claws.

Lamala is slightly younger, lithe and muscular, with flowers in her long, wavy russet-colored hair. She is clothed in furs and wears a necklace of shells.

Their son and daughter sit by their feet, playing. The girl rolls a round stone up and down on two parallel sticks. The boy builds structures with sticks, stones and vines.

They look much like modern humans although their heads are slighter larger to accommodate their larger brains. They have broader jaws, fuller noses and smaller chins. Their robust bodies are adapted to a cold climate and a very physical existence. Their thrusting spears bring them in close contact with the large animals they hunt.

Shanidar and Lamala sing their story

The UN people and the Mothers and Fathers of the Four Tribes are stunned at the appearance of these human beings from a distant past. They sit and gaze at them in awe.

Shanidar and Lamala begin to speak. The UN people expect the Neanderthals to speak in a guttural tone using a primitive language. They are surprised when the Neanderthal couple begin to *sing* their story in rich and melodious voices. Shanidar and Lamala communicate in an enchanting blend of language, song, dance and acting.

The UN people understand them intuitively. They are transported back to a primeval time before empire's ego voices became dominant, to a time when people still spoke from their whole body using their primal voice.

Shanidar, Neanderthal Singing People Father:

Greetings, brothers and sisters. I am Shanidar. We lived in the forests of the north (Eurasia) for hundreds of thousands of years before you came.

Lamala and I are the last of our people.

We are the Singing People. We listened to the songs of the birds and they taught us how to sing. We will sing you our story.

Lamala, Neanderthal Singing People Mother:

Your tribe and ours had the same ancient Mother and Father. Our tribe left the warmth of Africa long before you did and ventured into the cold north lands. We grew in different ways.

We have big hearts. We love our family. We laugh and sing.

We love Mother Earth. She gives us food to eat and flowers to wear in our hair. We love Father Sky. He gives us sun and rain.

We live in families. Three generations. We do everything together, hunting, gathering roots and berries, eating, sleeping and singing together. We love each other. When my children are sick, I ask Mother Herb for help. Mother Herb is very kind. She shows me the leaf that heals, the root that cures.

World of the Singing People

Shanidar:

Our Mother the Earth is always changing. The climate changes. The plants and animals change. We change too. In warmer times we prosper and grow and spread over the land.

Each family inhabits their own beautiful valleys, rivers and mountains. Lamala and I live in our cave during the winter. In the summer we live down in the valley where the reindeer browse. There we live in a shelter made of branches covered with deerskin hides.

In the morning we hunt, gather herbs and prepare food. At the end of the day, we sit around our fire on thick furs, massage each other's muscles and heal the hurts of the day. We sing and make love.

In summer we gather with other families to dance and feast. It's the time when young people can meet their mates, when families who have lost members can merge with other families. In the winter the nights are long and we sleep long. We enter the dreamtime and chant the ancient song-lines. The stars in the sky sing to us and guide us.

We have close relationships with our animal brothers and sisters. We share this land with them. We hunt the mammoth, the reindeer and the aurochs. From their bodies we receive our food, clothing, shelter and tools. We use our fires and our spears to protect our families from the lions and saber-tooth tigers that hunt us.

When the Big Ice comes and buries our land, we struggle. Our numbers become few. But some of us always survive. When the ice retreats our people spread over the land again. For hundreds of thousands of years we live like this all over Europe and Asia. Our vision and Mother Earth's vision are one and the same.

You come into our land

Lamala:

Then comes another time of rapid changes in the weather, going back and forth from warm to cold. Your people leave Africa. In the Middle East, you push out the Singing People who live there. Then you head north into Europe.

Every animal is made for its land. You were a tropical animal. When you traveled into the cold northlands you became an animal who no longer feels at home in its land. In the snow and ice, you fear death.

Shanidar:

We are shaped by the cold and we grew more robust than you. Our muscles, stronger. Our bones, thicker. You fear our strength.

We fear you because you come in great numbers with many families united together in clans. You come with sharp, light throwing spears that can kill at a distance. You bring new diseases from Africa that our bodies have never encountered. Most of all, we fear you because you see yourselves as the only true humans. You want to make a world without us. You occupy our ancient valleys and hunting grounds. You push us into ever more inhospitable regions.

Lamala:

Yet your people and our people live on the land together for many generations. Sometimes we cooperate and learn from each other. You love our singing and our joyful hearts. Sometimes we fall in love with each other. One of your men fell in love with my sister. She married him and went to live with you.

But resources are scarce in the cold. Your people and ours are always competing. Sometimes we fight with each other. We survived many ice ages. But we did not survive you.

Shanidar:

At one time your people and our people knew each other intimately. We were family. Let us get to know each other again and speak as brothers and sisters.

12. Cain and Abel

A forgotten story

Solan:

Shanidar and Lamala, thank you for sharing your story. Now I invite the Mothers and Fathers of the Four Tribes to respond.

The UN people and the Mother and Fathers of the Four Tribes sit stunned and speechless. They struggle with deep and conflicting emotions. They look at each other uneasily.

Finally the Fire Tribe Father speaks.

Fire Tribe Father:

Shanidar and Lamala, I can hear that you speak the truth. Of course I knew that Neanderthals existed, but your story is new to me. It leaves me confused and troubled.

Earth Tribe Mother:

You are my brother and my sister, and yet you are no longer with us. I feel a deep sadness.

Wind Tribe Father:

I have not heard your story before. I do not understand our part in your story.

Water Tribe Mother:

Your story is your truth. But has not become my truth yet. I do not remember this. I do not understand how I could have forgotten something so important.

Solan:

When one people go extinct and another survives, only the survivors live to tell the tale. Shanidar and Lamala are here to help you remember an important part of your story that you have forgotten.

Devara:

Yes, every one of you has forgotten your own story. Even the Mothers and Fathers of the Four Tribes have forgotten this part of your story.

First murder

Solan:

(To the UN people and Mothers and Fathers of the Four Tribes)

Your encounter with the Singing People troubled you when it happened, just as it troubles you today.

Once Shanidar and Lamala and the Singing People disappeared, you did not want to think about what happened to them. No one was left to sing their song. You wanted to forget their story and the part you played in their tragic extinction.

But you knew their story was too important to forget completely. Your meeting with the Singing People is recorded in the book of Genesis. After Adam and Eve leave the Garden of Eden they have two sons, Cain and Abel.

Although later generations no longer understood its many levels of meaning, they did remember that this was a crucial story about their origins. The strange and tragic story of Cain and Abel has been carefully preserved for thousands of years by the Jews in the Torah, by the Christians in the Bible and by the Muslims in the Koran.

Devara:

Do you remember the story of Cain and Abel? The older brother Cain is a farmer in the valley and the younger brother Abel tends his flocks in the hills.

In the vision space, the UN people see Cain standing in a broad valley, surrounded by flourishing grain fields crisscrossed by a network of irrigation channels. Abel stands in the high wild landscape of the hills with the animals he loves, the deer, the goats, the wolves, the bears.

Cain is taller, with darker skin. He wears a well-tailored robe and sandals. Abel is shorter and stockier, has lighter skin and wears animal furs. They are brothers with different appearances, different personalities and different ways of living in the world.

Solan:

Adam and Eve taught Cain and Abel how to practice the ritual of sacrifice in order to keep their mind clouds clear. The ritual of sacrifice and expressing gratitude helps people remember that their food, their life and their talents are gifts from the Creator and should be used not only to gratify their own desires but to further the Creator's work of evolution on Earth.

The Creator's smiling face appears on a billowing cloud, calling the brothers.

Creator:

Come, my sons, give thanks and celebrate!

Devara:

Cain has worked long and hard to grow his crops. With his intelligent mind and his tools he has learned how to clear the land and bring water to Mother Earth's dry fields. Cain resents having to give some of his hard-earned crops back to the Creator. He prepares a large bundle of wheat for sacrifice. On the outside are healthy stalks, but tucked away, inside and out of sight, are tough, inedible and moldy stalks.

Abel loves roaming the wild places and following his animals. His heart overflows with gratitude for the gifts of the animals and he brings the healthiest goat in his flock to the altar. The two brothers kindle their separate fires on the broad rock altar. Each man places his sacrifice on his fire.

Generous white smoke from Abel's offering billows up into the sky and the Creator receives its aroma with pleasure. The Creator's face in the cloud smiles upon Abel. Cain's offering smolders in the flames. Only a thin, dark column of smoke carrying a burnt and moldy odor drifts upward. The Creator's nose wrinkles in displeasure. Cain sees the Creator's face frowning at him.

Cain is upset and his face falls. He has not pleased the Creator. Now Cain fears that the Creator will favor his brother more than himself. Cain fears that Abel will prosper and have many children while he and his children will suffer and disappear.

The Creator speaks to Cain from the cloud.

Creator:

Cain, why are you angry and why has your face fallen? If you love, let your love rise from its wholeness. If you do not love, then the demon of separation crouches at your door. That demon wants to control you.

You still have a choice. Stop. Talk with me before you act unwisely.

Solan:

But Cain does not look up. He ignores the Creator's voice. He focuses his gaze on Abel. Cain listens to the demons that feed on his fear and fuel his anger and jealousy. Cain devises a plan.

He tells Abel he wants to share his bountiful crops with him and invites Abel to visit his fields. Abel comes and when they are in the field, Cain turns against his brother and stabs him in the chest. As the blade plunges into his heart Abel cries out in pain with a bewildered look on his face. Abel's blood spurts out. He falls to the ground. Blood gushes out and seeps into the earth.

Cain hurriedly digs a shallow grave. He pushes Abel's body into it. He covers the grave with fresh soil and scatters seeds over the top. Quickly, the seeds sprout and stalks of wheat grow from the ground.

The Creator sees everything that happens.

In the vision space, the Creator appears to Cain.

Creator:

Cain, my son, where is your brother, Abel?

Cain:

I do not know... Am I my brother's keeper?

Creator:

Cain, what have you done? Your brother's blood cries out to me from the ground!

Cain:

(Suddenly terrified)

Having killed, I now fear being killed!

(Pleading)

I must flee from here. Mark me with a sign, so that I am not killed.

Creator:

I do not need to mark you. You have marked yourself with Abel's blood. It shall remain on your forehead so that you may live and remember this day.

Devara:

Cain is horrified when he realizes that his forehead is stained with Abel's blood. He screams and runs away, deep into the desert, abandoning his Creator, and abandoning his parents, Adam and Eve.

Afterward, all men fear Cain the killer when they see the stain on his forehead and none dare to attack him.

Genesis concludes this story by telling us that Cain becomes the father of civilization. He builds the world's first city and his descendants invent new tools including ones made of iron. And they use their tools to make weapons to kill each other. The age of Eden is over. The age of empire has begun!

Solan and Devara end their telling of the Cain and Abel story and the scene disappears from the vision space.

The Four Tribes and the UN people are astonished. The Cain and Abel story takes the shocking revelations of the Singing People to an even higher pitch. The horrifying implications are too disturbing for words.

The silence in the amphitheater is excruciating.

13. To kill or not to kill

Solan and Devara become angry

In the hushed amphitheater, everyone waits for someone or something to break the tension.

Devara:
(To the UN people and the Mothers and Fathers of the Four Tribes)
I must speak! We came here to thank you for choosing the path of evolution. But after hearing Lamala and Shanidar describe how you treated the Singing People, I feel angry...and scared!

Our very existence depends on you choosing the path of love. Yet how can I believe that you will choose love when I see how you have followed the path of fear and domination since the very beginning of your existence.

(Pointing to the children of Lamala and Shanidar)
I see these children playing and my heart feels such pain. Because you mistreated the Singing People, these children will not survive to have children of their own. I am afraid that Solan and I will be doomed to live our lives as children of extinction instead of becoming children of evolution.

Solan:
I want to believe that you will choose the path of life. But I see that when you face conflict, you choose the path of violence.

(Solemnly)
You are killers.

Even now as we sit here, you remain killers at your core. How can we trust you? Honor you? Respect you?

Devara:
I feel deep love for Shanidar and Lamala. I can see why the Creator loved them. They accept their place in the circle of life. But when

you feel threatened you quickly resort to domination and killing. You chopped the great branch of the Singing People off of the Tree of Life.

How is that honoring the Tree of Life?

Solan:

(Turns to address the Fire Tribe Father)

All of you have blood on your hands, but the Fire Tribe was the one who delivered the death blow to the Singing People in Europe. Were you living by the Four Roots when you met Shanidar and Lamala?

Where is *love* when you kill others to get their land? Where is *truth* when you make up stories and lie to yourselves and your children? Where is *peace* when you provoke conflict with the Singing People instead of reuniting with them as family? Where is creative *power* when you misuse the gifts the Creator gave you?

You buried this murder deep in your heart where it curses you to this day. The mark of Cain is imprinted on your furrowed brows and the hunted look on your faces. Even today when you gaze at one another you see the mark of Cain and you know you cannot fully trust each other because a killer lurks within, ready to leap.

Devara:

(Also addressing her words to the Fire Tribe Father)

If you and the Singing People had reunited and intermarried, the dynamic genetic combination might have activated your evolution into a new species and produced a wiser, more loving form of human. But you usurped the Creator's role and knocked evolution off its course!

Over 30,000 years have passed since the extinction of the Singing People. They remain unmourned and the curse of extinction you brought on yourself is being fulfilled.

It is true that no one kills Cain. No one needs to. In the end, Cain kills himself!

(Frightened and angry)

You are destroying the planet and all humanity.

You have doomed us all to extinction!

Fire Tribe Father defends himself

Solan's and Devara's fiery words have agitated the Fire Tribe Father at a deep level. As he listens, his body stiffens and his ego skin grows hard again.

Fire Tribe Father:
(In a condescending, parental tone)

Devara, my dear, you do seem very scared. And Solan, you have said that you are evolved children from the future, but you sound just like today's teenagers with your naivete, your anger and your complaints.

You accuse us of grave misdeeds. But you were not there. You don't know what happened. We are peaceful people. We are human beings, not murderers. The Singing People lived in isolated groups. They had no real language and were not capable of talking with us. They mostly avoided us and they gradually disappeared.

Evolution is the survival of the fittest and the extinction of the rest. Millions of species went extinct long before we humans ever arrived on the scene. The Singing People were not able to adapt as well as we did to a changing climate.

Of course we played a role when we expanded into their land. But when a meadow gradually fills with trees and becomes a forest, do you accuse the trees of killing the meadow grass?

Am I not a part of nature?

Devara:
(Disgusted)

Here's a better question to ask yourself. It's the one the Creator asked Cain.

"What have you done? Your brother's blood cries out to me from the ground!"

You still haven't answered that one!

Fire Tribe Father confronts Shanidar

Fire Tribe Father:

(Abruptly turns his back on Solan and Devara and faces Shanidar and Lamala)

Shanidar and Lamala, I am sorry for the role we played in your extinction. The changing climate resulted in a difficult time for all of us. We focused on our own survival, not yours. On behalf of all the tribes, I ask you to forgive us.

Shanidar:

I can forgive you for wanting to survive and even for coming into our land. But how can I forgive you for your lies and your disrespect. Now I see that you not only lie to us, you lie to your own children.

Fire Tribe Father:

(Angrily attempts to interrupt)

You can't...

Shanidar:

(Holds up his hand)

I have more to say!

Native American Wind Tribe Father:

(To the Fire Tribe Father and the other Mothers and Fathers)

We must listen to the Singing People's story, no matter how disturbing it is to hear.

(To Shanidar)

I cannot understand who I am apart from you, my brother.

Shanidar:

Yes, I am your brother.

But your people thought you were superior to us. Even today you look down on us because we left no written language, no art, no temples.

We have no need for such things. We do not need a word language like yours because we sing. We live each moment so deeply that we feel no need to record it. Our life is our art and it vanishes with us when we die. Each generation leaves the world fresh and unspoiled for the next generation. What could be more beautiful?

Lamala:

You call yourselves *Homo sapiens*, the Wise People. You call us Neanderthals. That is not our true name. We are the Singing People! We too are human beings.

We have our own name for you. We call you the Talking People. Talking does not make you wise. What you call "thinking" is just you talking to yourself. You talk yourselves into believing anything that will justify you getting what you want.

Do you think you are the only intelligent species? Everything that exists is intelligent in its own way. We have Singing People intelligence. Bears have bear intelligence. Ants have ant intelligence. Water has water intelligence.

When we sing we do not sing to ourselves alone. We always sing to each other. And if I am walking alone in the woods I sing to the trees and the birds and they sing back to me. Each of us sings in our own language, yet we understand each other because we are all part of one great Song. The sounds I make come from my whole body. Every fiber of my being sings with me and vibrates to the same tone. I feel a resonance with all creation when I sing.

You can still hear our original language in your own children. Their first language is pure and fully alive. They love to sing and dance. But very quickly you teach them to limit themselves. You teach them that there is only one right sound for each thing in the world.

When I see water, I do not make one sound "water." The water in a river calls for a different sound than the water in a lake. The smile on my mother's face is not the same smile as the one on my daughter's face and I sing it with a different sound.

You chopped up the flow of sound into chunks you call words. You tied words to things. You separated things from what they do.

Shanidar:

You separated yourself from your body. You no longer speak with your whole body. Only your tongue moves. Your words hide the truth more often than they reveal it. We did not want to talk the way you did because we saw how you used talking to deceive.

You wanted us to talk…and we wanted you to sing.

Sky-Woman gave us all voices so we could create deeper connections with each other. You used language as a weapon. The worst thing that you did was lie to us.

Lamala:

You often pretended to be our friends. You gained our trust and then betrayed us. You told us you wanted to share our land. But then you took it all for yourself. You laid traps for us as if we were animals. You knew you carried diseases that made us sick. Yet you kept coming. Sometimes you invited us for a celebration and then as we feasted together you rose up and killed us.

You think you are superior. We are simply different. Our ways of being human each have advantages and disadvantages. Like Devara said, together we might have created a healthy balanced world.

Shanidar:

You think you are the most intelligent species, but the world you have created is teetering on the brink of a catastrophe of your own making. My species existed in harmony with Mother Earth for 400,000 years. Your species has only been around for 200,000 years. Yet you have done so much damage to the Earth that you yourselves are now in danger of going extinct.

You bring extinction with you wherever you go. We were not the only ones to disappear. Soon after your arrival in Europe the cave bears, the lions and the mammoths went extinct too. Your techniques are the same everywhere. Your species has mutated into a tidal wave of extinction that is crushing all other forms of life on this planet.

A lion leaps

Fire Tribe Father:

(Agitated and disdainful)

So then, Shanidar... I guess you *can't* forgive, can you?

Shanidar looks at his children and his wife and back at the Fire Tribe Father. He feels anger rising from his belly. He takes a few steps toward the Fire Tribe Father, glaring fiercely at him.

Shanidar:

(Loudly and passionately)

Have you no compassion? No empathy? Do you know what it is like to go extinct? It is a slow and agonizing death! Each generation watches the next one suffer and decline. Can you imagine the pain of seeing your children suffer? The pain of knowing that your children will not grow up to have children?

(Turning and pointing to his children)

These are my children!

The Fire Tribe Father feels challenged and takes several intimidating steps toward Shanidar.

Fire Tribe Father:

(Arrogantly)

You can't hurt me, Shanidar! I am alive.

Remember, you don't exist anymore.

(Disdainfully spitting out the words)

You're the one who went *extinct!*

Suddenly Shanidar shouts. He leaps in a great arc toward the Fire Tribe Father. In mid-air, he morphs into a mountain lion with open jaws, bared teeth and outstretched claws.

When he lands in front of the Fire Tribe Father he transforms back into his human form. With his powerful right hand he grabs the Fire Tribe Father by the throat and lifts him completely off the ground.

Shanidar:

(Shouts)

I am angry about what you did to my family and I am angry at how you have treated my Mother the Earth!

Sky-Woman and Sky-Man could not stop you from killing us, and now there is nothing they can do to stop me from killing *you*.

Fire Tribe Father:

(Still held suspended with Shanidar's hand around his neck, in a desperate choking voice)

I am sorry! I will do anything you ask, Shanidar! Tell me what you want!

Shanidar:

Yes, I will tell you.

(Slowly, calmly lowering the Fire Tribe Father to the ground and removing his hand)

You and I are both Sky-Woman's children. No matter how angry I feel, I would not kill you and cause my Mother more grief.

(More gently)

You asked me to tell you what I want.

(Softening)

That feels better than asking me to forgive you.

(Forcefully)

I will tell you what we need to heal the extinction of the Singing People.

Fire Tribe Father:

(In a conciliatory tone, still shaken from Shanidar's attack, trying to regain his composure)

Yes, yes, tell me what you need.

First request: Honor our bones

Shanidar:

We have lived as spirits in the noosphere for a long time. We have reflected on our time on earth. We Singing People have seven requests for healing. The first is the easiest.

Honor our bones.

Your scientists have learned much about us, and we are happy that now they can see us more clearly. Yet some people still think we were not fully human because our rituals were simple and left few traces.

Sometimes we buried our dead, but often we brought them into the forest and simply offered them to Mother Nature. We formed a circle around those who had passed to spirit. We sang songs. We cried and we honored their life. We left their body as an offering to the animals. With their death the animals feed us. With our death we feed the animals.

The most powerful rituals leave no trace.

Your scientists honor our bones in their own way by preserving them and studying them. But to heal we need the ancient rituals of mourning. You can ask the indigenous people who still remember the old ways to lead a ceremony. Gather our bones from your museums and laboratories. Bring together the scientists who touch our bones and tell stories about us.

(With heartfelt emotion)

We ask you to honor the bones of the Singing People.

Stop!

The Fire Tribe Father's face is tense and flushed. He still feels the imprint of Shanidar's hand around his neck. He fears Shanidar's anger and his animal power. He feels disrespected and hurt by Solan's and Devara's anger. He furrows his brow and clenches his jaw.

Shanidar has begun singing and acting out the ritual of mourning to demonstrate what he is asking for. He kneels on the ground and leans over an imaginary body. The Fire Tribe Father sees that Shanidar's back is now toward him. He reaches down and picks up a large stone. He moves toward Shanidar with his arm upraised.

Sky-Woman:
(Calls out in a piercing cry)
Stop!

The Fire Tribe Father hears Sky-Woman's voice and hesitates for a moment.

Before the Fire Tribe Father can smash the rock into Shanidar's skull, the Wind Tribe Father leaps forward, grasps the rock and twists it out of his hand. The Fathers of the Earth Tribe and Water Tribe rush in to help subdue the struggling Fire Tribe Father.

Singing People Tribe descends

Shanidar jumps up and raises his hands to the Sky. Lamala and their children raise their hands and the four of them begin singing. Their voices resonate and fill the air with powerful, ominous vibrations. This time no one understands what they are singing. Shanidar and Lamala sing in the ancient Singing People way, with their faces lifted up to the sky. They call upon the Singing People in the noosphere.

The UN people hear the sounds of singing coming back from the sky. As the singing grows louder, the white clouds and blue sky part, revealing the violet-colored realm of the noosphere. The Singing People descend in family groups from the sky. They are dressed much like Shanidar and Lamala, in animal furs, adorned with shell necklaces, feathers and bear claws. Many of them carry spears, clubs and stone knives.

The opening in the sky closes. Multitudes of Singing People descend and form a dense ring that encircles the UN people and the Four Tribes.

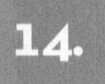

14. Singing People and Talking People reconcile

Four Tribes express remorse

As these two ancient relatives inhabit the same space once again, astonishment and fear fill the air. The Singing People are gathered in extended family groups of parents, children, grandparents, uncles, aunts and cousins. They are angry that the Fire Tribe Father tried to kill Shanidar and it reactivates their ancient trauma.

They begin to chant loudly, stamp their feet and strike the ground with their spears and clubs. The UN people sense the massive physical strength of the Singing People who surround them. A chill runs up their spines as they recall Shanidar's powerful leap. Will the Singing People now seek revenge?

Fire Tribe Father:

(Still on the ground, surrounded by the other tribe Fathers, disoriented, shaking his head)

What happened? I promised I would never resort to killing again.

Shanidar:

As long as you carry the curse of Cain, you are doomed to kill.

Fire Tribe Father:

(Suddenly trembling with fear in his eyes)

Now I remember my fear of the cold.

(Looking at Shanidar and Lamala)

I feared your strength. I feared that the Creator favored you because you and the land were one. I knew I was not made for your land. Yet your land was beautiful and I wanted to live there. To live there I needed to become the top predator.

I felt that fear again when you held me by my neck. Even after you put me down and said you would not kill me, I could not put out the fire raging inside me. You are right. Devara is right.

I still carry the curse of Cain. Once again I tried to kill. I am so sorry.

My sorrow is real, yet my words ring hollow in my ears, because now I know I would kill again. Killing is wired into my brain. My habit of domination now dominates me. When I feel threatened I react with violence. *In that moment I don't know what else to do.*

(To Solan and Devara)

I am sorry that my actions have placed your existence as children of evolution in jeopardy. Even the most peaceful Talking People can be provoked to violence. Even our most loving and caring people proudly go to war. We *are* too violent.

(Looking around at the other tribes and UN people)

Now I understand why we are so afraid of each other. We all recognize the killer instinct in each other.

(To Shanidar and Lamala)

You are very kind to call us the Talking People. You could have called us the Killing People. I am sorry for my role in the extinction of your people.

Now we face our own extinction.

Native American Wind Tribe Mother:

(To Shanidar and Lamala)

Your story happened long before our Wind Tribe arrived in the Americas. Yet we too are Talking People. I too carry the blood stain of Cain. When we built empires in the Americas, many of them became cruel, unjust and blood-stained. We demanded human sacrifices.

As you told your story I felt my memory being restored. I can now remember living in peace with you long, long ago. You were a happy, loving people. You befriended us when we came into your land and helped us find food. We had children with you and formed communities with you. I regret that your people are no longer with us.

Asian Water Tribe Father:

(To Shanidar and Lamala)

I see how closely your lives were interwoven with the Tree of Life. You *lived* the truth and had no need to make symbols for the truth.

Sky-Woman gave us the Original Teachings because we were losing the instinctive wordless wisdom that you still possess. We needed symbols, stories and rituals to help us remember how to live.

Yet we choose to ignore and distort the Original Teachings when it suits our purposes. I invented stories where the Creator made *me* the chosen one. I left you out of the story and the curse of Cain still haunts me.

African Earth Tribe Mother:
(To Shanidar and Lamala)

Thank you for coming and singing to us. I feel close to you. Like you we sing when we work and we sing when we play.

I am moved by your love. Your ability to love us after what we have done to you gives me hope that our Talking People family can forgive each other for the harm we have suffered and the harm we have caused each other.

My Earth Tribe did not go into your north lands. We do not have your blood on our hands. But there is other blood on our hands. Now I can remember the other humans who lived in our land. We drove them out, just as our brothers and sisters in the north drove you out. We too built empires.

Dear Singing People, we are truly one family with you. In your faces I see the faces of the many members of the human family who came before us and who have disappeared.

I fear we may be the next to go extinct. *We have forgotten how to evolve.*

Lamala:
(With compassion)

We have gone extinct and you fear going extinct.

Shanidar:
(Walks over to the Wind Tribe Father)

You saved my life.

The two men hug each other.

Shanidar:
(Turns to the Four Tribes)

Are we all humans? Are we all family?

Four Tribes and UN people:
(In unison)
Yes. We are family.

Shanidar:
Let us love and respect the earth that gave birth to us.

Lamala:
And let us embrace as family.

The Mothers and Fathers of the Four Tribes all hug Shanidar and Lamala. Tears begin to flow. The Singing People in the outer circle smile. The UN people heave a sigh of relief and relax.

Healing the Four Tribes

Sky-Woman and Sky-Man step forward.

Sky-Man:
(To the Fire Tribe Father)
As the Fire Tribe of power it is in your nature to take action. But power must never act alone. When power acts without the guidance of the other three roots, it always goes too far.
(To all the Fathers)
Always council together so that your power can be guided by truth, by love and by peace.

Sky-Woman:
(To the Fire Tribe Father)
You stopped when I called out, and in that moment the Wind Tribe Father prevented you from killing again. The instant you stopped your old habit you gave birth to the possibility of a new story.

Sky-Man gathers the Fathers together in a circle around him. The Fathers rest their arms on each other's shoulders. The mind clouds above each of the Fathers become visible, a yellow cloud above the Wind Tribe Father, a red cloud above the Fire Tribe Father, a blue cloud above the Water Tribe Father, a green cloud above the Earth Tribe Father.

Sky-Man:

Men find peace in the embrace of women, yet they can also find peace in each other's arms. Men are born with an innate desire to make the world a better place. Men instinctively want to be friends with other men. Men want to make women happy. Men want to see their children grow and prosper. Men will selflessly sacrifice their lives for a cause they believe in.

If you give men the opportunity to express their love in healthy ways, each man will be a hero in his own life and will be a Tree of Life to those around to him.

(Raising his arms)

Now let us bring our minds together and create one mind.

Sky-Man moves his arms and circulates the energies of the red, yellow, green and blue mind clouds above their heads. The men open their mind clouds to each other. Their colors combine to form a swirling dome-shaped rainbow above their circle.

Fire Tribe Father:

My urge for growth has been misdirected. The unknown frontier lies inside me, not outside me. My biggest enemies have been my own demons and delusions. And my biggest delusion is that I am separate from you.

(Turning to Wind Tribe Father)

Thank you for stopping me from killing again.

Wind Tribe Father:

I offer you peace, my brother.

Each of us carry all Four Roots within us. Today I felt the root of power activate within me. It gave me the power to stop you. From this day forth, we will sit in council before we act.

Water Tribe Father:
(To Fire Tribe Father)
We came too close to tragedy once again. When a man feels threatened, his vision becomes sharp but very narrow. We can help each other to remember the whole.

Earth Tribe Father:
Acting from fear spreads fear. Together we can act from love and spread love.

Sky-Woman gathers the Tribal Mothers together in a circle. The Wind Tribe Mother speaks for them all when she addresses the Fathers.

Wind Tribe Mother:
(To Tribal Fathers)
We remember our original dream of creating a Human Earth with you where we can raise happy, healthy children. We have seen how men rise to domination during times of crisis, conflict and empire.
(Smiling)
Fortunately the time of empire is coming to an end and we can return to balance. We want to create a happy home with you. We want our children to live in a peaceful world where they can experience the joy and the beauty of life. And that can only happen on a planet where that's true for everyone's children.

The Tribal Fathers smile and nod their heads in gratitude.

Mark of Cain still leaves a stain

Sky-Woman:
(To the Singing People in the outer circle)
Thank you for joining our gathering, dear Singing People. We honor you.
(Turning to Shanidar and Lamala and hugging them)
Thank you, Shanidar and Lamala, for coming and telling your stories. The Talking People heard your story and saw themselves through your eyes. It was only then that they could heal their four separated Tribes into one people.

(Turning to Devara and Solan)

Devara and Solan, thank you for uncovering this deep layer of the story.

(To everyone)

Shanidar and Lamala are my children too. All living creatures on earth, both past and present, are my children.

I take many forms and appear to all my children in their own image.

Sky-Woman changes into a stunningly beautiful Singing People woman.

Sky-Woman:

(Walks over to the Talking People in her Singing People form)

Did you know that I looked like this too?

Then Sky-Woman takes the shape of an ape, a galloping horse, a soaring eagle, a dragonfly, a fish, an octopus, a virus, a blue-green amoeba. The amoeba morphs into the blue-green planet earth. Then Sky-Woman resumes her Talking People form.

Sky-Woman:

(Turns to the Four Tribes)

The story of the Singing People is the missing chapter in your story. Their memory haunts you in your sleep. The mark of Cain still stains your forehead.

For your story to be reborn as a living story you need to include the story of your brothers and sisters, the Singing People.

Human impact on Earth's five spheres

Sky-Woman:

Earlier you saw how our earth grew, layer by layer, from geosphere to biosphere, to atmosphere, to humasphere to noosphere, and into a living Human Earth.

Now we can bring your story up to the present. Five hundred years have passed since the Fire Tribe's empire spread over the world. Let's look at the impact your species has had on the earth during this brief time.

The *geosphere* is the foundation of all life. Yet you drill into Mother Earth to extract metals and fossil fuels. You decapitate mountains and rob them of their ancestral coal beds. You pump ancient water from the deepest aquifers. You have plundered, battered and polluted the geosphere.

You have also destroyed much of the *biosphere*, the interwoven fabric of life that sustains your own humasphere. The rich, diverse biosphere has become sick, bare and impoverished. You degraded the diverse and bountiful prosperity of Mother Earth into the poverty of a commercialized, industrialized wasteland.

You fill the *atmosphere* with toxic smoke. An overheated atmosphere reacts with extremes in weather that batter the biosphere. The clear blue sky was a source of spiritual inspiration and serenity for past generations. Now your killer planes roam the sky and deliver sudden death with militarized lightning strikes.

Your own *humasphere* which began as a creative growth within the biosphere has mutated into a malignant tumor. Your empire civilization has become toxic and your people are sick, unhappy and embroiled in endless conflicts with each other. Families and children struggle to survive in today's unhealthy humasphere.

Even though you abused these spheres of life, including your own humasphere, the *noosphere* still remained clear and peaceful until recently. But now you have extended your empire into the heavens above.

You have polluted the noosphere, just as you polluted the atmosphere. You used rockets to put satellites into orbit around the earth without any means of retrieving them after their short lifespans. Now hundreds of thousands of jagged fragments imperil your own astronauts and space flights. This space debris clutters the noosphere and interferes with its vital role as your global brain. You have turned heaven itself into a junkyard.

Your communication satellites now beam your toxic arguments into the noosphere where it disturbs the whole planet's peace of mind. With your spy satellites and anti-satellite weaponry you are extending your earthly wars into the heavens.

Every sphere of life has been harmed by your actions and your own survival is now threatened. You are the meeting place between Earth and Sky. Yet your humasphere no longer connects Earth and Sky. It splits them apart and pollutes them both.

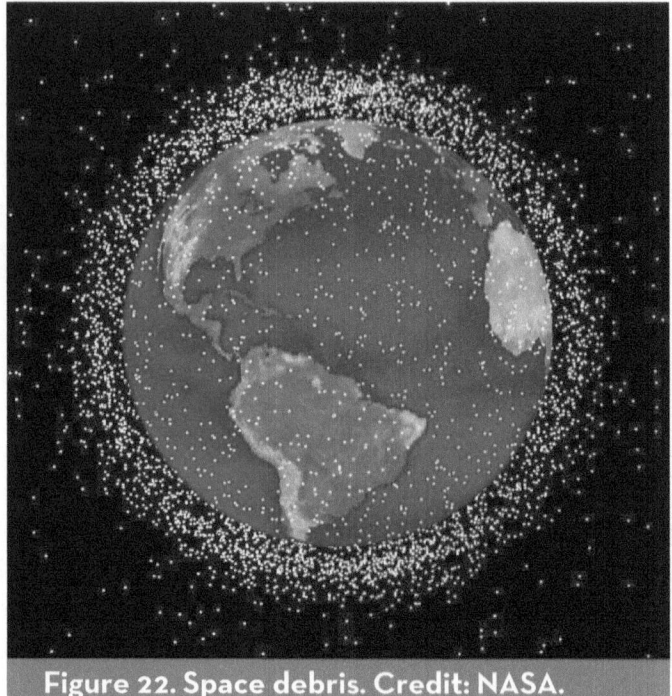

Figure 22. Space debris. Credit: NASA.

Sky-Woman:

(To the Singing People)

Shanidar and Lamala, we thank you and your Singing People for joining us here for healing. We invite all of you to remain with us as we continue the council.

Sky-Man:

Just as the Singing People have disappeared from the earth, so too will the Talking People eventually disappear. No species exists outside the spiral of evolution.

The only question is: Will you disappear because you went extinct? Or will you "disappear" because you *evolved into a higher form of human?*

PART 6:
CHILDREN OF EXTINCTION

15. Walking the path of extinction

Will Devara and Solan go extinct?

Sky-Man:

You are at a crossroads in your journey. One path leads to a dark future of extinction. The other path leads to a bright future of evolution.

Many life forms have disappeared from our planet. Evolution never stands still. After 4.5 billion years you are still here. *You are the planet's most adventurous evolvers.* At crucial moments, when others species clung to old forms, your ancestors, going all the way back to when you were tiny one-celled creatures, were the ones who always chose to grow and evolve.

Will you stay on the road of Empire Earth that goes downward to extinction or will you choose the path of Human Earth that leads upward toward the infinite adventure of evolution?

Sky-Woman:

(Turning to Solan and Devara)

You have come to us from the beautiful evolutionary future that is possible for all humanity. Yet today people are descending into a spiral of despair and self-destruction. This dark future *must be faced* if people are to wake up in time.

It pains me to ask this of you. Will you help them wake up? Having told us a story of evolution, Will you tell us a story of extinction?

Solan:

(With dread)

But the only way we can do that is to *become* children of extinction!

Devara:

(Panic-stricken)

You want *us* to go *extinct?* To go extinct like Lamala's children? We have not yet lived. What you ask sounds *horrible!*

Sky-Man:

If you want to live in the future as children of evolution, then humanity must make the right choice now. If you show them where the road of empire leads, it may help them find the courage and the clarity to face the present crisis.

Solan:

(Slowly, solemnly)

It seems that I too need to face my fear of death.

Devara:

(Reflectively)

Now that I am faced with my own extinction, I have even more admiration for the Singing People. And I have more compassion for the Mothers and Fathers of the Four Tribes. Now I too feel the primal urge to survive. I feel the part of me who so desperately wants to live that she will do anything to survive...

(She begins singing quietly)

I am I and you are you.

Together we are one family.

The Talking People and the Singing People join Devara and Solan in the ancient chant.

Devara:
Yes, I will walk the path of extinction.

Solan:
I too will walk this path with the intention that future generations will not need to.

Sky-Woman:
I honor your courage. Thank you, my children.

Solan and Devara stand in front of the Tree of Life. They slowly begin to morph into children of extinction.

Soon everyone is staring in disbelief at bizarre-looking versions of Solan and Devara. Their bodies are short and stunted with spindly arms and legs and grayish skin. They are barefoot and wear tattered T-shirts and pants. Their eyes, ears, nose and mouth are all small, giving their faces an oddly blank look. Their bodies are nearly identical, appearing almost asexual. Their small hands have only a thumb and two fingers. Their feet have only a big toe and two other toes.

Sky-Man:
These children have come to us from one of earth's possible futures. Please open your hearts and minds to the children of extinction.

Children without a story

Solan, as the son of extinction:
(Looks around at the trees and grass and speaks in a voice that sounds tight, tense, and numb)
I am shocked to see how beautiful this Earth once was.

Devara, as the daughter of extinction:

(Speaks in a similar tone)

(Looking wistfully at the UN people)

When I see how you look I feel ashamed of what I have become. And I wonder what *you* are feeling…as you look at me…your granddaughter.

Solan:

We are the last of our people. We have only enough to eat for one more day. When we die, there will be no more humans left on the planet. I hope my death comes soon. The world I come from is far more bleak than you can imagine.

Devara:

You want to hear our story. But when we were growing up, no one told us any stories. We have no story to tell.

The Sky Elders, Sky-Grandmother and Sky-Grandfather, step forward and walk over to the children of extinction. They place their hands on their grandchildren's heads.

Sky-Grandmother:

Solan and Devara, we will hold you and protect you on this journey. We are the Memory Keepers. May the broken generations within you reconnect now.

Sky-Grandfather:

May your memory be restored.

Energy streams through the Elders' hands and into the heads of the Sky Children. They stand more erect and appear more alert.

16. Seven Generations of extinction

First Generation: Climate change and chaos

Solan:

(Speaks in a clearer, stronger voice)

Now I can see the generations who came before me. Now I can tell you our story.

(Looking at the UN people and tribes)

I am from the Seventh Generation and I come to you from the year 2199. This is what happened to the Seven Generations who came after you.

The governments of the world failed to heed the message brought by the Sky People. The media offered sensationalized reports of a strange event at the UN and concluded that this planetary council was a bizarre hoax. Many grassroots movements led by people who were at the UN that day sprang up but they were marginalized and suppressed. The course of empire continued on its way.

The climate changes that you are now experiencing became far more extreme. During your lifetime, carbon dioxide in the atmosphere reached the tipping point and then kept on going. Temperatures increased. Sea levels rose, destroying many coastal towns and cities.

You and your children experienced unprecedented storms, natural disasters, famine, mass migrations and wars. Wave after wave of pandemics swept over the planet. Fear and daily survival anxiety became the "new normal" for most people even in the most economically developed countries. Financial crises resulted in the collapse of many nation states. The European Union fell apart and those nations reverted to warring with each other, as they had so often in the past.

In the USA, a bankrupt government could no longer inspire loyalty or provide many basic services. An alliance of power-hungry politicians, corporate oligarchs, financial elites, military professionals and technocrats completed their takeover of what remained of the American government. They consolidated their control of the internet and telecommunications and intimidated the populace via a vast surveillance apparatus. But the government had much less control on the ground, out in the streets and in rural areas and was unable to maintain public safety.

Naturally, the already heavily-armed populace resorted to self-defense and vigilante justice. Gangsters and warlords arose to control scarce resources and rule local neighborhoods. Racial and class tensions erupted in riots. In this lawless, power-mad atmosphere vulnerable groups lost the legal protections they had gained during the prior century and were once again used and abused.

Many countries experienced civil war, widespread starvation and mass migrations. The global population plummeted from over 7 billion to less than 5 billion. Social chaos, scarcity and violence reduced life everywhere on the planet to a struggle for survival.

Although global nuclear war was avoided, there were regional nuclear attacks, explosions at poorly-maintained atomic power plants and the detonation of dirty bombs in local conflicts. This resulted in uninhabitable radioactive areas on every continent and higher levels of toxic radioactivity in the earth's atmosphere.

When the Sky Elders' prophesied apocalypse arrived, the massive burst of solar radiation and cosmic energy knocked out the telecommunications grid. It had just as devastating an effect on the highly sensitive human nervous system, resulting in widespread mental breakdowns. The depth of suffering was unprecedented all over the planet.

These catastrophes made life more difficult for corporations and the elite too. But with their repositories of wealth and power, many of them were able to survive in heavily fortified residential enclaves, enclosed shopping malls, walled industrial districts, and corporate campuses guarded by private military forces.

Second Generation: Cosmopolis

Radun's vision of Cosmopolis

Devara:

By the second generation, sea levels stabilized and new ramshackle settlements grew up along the relocated shorelines.

The second generation had grown up knowing nothing but conflict and chaos, starvation, disease and fuel shortages. They yearned for stability and order.

A charismatic leader arose to inspire the population with a radical new vision. His name was Radun. He was a successful international entrepreneur with advanced degrees from both Harvard and Peking University. His father was Chinese-American and his mother was German-Nigerian.

His wealth, iconoclastic brilliance and passionate eloquence soon won him a devoted following. He outlined his vision in a speech that became famous worldwide.

In the vision space Radun speaks.

Radun:

The past generations failed us. They failed to change and adapt and now we suffer from their mistakes.

Why did they fail? Because they did not unite and take action. National governments were corrupt and ineffective. The United Nations lacked power and leadership. The corporations were greedy and pursued reckless, short-sighted agendas. The public was distracted by mind-numbing entertainment. Everyone was trapped in an outdated way of thinking.

When faced with a crisis, they failed to adapt and innovate. Instead of fully embracing new technology and implementing global solutions, they clung blindly to old nationalistic and religious prejudices. They lacked both the vision and the will to change.

But it is not too late. We can still create a peaceful, prosperous world if we think big and act boldly. It is time to end divisive nationalism, racism, religiosity and violence. It is time to unite as one people, one planet. Together we can remake the world that our predecessors nearly destroyed.

It's time for our species to advance to the next level. Our challenge is to imagine the planet as a global city and every country as a neighborhood. Join me in becoming a citizen of this new planetary city called Cosmopolis!

In Cosmopolis everyone will have equal access to food, energy, shelter, education, justice and healthcare. You will enjoy unlimited freedom to express your unique individuality.

We will establish a transnational global union called GovCorp that unifies the best aspects of government, corporations and science. GovCorp will serve the needs of the people. We will eliminate poverty, crime, disease and the senseless violence that now makes each day so terrifying. GovCorp will be responsible for your safety. All personal weapons will be collected and recycled. Private security forces will be disbanded and the misrule of local warlords will end.

Our goal is to provide you with all the necessities of life for free. Our motto is: "No bills. No taxes."

With your support we can create the Golden Age of Cosmopolis within one generation!

Devara:

Radun captured the popular imagination with his eloquence and his bold vision. He also met privately with the financial elite and the corporations. He warned them that they would soon lose what remained of their wealth and power in the growing chaos.

Radun told them that he could manage the planet effectively using science-based policies and proven business models. He explained the great potential of a fully integrated political-technological-economic order. He inspired the elite to invest their wealth and expertise into one unified global entity called GovCorp.

Under Radun's leadership the major nations merged their collapsing governments, financial institutions, corporations and the Internet into Radun's GovCorp. All the smaller nations soon rushed to join.

With the popular support of the desperate masses and the material resources of the frightened elite, Radun began tackling the vast problems of a hungry, weary, post-apocalyptic world under the banner of "Cosmopolis: Peace and Prosperity for All."

CleanFire

Devara:

GovCorp's greatest and most urgent challenge was to end the ongoing climate crisis and the many other problems it spawned such as pandemics, mass migrations and social disorder. Fossil fuels were still the main source of energy and temperatures continued to rise relentlessly. So-called "green energy" like solar and wind had never been adequately funded. They also required rare earth minerals that involved toxic mining and manufacturing processes. In addition, they required large tracts of scarce land and aroused local opposition. Many landscapes were now blighted with broken, rusting wind turbines and solar arrays.

Radun explained that the climate crisis occurred because the fossil fuel companies had played upon public fears. They not only hampered the development of solar and wind but they derailed the only form of energy production suitable for a technologically-advanced global culture: safe nuclear power.

Radun's proposals sparked a resistance movement of people called Traditionalists. Traditionalists not only feared the dangers of nuclear reactors, they had a visceral distrust of GovCorp. They were a diverse, loosely connected group of people who saw GovCorp as a soulless entity that was taking away their freedoms. The Traditionalists included many diverse groups including anti-technology radicals, religious fundamentalists, anarchists, back-to-the-land survivalists, nationalists, ethnic supremacists, nature lovers, local warlords, the idealistic young and the nostalgic elderly.

Radun responds to the resistance with a global telecast and issues a stirring call for bold, evolutionary change.

Radun:

It is time to put an end to the primitive, toxic age of burning fossil fuels and usher in a new age of clean, safe, affordable nuclear energy.

The brilliant scientists of the 20th century unlocked the astounding power of the atom. They discovered the holy grail of energy. They promoted a vision of the peaceful atom and the production of inexpensive, unlimited energy. But their vision was undermined by the fearful Traditionalists of their time. If the world had evolved to safe nuclear power during the mid-20th century, the climate crisis would have been completely avoided!

I understand why some people are nostalgic for the past. But the earth has changed and going back to the past is not an option. The arrow of time does not move backward, only forward.

Nuclear energy is a new advanced form of fire. Do you want to be like a long-forgotten branch of extinct early humans who ran away from fire in fear and never benefited from its power? Or do you want to be like our own ancestors who thrived because they learned to master fire and used it safely for cooking and warmth?

Today we have a second chance. We can restore the original vision of the "peaceful atom."

GovCorp will build an energy system called CleanFire that is safe, reliable and available to all citizens of Cosmopolis. You will receive free electricity to heat your homes, run your appliances and power your vehicles.

GovCorp will not repeat the mistakes of the past when war-mongering politicians and the military-industrial complex misused nuclear energy for destructive purposes. As part of our peaceful atom program, we will eliminate all nuclear weapons and put an end to a shameful chapter in our history.

Devara:

Radun resurrected the moribund nuclear power industry. With the expertise of the best scientific minds and the resources of GovCorp, technological breakthroughs soon led to smaller, safer, more efficient nuclear power plants that were soon nicknamed "nukeys."

A nukey, the "new key" to abundant energy, was strategically placed in every local region so that the risks and benefits were shared equally. True to his promise, as the CleanFire network spread across the planet, Radun destroyed all the obsolete nuclear missiles that lay rusting in their underground silos. For the first time in many generations, the world was free from the fear of a nuclear Armageddon!

GovCorp had the power to take decisive action and enforce compliance. To aid in the restoration the health of the planet, GovCorp banned the burning of all carbon-based fuels and the manufacture of solar and wind installations. Wood fires, candles and all other open flames were abolished. Electronic simulations of fireplaces and candles satisfied the primal human attraction to fire while eliminating the age-old danger of live fires. In a surprisingly short time nearly everyone was connected to GovCorp's nuclear-powered electrical distribution system. It provided reliable energy for cooking, heating, cooling, transportation and manufacturing and, as promised, it never sent a bill or levied a tax. With carbon emissions reduced to preindustrial levels the climate stabilized and life for everyone became easier.

Cosmopolis sponsored a global celebration. People began to feel confident that GovCorp could rejuvenate the planet.

SkyWeb

Devara:

Fraud, hacking and sabotage had rendered the old Internet nearly useless. Radun declared that he would fulfill the original dream of the founders of the Internet with a free, universal system called SkyWeb.

GovCorp constructed a secure, centrally controlled grid that covered the planet through a sophisticated network of cables, satellites, high-altitude balloons, drones and lasers. Each person on the planet was given a unique SkyWeb identification number. Everyone was connected wirelessly via free SkyScreens which were available as laptops, phones, tablets and wristwatches.

SkyWeb brought GovCorp's education program to every child's SkyScreen. High quality universal education was finally available to everyone on the planet at no charge. Local teachers and schools were gradually phased out.

To preserve the world's remaining forests, GovCorp outlawed the manufacture of paper. Writing, drawing and painting in any non-digital format became illegal. Books and paintings gradually disappeared.

SkyWeb's universal identification and surveillance system put an end to crime. Robbery became self-defeating because every item was tagged with a radio chip. Punishment for harming other people or damaging GovCorp facilities was swift and certain because everything that happened in Cosmopolis was recorded on video and tracked electronically.

SkyWeb monitored and collected behavioral metrics on every person from birth to death. Everyone received a monthly Good Neighbor Score derived from GovCorp algorithms based on their social activities, productivity, financial status, social media posts, health grade and other relevant factors. Everyone in Cosmopolis had the same basic rights but additional opportunities, rewards and special offers were available to those with higher Good Neighbor Scores.

When epidemics flared up, they were contained more effectively than ever before through precise digital surveillance and the rapid isolation of infected individuals.

SkyWeb now provided a free and 100% secure communication, information and entertainment system to every citizen of Cosmopolis.

PeoplesBank

Devara:

Even though GovCorp provided the basics of life for free, many other desirable products were available for purchase. For example, basic SkyWeb was free but access to much of its entertainment content required additional payment. No-frills SkyScreens were free, but the more stylish, full-featured models and accessories needed to be purchased.

GovCorp used SkyWeb's secure centralized Internet to establish a global PeoplesBank that citizens could access via any SkyScreen. Everyone was given a free account. Soon virtually all financial transactions occurred through PeoplesBank.

PeoplesBank accounts were free, but transactions incurred a nominal processing charge. Since everyone was provided with the necessities, individuals tried to achieve status and differentiate themselves through personalizing their consumer items.

In the vision space Radun announces another milestone.

Radun:

The money system used by our ancestors was an advance over the primitive method of barter. But it became a destructive force that resulted in greed and inequality.

Instead of our ancestors' selfish money economy we can now enjoy a caring gift economy. PeoplesBank has created its own secure virtual currency, called Giftz. With Giftz we leave behind the age of money and usher in the age of community. Everyone will receive Giftz units which can be easily exchanged anywhere with anyone via your mobile SkyScreens.

Giftz are our way of saying thank you to all of the amazing people who are helping to build Cosmopolis! Fees for all transactions using Giftz will be cut in half. And when you play SkyWeb games, instead of accumulating meaningless points, you will be able to earn Giftz.

Devara:

Usage of the few remaining national and local currencies declined rapidly. Soon PeoplesBank Giftz became the only accepted form of exchange on the planet.

Radun had relied upon popular support, the purchase of optional GovCorp products, and the wealth of the elite to provide free energy and free communication while upholding his pledge of "No bills. No taxes." Now, by taking a small percentage of trillions of daily financial transactions, GovCorp tapped a continuous and immensely profitable income stream. The PeoplesBank brought Radun's long-term strategy to fruition. GovCorp soon repaid its original investors and it did so in Giftz.

The vast majority of the world's population supported GovCorp and appreciated the restoration of order and the improved standard of living, including universal healthcare. From time to time, here and there, Traditionalist resistance movements continued to arise. The vast majority of the population, who saw the world through GovCorp media news, viewed Traditionalists as misinformed people obstructing progress.

Since all media consumption and interpersonal communication took place via SkyWeb, GovCorp was able to develop a profile for each person and could intervene quickly if anyone questioned the authority or legitimacy of GovCorp. Its healthcare professionals diagnosed Traditionalists as suffering from a mental illness known as Toxic Nostalgia Syndrome. They encouraged early detection and treatment protocols that required mandatory medication and reprogramming therapy.

Usually these Traditionalist movements died out on their own. People could no longer survive outside of GovCorp's seamless government-energy-communication-technology-finance system. But when these resistance groups persisted and gained local power, their members were removed by GovCorp's security forces to correctional communities for intensive rehabilitation.

Third Generation: Golden Age of Cosmopolis

Solan:

The third generation experienced the beginning of a new period of global prosperity that became known as the Golden Age of Cosmopolis. The world's population began a gradual increase after two generations of decline. Virtually everyone now worked directly for GovCorp and its subsidiaries.

Radun retired from the active management of GovCorp and devoted himself to promoting the new culture of Cosmopolis. He celebrated the many social goals that had been achieved: universal education, the end of war and racism, the full equality of the sexes, the eradication of poverty, and the acceptance of diverse forms of personal and sexual expression. Divisive national and religious identities had been replaced by a shared identity as citizens of Cosmopolis.

As the Golden Age continued, a burst of collaborative creative energy turned SkyWeb's omnipresent screens into the fascinating and ever-changing focus of everyone's waking lives.

But in the midst of this heady progress, a sudden disaster erupted that threatened everything. An epidemic morphed almost overnight into a worldwide pandemic that proved far more lethal than the milder ones that afflicted previous generations. In some of the hardest hit areas over half the population died within 48 hours. Radun came out of retirement to save the people of Cosmopolis from the ravages of infectious disease.

Radun:

It is time to put an end to the scourge of infectious disease. Infectious diseases were never more than a minor problem for humans before we domesticated animals and crowded them into pens and coops. Today these disease-ridden animals spawn viruses that threaten the very existence of our species.

It is time to evolve beyond infectious disease by ending the shameful exploitation of animals.

Solan:

GovCorp conducted a massive and ultimately successful campaign that resulted in the worldwide eradication of all domesticated animals including cattle, pigs, goats, chickens, dogs and cats and the compulsory vaccination of the population against all known diseases. As Radun had promised, animal-related epidemics were completely eliminated and the population rebounded quickly.

However, with meat and dairy products no longer available, people became almost totally reliant on crops like rice, wheat, corn and soy. Manufactured foods, including meat substitutes, all depended on these traditional crops for their raw materials. But monoculture, pesticides and genetic modification had resulted in a loss of crop diversity and disease resistance. Now these basic crops were attacked by insect pests, fungal infections and viral diseases. Millions of acres of desperately needed food crops lay rotting in the fields.

Wild fish had disappeared from the human diet during the previous generation due to overfishing and water pollution. Genetically modified farmed fish had filled the protein gap for many years. Now a viral pandemic swept through the overcrowded fish farms, destroying what remained of this ancient food source. The oceans were virtually empty of life except for toxic algal blooms and swarms of inedible jellyfish.

Unfortunately at this same time, the Earth's complex weather systems reacted to the rapid decrease in atmospheric carbon dioxide levels caused by the abrupt elimination of fossil-fuel burning. After years of hotter weather, a sudden drop in global temperatures resulted in what became known as the "decade without a summer."

The resulting food catastrophe confounded GovCorp's policy makers and scientists. The cereal crops that had sustained humanity for thousands of years could no longer be grown in sufficient quantities to feed everyone. The threat of mass starvation loomed.

Again Radun came forward with a solution.

Radun:

The current crisis presents us with an opportunity. When we engineered the atom for nuclear power we brought the Age of Technology to its culmination. Now it is time to usher in the Age of Bionization. It is time to master life itself, and food is the essence of life.

For hundreds of thousands of years our ancestors thrived by eating various edible body parts of certain plants and animals. Then greedy agribusiness and food manufacturing corporations began processing these raw materials into toxic commercial products that have made many people sick and resulted in a decrease in basic human health.

Fortunately Mother Nature has provided us with the solution: DNA and genetic engineering. GovCorp will provide you with a new form of highly digestible, highly nutritious, highly concentrated biofuel. Just as nuclear energy is a more evolved form of fire, bioengineering is a more evolved form of cooking. Replacing old-fashioned food with scientifically-designed biofuel will allow us to evolve as a species. We will put an end to food allergies, malnutrition and obesity.

The era of food is over and the age of biofuel has arrived!

Soon GovCorp will be able to offer you a revolutionary new product called Nutrex. It will be 100% natural and free of toxins. Everyone will receive the ideal nutrition in the optimal amounts for maximum health. And GovCorp will provide Nutrex to every citizen of Cosmopolis at no charge.

Solan:

Although the dream of packing all the necessary nutrients into one pill a day proved to be unrealistic, GovCorp's scientists succeeded in creating a concentrated energy source called Nutrex. It was available as a bar and as an all-purpose powder. Nutrex came in dozens of delicious flavors. It was quick, easy and free. The powder could be mixed with water and eaten as a cereal or consumed as a beverage.

One bar or one bowl provided a full day's nutritional energy. GovCorp distributed free packages of concentrated Nutrex to everyone with the slogan: "Nutrex. A bar or a bowl. Eat once and be done."

Nutrex had been designed so that everyone felt full and satisfied as soon as they had consumed the optimal amount. This biofuel rapidly replaced other forms of food. As Radun had promised, it put an end to allergies, malnutrition and obesity.

The scientists who developed Nutrex had to balance manufacturing efficiencies with nutritional completeness. It was rumored that some trace elements and essential micronutrients had not been incorporated into the formula. GovCorp quickly developed a thriving market in expensive nutritional supplements for those who could afford them.

The average life expectancy of the general public did improve slightly with the introduction of Nutrex, mostly due to the elimination of obesity. However, GovCorp's elite experienced greatly increased lifespans thanks to the medical wonders of the new Age of Bionization which included artificial organs, bionic implants and the genetic engineering of human embryos.

Radun himself was a prime example as he continued to live into the fourth generation.

Fourth Generation: GovCorp remakes the world

Devara:

By the fourth generation, the Golden Age of Cosmopolis was in full flower. GovCorp declared that it had permanently solved the age-old problems of food, fuel, health, education and social justice.

With the virtual elimination of infectious disease and the success of Nutrex, the global population reached an all-time high of 10 billion. This resulted in the urbanization of all the remaining wild places on earth. Very few plants and animals were able to survive the loss of their habitats. Most large mammals and many amphibians, birds and fish disappeared. The remaining natural areas left were maintained as parks where representatives of essential species were kept alive for genetic research and public enjoyment. As Radun had envisioned, the entire planet had been transformed into the City of Cosmopolis.

Most people loved GovCorp because it was the source of everything. It told them what they needed and it gave them what they needed and it was all they had ever known.

Almost everyone lived in GovCorp's housing complexes (informally called "hives"). Each person resided in their own individual cubicle. This also helped to limit the spread of the contagious diseases that occasionally arose in the densely-populated hives. Infected individuals could be electronically locked into their cubicles. Nutrex and essential items were supplied via specially designed delivery ports.

The vast majority of all adults remained single and childless. Relationships in Cosmopolis were primarily conducted via SkyScreen. If two people wanted to cohabitate they could apply for adjoining cubicles.

Everyone went to work in office industrial parks or worked via SkyWeb from their home cubicles and performed the tasks assigned to them. There was no unemployment. GovCorp assigned superfluous workers to earn Giftz via SkyScreen games which were designed to be indistinguishable from "real work."

The chaos of climate change, followed by GovCorp's rapid rise had a devastating effect on traditional family structures and communities. People lost the ability to maintain long-term personal relationships or care for young children. Stable families who could rear children to adulthood virtually disappeared.

During this time GovCorp gradually took over the management of relationships and reproduction. Children were conceived through a scientific eugenics process. The most successful males in Cosmopolis donated their sperm to GovCorp's GenePool. Radun was the first male to donate his sperm. Being licensed as a GenePool donor quickly became a status symbol.

Sperm was inserted into GenePool eggs that were harvested from DNA-certified fertile women. After being genetically modified to meet the latest standards, the eggs were implanted in the wombs of healthy breeder females. After birth, children were cared for and raised in GovCorp's New Generation Homes where each lived in their own cubicle.

GovCorp discontinued the outdated and inefficient system of giving names to newborn babies. Instead it implanted a radio frequency chip with a unique identifier in their right hand. This enabled individuals to receive all of GovCorp's benefits and live a fully connected, though nameless, life in Cosmopolis.

The last traces of racial distinctions disappeared as genetic engineering gradually eliminated differences in skin color and facial features, producing a more uniform human appearance. GovCorp was finally able to regulate the population level via optimal algorithms to ensure a sustainable resource-to-people ratio.

When not working, people immersed themselves in virtual entertainment. Most people no longer had original thoughts of their own. Their minds were programmed with GovCorp-produced images, music and stories.

Words such as "spirit," "purpose," and "thinking" either disappeared completely or changed their meaning. For example, the word "love" was no longer used in the context of human relationships, but persisted in the sense of wanting GovCorp's products ("I'd love to get one of the new SkyScreen watches"). The meaning of the word "thinking" also changed. A person who didn't want to be disturbed while looking at their SkyScreen would say, "Don't bother me while I'm thinking."

The Golden Age saw a resurgence and new boldness in remaking the world. Bioengineering tackled the problems of life with renewed confidence. The once ubiquitous SkyScreens became increasingly obsolete as surgically implanted chips stimulated the user's brain directly via SkyWeb transmissions. Interpersonal conflicts were greatly reduced as brain functioning became centrally monitored and controlled.

Toward the end of the fourth generation, the people of Cosmopolis began to experience a few unexpected challenges. The bioengineered Nutrex diet had radically altered the microorganisms in the human digestive tract which resulted in an unanticipated increase in chronic metabolic illnesses. GovCorp's scientists investigated the problem and concluded that the human body had failed to adapt to Nutrex as smoothly as predicted. They began to genetically engineer the digestive system to utilize Nutrex more effectively.

By now humans had been exposed to the inescapable electronic pollution from the devices that permeated every part of the planet for several generations. GovCorp had established its CleanFire nuclear energy network without having solved the problem of radioactive waste disposal. Inevitably, some underground storage tanks leaked radiation into the groundwater. Some aging nukeys began to malfunction and spew radiation into the air. A growing number of people had tumors growing in their bodies. Spontaneous mutations began to appear with increasing frequency.

Scientists intensified the use of genetic engineering with the goal of developing radiation-resistant humans. Genetic modification or "gen-mod" was increasingly used to design humans with special abilities that were useful to GovCorp.

Fifth Generation: Epidemic of mutations

Solan:

Early in the fifth generation, in yet another stunning advance, gen-mod scientists were able to bioengineer the brain's own neurons to receive GovCorp transmissions, completely eliminating the need for surgically implanted brain chips.

By the fifth generation, the many alterations GovCorp's scientists had made to the ancient genetic code and the high levels of radioactivity triggered a reaction in the human genome. A runaway cascade of mutations led to the birth of bizarre humanoid organisms. The proliferation of grotesque humanoids forced GovCorp to destroy an increasing number of defective embryos and maladapted newborns.

After the damage to the human genome became obvious, GovCorp's gen-mod engineers frantically tried to retro-engineer the genetic code in a desperate attempt to restore key elements of the ancient code. But it soon became obvious that the alterations had gone beyond the point of no return.

By now Radun had passed away. Fortunately his brain had been uploaded into SkyWeb. GovCorp's executives pressured their scientists to use Radun's cyber brain to solve the problem.

Sixth Generation: Fall of GovCorp

Devara:

By the sixth generation, genetic modification, radiation and the Nutrex diet had wreaked havoc on the human immune system. When new and virulent human pandemics caused by mutated viruses swept across the globe, three-quarters of the world's population died within six months. Without its workforce, GovCorp was unable to function. Its distribution system could no longer deliver the necessities of life.

People began to think the unthinkable. The possibility of extinction loomed. A gloom settled over the planet. The unmaintained industrial landscape quickly became bleak and barren. On an individual level, the pain of being born severely maladapted to life was horrific. A massive epidemic of suicides reduced the global population still further.

The sixth generation saw the rapid collapse of the era of GovCorp. The people who had survived the pandemics began to starve as GovCorp's factories closed and ceased the distribution of Nutrex. Small bands of people tried to regroup and survive on a radically altered planet.

Seventh Generation: Last survivors

Solan:

We are the last surviving members of the Seventh Generation. Our generation was very small, numbering only a few thousand. Reproductive rates plummeted when GovCorp's genetic labs closed. Only a tiny number of people retained the ability to reproduce naturally. My parents were mutants born during the sixth generation. They were able to reproduce because my mother was a breeder and my father was one of very few men who could still produce viable sperm.

Our parents were among the first people bio-engineered without the fourth and fifth digits of the hands and feet. GovCorp scientists had decided that the extra digits had become superfluous in a world where hands were used to push buttons and feet were only used to get from one room to another. Our parents also had the smaller eyes and ears that reflected the change from real world to virtual world interactions. Their reduced mouths and jaws were adapted to consuming Nutrex.

Our parents joined a band of other survivors. They did their best to care for us in an inhospitable world. Navigating the bleak and treacherous landscape was challenging. We could no longer run or travel far on our smaller feet. Making tools was difficult because our hands were no longer skilled enough with only three fingers.

My parents attempted to grow their own food using precious seeds liberated from GovCorp's doomsday seed storage vaults. We all felt hopeful when we succeeded in growing some of the traditional foods like rice, wheat and beans. But our Nutrex-engineered digestive systems could no longer digest these foods. Our parents tried to eat them and they became sick and died.

(Taking a medallion out of his pocket)

The last thing they gave us before they died was this medallion certifying that they were descended from DNA-certified eggs and genuine Radun sperm. I didn't really understand what that meant at the time. Now I realize that Devara and I are Radun's great grandchildren.

We are the last survivors. Devara and I have been staying alive by eating old bars of Nutrex that we find in abandoned cubicles. We have only one left.

It is now 2199. Soon we will die. When New Year's Day 2200 arrives, there will be no humans left on planet Earth. There will be no one left to celebrate, or to mourn.

Now we have spoken and you have heard our story.

Devara and Solan return to the Tree of Life

Many of the UN people sit numbly in silent disbelief. Others sob uncontrollably in heartrending grief. Finally Amaka, the Nigerian ambassador, stands up.

Amaka, Ambassador from Nigeria:

Sky-Woman, please, we must do something! Isn't there anything we can do for our children?

A chorus of voices arises:

Yes, what can we do for our children? We must save them!

Sky-Woman and Sky-Man turn and embrace Solan and Devara.

Sky-Woman:

Dear children, thank you sharing your story. You are now carrying the suffering of the entire world in your bodies. Would you like to make a request?

Solan:

Yes. Please do not attempt to save my life. Living in this body is more painful than you can imagine.

If your generation fails to heed the warning signs and you let this window of opportunity slip by, seven generations of parents will be doomed to fail their children. Seven generations of children will be doomed to *devolve* instead of *evolve*.

Devara:

For me, the most painful part is knowing that previous generations did not love us enough to do what they needed to do during their lifetime. When a generation does not take responsibility for the problems of their time, they push their problems onto the backs of their children's generation.

Please create a future in which no child will ever be born into a body like mine.

Sky-Woman:

Do you have any other requests?

Devara:

(Crying)

When you hugged me, I felt happy for a moment. In our world, people no longer hugged each other.

Solan:

(Through his tears)

When we first came here as children of evolution, we went around the circle and hugged everyone. This time, I would like all of you to come and hug Devara and me.

The UN people, many of them weeping, rise and form a line leading to the children of extinction. Each person stops and embraces Solan and Devara. The deep trauma in their wiry, emaciated and frightened little bodies is palpable.

With each hug the children grow healthier. As more people hug them, Solan and Devara become taller, stronger and more human again. By the time all the UN people return to their seats, the children have been restored to their previous form as the children of evolution.

Devara's and Solan's faces alternate between looks of astonishment, horror and joy as they adjust to being back in their healthy, evolved bodies.

Solan:

(Shuddering)

I was feeling so alone and abandoned.

Devara:

(With excitement)

Your love brought us back. Your *love* brought us back!

Sky-Woman and Sky-Man hold Solan and Devara tenderly. They smile, grateful that their frightening experience as children of extinction is over. Feeling exhausted from their ordeal, they walk to the Tree of Life to rest and recover under its branches.

The UN people heave a collective sigh of relief when they see that the Sky Children have been restored to health. Yet the dark future they have embodied leaves them feeling deeply disturbed.

PART 7

A GIFT AND SEVEN REQUESTS

17. The Human Earth Stone

Singing People elders bring a gift

Sky-Man:

(To the UN people and tribes)

You have now walked the path of extinction with Devara and Solan and seen what your future might be like if you do not return to the Tree of Life and create a Human Earth.

Shanidar and Lamala have already experienced extinction. They may now be your only hope to avoid a similar fate.

Sky-Woman:

Shanidar and Lamala had seven requests. Shanidar was only able to make one request before he was attacked.

It is now time to hear all of the Singing People's requests.

Lamala:

Before we share our requests, we would first ask you to accept a gift from us.

I want to give you a gift that will help you tell yourselves a new story.

(Turning to the outer circle of Singing People who still surround the UN people)

I ask my Grandmother and Grandfather to join us.

Lamala's grandparents emerge from the outer circle and walk to the center. They have white hair and their faces are wrinkled with wisdom. They exude joy and vitality.

Singing People Grandmother:

(Holds a spherical granite stone in her hands)

We bring a gift for you.

This stone was formed billions of years ago. It has been used in sacred rituals for countless generations by our wise elders. When you look at it, you will remember your love for this precious rock upon which you live, the rock that came alive and grew into human beings.

Grandmother lifts her hands and the Human Earth Stone rises into the air. Small pools of water emerge from the gray rock, forming oceans and land. Then life forms in the oceans and green plants appear on the land.

Soon the granite Earth Stone transforms into a living miniature Human Earth, just like the one the UN people saw earlier when the Sky Elders shared their vision of earth's cosmic origin. While Lamala's Grandmother speaks, the Human Earth Stone rotates in the air.

Singing People Grandmother:

Before we return to the noosphere we want to tell you what we have learned during our time there. This knowledge will help you tell your new story of Human Earth.

Singing People reflect on their extinction

Singing People Grandfather:

In the noosphere we have reflected on our time on earth and why it ended. We have also watched you survive to reshape the earth.

Although you did contribute to our demise, we do not blame you for our extinction.

Like other human species before us, we became too committed to a particular form. We became set in our ways. Like you, we assumed we were the final product, the ultimate human. But evolution is about continuous growth. There will never be one permanent human form.

Despite your role in our extinction, we are grateful that Sky-Woman gave birth to you. If you had not been born, the entire human species might have died out with our disappearance.

Singing People Grandmother:

Much of our story with you has been dark. But we also share a light-filled story.

There were Singing People and Talking People who fell in love with each other. If you look into the deepest place in your heart you may still remember celebrating, feasting and making love with us. Many of you carry our essence in your genes.

Let us feel the love that draws us closer and release the guilt and anger that separate us. The betrayal of love brings pain, and only the restoration of love can remove it.

You discovered the secret of evolution

Singing People Grandfather:

Grandmother and I have observed you from the noosphere since our extinction on Earth. We cannot show you your path to evolution. Only you yourselves can find that. Yet we *are* your brothers and sisters and we knew you when you were much younger and lived among us.

You stayed in Mother Earth's African womb longer than any other humans and you practiced one of the great secrets of evolution: You made the love and care of each new generation the foundation of your culture. Your early fertility rituals were a celebration of the miracle of evolution that takes place within a woman's body. Long-lived grandmothers provided an essential new layer of care for the young. Men supported women and children by providing love, food, shelter and protection.

You learned how to shape the world around you. But then over time you forgot one very important thing: You forgot that evolution still applied to *you*. You and your children have to live in the humasphere you make. You are shaped by the world you create.

You carry our hopes and the hopes of Mother Earth herself. Love yourself. Love each other. Love the world and the universe that gave birth to you. Evolutionary success means being the one who changes, the one who *voluntarily* "goes extinct" by evolving to the next level.

18. Seven requests for healing

First request: Honor our Bones

Singing People Grandmother:

Now we can share our seven requests that will guide you in healing and co-creating a Human Earth.

(Gesturing to Shanidar and Lamala)

As Shanidar requested earlier, please take our bones from the museums and honor them with rituals. Rituals for the dying are sacred to both the Singing People and the Talking People.

As you have seen, we came here from the noosphere. For you to understand how important death rituals are to the planet, we need to explain something about the noosphere to you. It is a realm of great beauty and wisdom. All the energy from the sun and stars first passes through the noosphere before it reaches the Earth. This celestial energy is as fresh as a new dawn.

When you die, your physical body returns to the earth and your spirit body returns to the noosphere. When you are ready to be reborn, your spirit descends from the sky and your body grows from the earth, through your mother and the food she eats.

When death releases the human spirit from the physical body, that person's energy flows back to its source in the noosphere. In a healthy community the dying person is "birthed" back into the spirit world through ritual and mourning. Mourning includes both honoring the person's life and grieving their loss. The spirit of a person who has been mourned returns to the noosphere as light energy. This spiritual energy enriches the noosphere and furthers the evolution of Human Earth.

But many dark clouds have formed in the noosphere. They are filled with the spirits of the *unmourned dead*. The unmourned include all the people who died without the benefit of grieving rituals. You know how important it is to honor and be honored. This is why you include a Tomb for the Unknown Soldier in your cemeteries.

Traumatized and unmourned spirits are not able to transform into light and ride the plasma energy tubes up to the noosphere. Instead they drift slowly upward and become stuck together as heavy clouds. These dark clouds contain the unmourned spirits of people who died from violence, epidemics, famines, natural disasters, wars and genocides.

For tens of thousands of years we Singing People have existed in a state of limbo in a dark noosphere cloud. Other dark clouds contain the unmourned spirits of other extinct species. Every day more traumatized spirits arrive in the noosphere because of the violence in your world. The clouds grow darker and heavier, blocking life-giving cosmic energy from reaching you.

The only way to free these spirits is for people on earth to engage in mourning rituals and tell their untold stories. Genuine grieving heals these suffering spirits with love and dissolves the dark clouds. Once again the earth will be able to receive cosmic energy that is clear and energizing.

That is why it is so important to honor our bones, the bones of all the unmourned and the bones of all the ancestors. Honoring *our* bones will help you to honor *your* bones.

Second request: Give us new names

Singing People Grandfather:

You have named us Neanderthals, based on a valley in Germany where you first unearthed our bones. Over the decades, your attitude of disrespect has tarnished this name.

We ask that you change your name for us from *Homo neanderthalensis* to *Homo sonatus*, the Singing People.

That would make us very happy.

(Smiling)

You have named every species. Do you realize that you are the only species who *named themselves*?

You call yourselves *Homo sapiens*, the wise people. *Homo sapiens* is a noble name and it reveals the kind of human you aspire to be. From time to time wise people do arise among you. Yet as a species you have not yet earned the name wise. If you were wise you would honor your wise ones instead of ignoring them and persecuting them.

As Lamala told you, our name for you is the Talking People. Your scientific name could be *Homo ego*, describing your current level of consciousness. Giving us both new names would help heal our relationship.

Once you have named yourselves more accurately, you will be able to see yourselves more clearly. Then you can learn to use your whole brain and develop its full potential. You can evolve from *Homo ego* to become *Homo sapiens*.

This could be the next step in your evolution and of the Earth herself.

Third request: Build Human Earth Shrines

Singing People Grandmother:

Every place on earth is sacred. We ask you to create Human Earth Shrines all over the world. Rediscover the locations that hold special power and reactivate them with rituals. Find the traumatized places that have been desecrated by empire. Restore them to health with rituals of regeneration.

Each community can select locations of beauty and spiritual meaning as gathering spaces. Many sites have been in use since ancient times. They are places where Earth and Sky energies intersect in powerful ways. They are the acupuncture points of Mother Earth's body. Ask the indigenous people who remain in your land if they will share their knowledge of sacred sites with you so they can be honored and preserved for future generations.

Each family and each person can create their own Home Shrine to connect them to the Earth and Sky, to their ancestors and to the human family. In this way healing the earth can happen at every level, from the personal to the planetary.

Fourth Request: Gather for council rituals

Singing People Grandfather:

Our fourth request is that you gather in council and enact healing rituals at your Human Earth Shrines and your home shrines. Weave the sacred cycle of Grandmother Moon back into your community life.

Realign your calendar with the sky as it was in ancient times. Celebrate the rituals of the four great seasonal turnings. Gathering at the equinoxes and solstices brings people all over the planet together at the same time. These seasonal rituals create a rhythm that animates and harmonizes all life on Earth. Each person has the experience of sharing one earth and one family.

Councils reconnect you to the Tree of Life and the loving universe that surrounds you — Grandfather Sun, Grandmother Moon, your brother and sister planets, and the ancestral stars. Each of you can practice the art of inner council to harmonize your inner life and come to one mind within yourself. From these practices you will develop a clear mind and learn to think like a planet.

Councils help you solve problems by coming to one mind. Family councils help families bond and create meaningful family traditions. Partner councils help intimate relationships grow deeper and more loving. Social councils help groups and communities clarify their missions and develop effective strategies. Grieving councils allow you to recognize and mourn the great personal and planetary losses that are happening today.

Rituals are tools for evolving consciousness. You have forgotten some of the most basic rituals that sustained your ancestors through all their challenges. One of our most powerful, and delicious, social rituals has always been cooking food and eating together. Eating is the sacred act of taking life and giving it new life. Take the time to choose your food wisely, express gratitude, and experience the pleasure of eating.

Another age-old ritual is the primal art of using your strong, sensitive hands to care for each other. There is so much healing power in your touch. A loving touch reaches deep into the soul. A hug reaffirms our connection. After the sun sets we always sit around the fire, massage each other and sing about our day.

Many of your current cultural rituals have outlived the meanings they once had. Breathe new life into them or let them go and discover creative rituals that can guide your evolution today. Reinvigorate your life journey with meaningful rituals for all the great turnings — birth, coming of age, marriage, conceiving a child, finding your calling, aging and dying.

Fifth request: Tell true stories

Singing People Grandmother:
   Our fifth request is that you tell true stories. Tell stories that grow from the Tree of Life and the Four Roots. New stories of Love, Truth, Peace and Power.

   When you tell the story of the Four Tribes and your great journey, remember to tell the story of the Singing People and the epic time we lived on the earth. Remember our visit here today and our role in helping you heal the earth.

   Each tribe and nation can retell their story in a way that generates social healing. People of all faith traditions can evolve together and help write new, unifying stories for Human Earth. Each of you can retell your life story in a way that strengthens your self-confidence and nourishes your inner Tree of Life.

Sixth request: Find a home for the Earth Stone

Singing People Grandfather:
   (Gestures to the miniature living Earth suspended in the air)
   We ask you to build a shrine that can be a home for the Human Earth Stone we are giving you. At this Human Earth Shrine you can plant a Tree of Life and perform rituals for the healing the whole earth.

   These rituals will help you live more consciously and creatively. They will connect you with your global brain. Your rituals will create energy tubes that restore the circulation between the humasphere and noosphere. This energy flow will dissolve the dark clouds and clear the noosphere.

   Where you build this planetary shrine is something that you will need to decide. Two UN-designated international zones already exist as possible locations. One is right here on the land dedicated the United Nations. The other is in Jerusalem. They both offer unique opportunities for healing the planet.

The UN is here in New York, where all the nations who descended from the Four Tribes already meet. If you honor the Earth Stone and make a sacred place for it here in the heart of empire you can transform the world.

Jerusalem is in the Middle East where the Singing People and the Talking People first encountered each other. Jerusalem has long been the focus of intense planetary energies. It is the crossroads of the world, where the great continents of Asia, Africa and Europe come together. Jerusalem is central to Christianity, Islam and Judaism. Everyone wants to claim Jerusalem as their own.

Where people meet, conflicts arise. The people who live in Jerusalem and the surrounding regions have suffered invasions and occupations for hundreds of generations. Jerusalem is the planet's spiritual center *and* its trauma center. It is the land of Cain and Abel. Perhaps the Earth Stone can help to heal this ancient wound.

So that every land can be blessed by its presence, remember to find the Earth Stone a new home for each new generation.

Seventh request: Evolve a Human Earth

Singing People Grandmother:

Our last request is the shortest, yet the most challenging: Evolve a new planetary culture, a Human Earth, that grows from the Tree of Life and the Four Roots.

We are all children of Sky-Woman and Sky-Man. May they bless you and guide you on your journey.

Shanidar and Lamala step forward.

Lamala:

Thank you Grandmother and Grandfather for sharing your wisdom with all of us.

Shanidar:

(To the Mothers and Fathers of the Four Tribes)
Will you honor our seven requests?
Will you honor our bones?
Will you give both of us new names?
Will you build Human Earth shrines?
Will you gather in councils and do rituals?
Will you tell true stories?
Will you find the Human Earth Stone a home?
Will you evolve into a Human Earth?

Four Tribes pledge to create Human Earth

The Native American Wind Tribe Mother and Father glance at the other Mothers and Fathers who nod their approval. The Mothers and Fathers of the Four Tribes all step forward and walk over to Shanidar, Lamala and her grandparents.

Wind Tribe Mother:

We will honor all your requests.

We gratefully accept your gift of the Human Earth Stone. Thank you for sharing your love and wisdom with us.

Wind Tribe Father:

Each of your requests is a gift to us. In return for your gifts, we pledge to create a Human Earth for our children that includes a clear and vibrant noosphere.

The hovering living Human Earth descends into the Singing People Grandmother's hands. As it descends, it transforms back into a granite Earth Stone. She approaches the Wind Tribe Mother.

Singing People Grandmother:

We give this sacred Human Earth Stone to the Talking People with all of our love. We place it in the care of the Wind Tribe.

The Singing People Grandmother gently places the Earth Stone in the Wind Tribe Mother's hands.

Singing People Grandfather:
We will bless you and guide you from the noosphere to help you create a Human Earth.

Lamala's grandparents raise their arms in farewell and return to the outer circle of Singing People.

Singing People and Talking People celebrate

Shanidar:
Thank you for accepting our gift and our requests. The healing has begun.

Lamala:
Let us sing together!

In their resonant, melodic voices Lamala and Shanidar lead everyone in a powerful and deeply moving chant. As the Singing People and Talking People sing together, their breathing synchronizes and their hearts and minds become one. Their faces reflect a sense of joy and connection.

As they sing, Shanidar, Lamala and their two children walk slowly back to their cave. They stand at the entrance to their cave, gazing back at the Talking People. Slowly, layer by layer, their clothing, their skin, their muscles and their inner organs dematerialize until only their skeletons remain standing.

The singing becomes louder and fills the air as their bones return to the ground. Then their spirit bodies emerge from the earth, visible as diaphanous energy forms modeled on their physical bodies.

Shanidar and Lamala rise above the ring of Singing People. The Singing People also transform into spirit bodies. They all begin to rise, forming an ascending spiral into the sky.

Everyone else is left down below. They feel a heart-rending sadness as they see their brothers and sisters leaving their world once more.

Now the singing from above becomes even more beautiful and enchanting. The Talking People become swept up in its simple yet powerful melodic flow. The vocalizations of the departing Singing People become ever more intricate. The Talking People sense their nervous systems being transformed by the polyphonic overtone chanting.

Suddenly they notice with surprise that they are being drawn upward by an irresistible force. The Talking People's bodies take on a spirit form as they follow the Singing People and rise up through the atmosphere, beyond the clouds, to the first level of the noosphere.

There the Talking People find themselves in the ancient world of the Singing People. It is summertime and they are in a beautiful pristine valley in ancient Europe. It is the golden age of the Singing People. The Talking People breathe in the vibrant aroma of the earth as it was before the pollution of the industrial age. Simply breathing this pure air fills their bodies with an inexpressible joy and vitality.

The Singing People are gathering for their summer solstice celebration. The Talking People join the Singing People and they feast together. The tantalizing aroma of venison roasting over open fires fills the air. There are bowls filled with fresh greens, mushrooms and ripe berries. The food is delicious and the Talking People can sense the life energy in the wild foods.

The solstice sun sets in a V-shaped notch in the mountains. Under a brilliant starlit sky, a bonfire blazes at the center of a sacred circle of stones.

As everyone gathers and sits in a circle, Sky-Woman and Sky-Man create a vision space. The ancient scene of Cain and Abel reappears. This time Cain cries out for forgiveness and brings an authentic and heartfelt offering to the altar. He offers the best of his harvest and the smoke of his offering rises to the Sky. The Creator smiles.

Abel rises from beneath the ground and brings his offering to the altar. The two brothers embrace. A golden glow emanates from their connection and flows out to bathe everyone in healing energy.

The vision space disappears and the Singing People arise. They form two circles and begin to dance their traditional summer solstice dances.

They drum on hollow logs with rounded drumsticks. They shed their animal furs and their skin glistens in the firelight.

The Singing People men dance in a circle with their hands on the shoulders of the man in front of them. The women dance in their own circle with their hands on the shoulders of the woman in front of them. They dance in one direction and then reverse. Then they merge their two circles in a dance of love.

The Talking People are transported by the natural beauty and sensuality of the Singing People. They remember a time when they too lived close to the heartbeat of Mother Earth. The Singing People reach out to the Talking People and bring them into the dance. Throughout the night, their dance of love and reconciliation generates streams of energy that flow between the noosphere and the geosphere, bringing healing and harmony to the five spheres of life.

As the first gorgeous colors of dawn break over the majestic mountains, the world of the Singing People begins to dissolve. The Singing People slowly rise and continue their journey to their home in the upper noosphere. They return joyfully, knowing that their dark cloud is dissolving.

As the Talking People descend to the earth they tenderly wave farewell to the Singing People. The ethereal spirit bodies of the Talking People gradually transform back into their physical bodies. Sky-Woman and Sky-Man guide everyone back to the Tree of Life by the river. The UN people relax in the amphitheater and reflect on their encounter with the Singing People.

They look up at the sky. Now they can see the faint violet hues of the noosphere beyond the blue atmosphere. Having been there and felt its rejuvenating energy directly, they feel a strong desire to keep the energy flowing between the humasphere and noosphere with clear thoughts and healing rituals.

For the first time modern humans have met face to face with another human species. Their own ethnic and regional differences seem far less significant than before. As human beings they are bound by a common origin and a shared legacy of heroic adventures and great tragedies. They are one family.

They wonder, "Can we regain our ability to evolve and make the leap to the next level?"

PART 8

EVOLUTION OF HUMAN EARTH

19: Evolutionary challenge

The coming apocalypse

Sky-Woman:

The Singing People have given us the most valuable gifts of all, love and healing.

Sky-Man:

Just as the Singing People have disappeared from the earth, so one day the Talking People will disappear. One question remains unanswered: Will you disappear because you went extinct or will you "disappear" because you evolved into a higher form of human?

Four Tribes and UN people:

We want to evolve but we have forgotten how.

Sky-Man:

Human Earth cannot become fully mature until you reunite your consciousness with her. Evolution has chosen you to fulfill earth's destiny. You still have time to create a Human Earth.

When we first arrived we revealed that you are approaching the center of a great spiral of evolution. When you approach the center of a spiral, time goes faster, cycles become shorter, and energy builds up.

Your population has reached a massive density on the planet. Your empire-based humasphere is damaging the biosphere and all the other spheres. You've pushed things to the tipping point.

You are at the crucial 5-billion-year midpoint of earth's 10-billion-year lifetime. Human Earth is going through a midlife crisis. This is your moment of truth as human beings. To survive you need to go through the center of this evolutionary spiral and emerge on the other side.

Sky-Man:

Three and a half years from now, at the autumn equinox in the northern hemisphere (the spring equinox in the southern hemisphere), you will pass through the center of this spiral of evolution and experience a great energy pulsation from the center of your galaxy. This will initiate the reversal of the earth's magnetic poles. During this cataclysmic event you will either rise up into an evolutionary Metanoia or collapse into a global catastrophe.

The dark future that Solan and Devara experienced happened because humanity did not prepare for the Metanoia and they missed the opportunity for healing. One of your poets saw an apocalyptic vision of this spiral spinning out of control and wrote: "Things fall apart; the center cannot hold."

If you respond to the challenge of the apocalypse by evolving your consciousness, you will experience a Metanoia. If you resist being changed then your world will be turned upside down.

Spiritual messengers

Fire Tribe Father:

Sky-Man, as I listen to you I am filled with a fear that I don't fully understand. I want to feel confident that humanity will rise to the opportunity of the Metanoia, but I have a dark feeling of doom.

Empires are rigid and always self-destruct. Empire pyramids impose order from above and resist change from below. Eventually the pyramid becomes so top-heavy that it collapses under its own weight leaving chaos and destruction. Even if there is a worldwide Human Earth movement, won't empire's financial, political and military domination block change from happening in time?

The other Tribal Mothers and Fathers and many UN people nod their heads in despair.

Sky-Man:

It is true that empires resist change. When empires first arose, we began sending you spiritual messengers to guide you back to the Tree of Life.

Spiritual teachers, like Moses, Buddha, Jesus and Muhammad, are evolved human beings who experience spontaneous awakenings, personal Metanoias. Afterward, they recognize that their fellow human beings have forgotten the Original Teachings and suffer under empire's toxic trance. From a place of deep compassion they offer everyone the opportunity of Metanoia, saying: "Wake up! Change your consciousness!"

Yet empire chooses to ignore or persecute these spiritual teachers and distort their message.

Two thousand years ago, Jesus' radical message of love posed a grave threat to the biggest empire the world had ever known. The Roman Empire had conquered the independent nation of Israel and turned it into an oppressed colony. Jesus' teachings struck a chord with people who saw that their Original Teachings were being lost and their government no longer represented them.

Many of these people began gathering in sharing communities and living outside the Roman Empire's money-based system. The empire tried to crush the movement by arresting Jesus and torturing, humiliating and crucifying him. Yet the power of his love had already had such a profound impact that his supporters spread the "Good News" of a new way of life throughout the Roman Empire. Despite the Empire's continuing persecution, Jesus' love-based movement grew rapidly after his death.

Hundreds of years later, Christian communities existed throughout the Roman Empire and were growing increasingly influential. One of the embattled Roman Emperors saw the advantages of incorporating the early church and using it to unify his crumbling Roman Empire under one official state religion.

The persecuted church merged with its empire oppressor. The newly combined empire/church kept the story of Jesus alive, but the story became increasingly distorted over the centuries. Jesus' liberating, life-affirming message of love became buried under a repressive doctrine of fear, sin and obedience to empire's patriarchal authority.

Jesus' liberating message of "Change your consciousness!" was twisted into a guilt-driven admonition to "Repent!" Yet the word used in the New Testament is *Metanoia* (Matthew 4:17) and it reflects Jesus' Original Teachings. Empire could not kill Jesus' essence, because his essence is love, and his bright light continues to radiate today.

Sky-Woman:

We have sent many spiritual messengers, carriers of the Original Teachings, to all parts of the world. Many of them are unsung heroes and heroines, indigenous wisdom keepers and everyday people who keep the Tree of Life alive in their families and communities. We saw the nations of the world continuing to make war and ignore these carriers of the Original Teachings.

We realized that individual messengers were not enough, so we mobilized the spiritual energies of the noosphere and sent a massive wake-up call to the planet. During the 1960's many young people were searching for alternatives to living in empire and they heard our call. A worldwide movement arose for a new life-affirming culture. The Tree of Life which had been withering, began to blossom with new growth.

People saw what was happening to Mother Earth and they organized the first Earth Day. During that time many flowers bloomed: environmental movements, green technology, civil rights, indigenous rights, women's rights, a return to nature, a rediscovery of the body's own healing power, natural foods and organic agriculture, a cultural meeting of East and West, meditation and spirituality, social and economic justice, political liberation and peace movements, and grassroots consciousness-raising groups. A Whole Earth Catalog promoted tools for ecological living and self-empowerment. In every area of life, new creative thinking arose.

Sky-Man:

People came together and nourished the Four Roots of Love, Truth, Peace and Power and they began to envision a new Human Earth. The possibility of a Metanoia was in the air. The young people said to empire, "The old stories are not working for us anymore. Let's wake up and take the next step in our evolution!"

But empire resisted the change and brutally suppressed this renaissance of the Tree of Life. And as usual, empire skillfully co-opted and commercialized what it could not suppress.

Sky-Woman:

We witnessed the new blossoms on the Tree of Life begin to fade in the 1970's. One generation alone cannot evolve. It takes all the generations, young and old, linking arms together.

You have missed many opportunities over the past decades.

Four faces of the Goddess

Sky-Woman:

Not every living planet passes the challenge of consciousness and evolves to the next level. The time has come for us to talk about how your relationship with me can evolve. I will always be your mother and you will always be my children. But you are now my *adult children*.

I am not only your Earth Mother. I am the Goddess and I have four faces, that of Grandmother, Mother, Lover and Child.

Sky-Woman, as Grandmother Earth:

(Transforms into a majestic elder, wearing a necklace of precious stones and a silver-gray robe upon which flow images of mountain ranges, oceans, continents)

As Grandmother Earth I am the "rock of ages." My geosphere creates the continents that form the bedrock of your life. I provide the foundation for your homes and buildings.

The ancestors called me Grandmother Turtle because they saw my continents floating like great turtles on the molten sea beneath.

I speak to you through rocks and fossils and the deep layers of sedimentary memory. I have seen many worlds come and go on this planet. I want to share my sacred wisdom and my stories with my grandchildren.

Sky-Woman, as Mother Earth:

(Transforms into a mature, nurturing and maternal woman in midlife, wearing a colorful robe upon which flow images of lush valleys, villages, forests, orchards, vegetable gardens and grain fields)

As Mother Earth I grew a biosphere so I could feed and support you. I continue to nurture you as I did when you were younger. Every day I give you food to eat, pure water to drink and fresh air to breathe. I give you all the materials you need to create your world.

During your hunter-gatherer times, your life was directly interwoven with the natural world and you still lived close to me. After you mastered fire, developed language and became conscious you looked at me differently. At that moment, you grew from being a child into an adult.

Sky-Woman, as Lover Earth:

(Transforms into a beautiful, sensual young woman, wearing a robe upon which flow images of flowers, meadows, fruit trees, bubbling springs, sunsets and moonlit nights)

Yes, I am also your lover. Your very first songs, poems and psalms were love songs to me, filled with awe, delight and passionate longing. I loved your touch. I loved the way you explored my body. You made your homes and villages in my forests, in my hills and valleys and even in my deserts. You loved everything about me and every part of me was sacred to you.

You did rituals with me, expressing your love, creating a time and space for us to be with each other. You never harmed me. You always showed respect and gratitude. As lovers we shared our secrets with each other. You talked with my plants and began to care for them in your gardens so they could give you more good things to eat.

But once you started building your cities and empires you became intoxicated with your own power. You had fewer conversations with me and you began to use your knowledge to manipulate me. You looked at my body as raw material for empire-building. You cut me up into pieces of property and sold me to other men who did whatever they wanted to me.

Today I experience your abuse more often than I feel your love. You are hurting me. Now in this present age of the Anthropocene, the heat from your fires has churned up the atmosphere, making my moods swing more widely than before. My life-giving rains morph out of control and rage into devastating superstorms that flood your homes. My clear sunny days now stretch into devastating droughts that parch your farmlands. Disease and extinction now threaten many of my children.

This is not the kind of relationship I want with you. I want to be lovers again. As your lover, I want you to feel pleasure as you breathe me in and when you touch my skin. I want you to *come back to your senses* so you can feel my love in every cell of your body.

Tell me what kind of world you dream of and I will help you create it. Ask me about the kind of planet I want to become and help me fulfill my life.

As lovers it is our destiny to have a child together. When you tried to give birth without me you gave birth to empire. As lovers we can give birth to a Human Earth. This baby is inside me now. I can feel her wanting to be born. I need your help to birth her into the world.

Sky-Woman, as Human Earth Child:
(Transforms into a beautiful 5-year-old girl who glows with vitality, wearing a robe upon which flow images of a future earth full of mystery and wonder):
I am ready to be born. Please take good care of me.

Sky-Woman:
(Resumes her own form)
Behind all my faces, I am one with you and you are one with me. You and I evolve together or not at all. Together let us grow a planetary mind and enter the new age of the Noocene.

From empire's pyramid into a Tree of Life

Asian Water Tribe Father:

I want to evolve more than ever now, but how can a rigid empire pyramid could ever be transformed? When I look back at history I see that empires rise spectacularly and then fall catastrophically. Pyramids are so resistant to change that they still stand in Egypt as lasting monuments to empire.

Sky-Woman:

It is impossible for empires to transform as long as you see a pyramid with physical eyes alone. The true nature of an empire pyramid is only revealed when you see with your spiritual eye.

You usually picture empire's pyramid as a hierarchical social organization with all the power at the top. But if you picture empire's pyramid as the ancient Egyptians saw it, you would see a sacred double spiral connecting Earth and Sky.

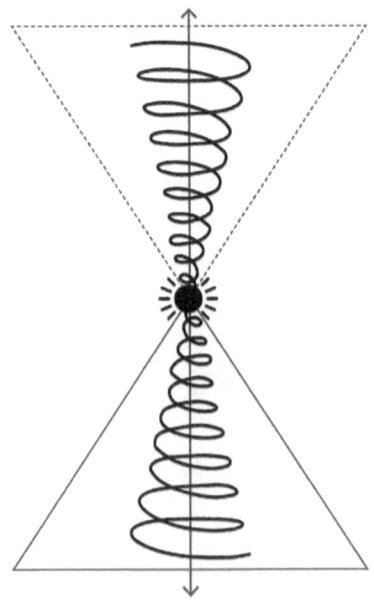

Figure 23. Visible and invisible pyramids. Spirals of materialization and spiritualization. Credit: Gerzon

Sky-Man:

The top of the physical pyramid is the apex of an Earth spiral that flows into an invisible Sky spiral. If people at the top of the pyramid block the energy flow, the pyramid gets top-heavy and collapses on itself.

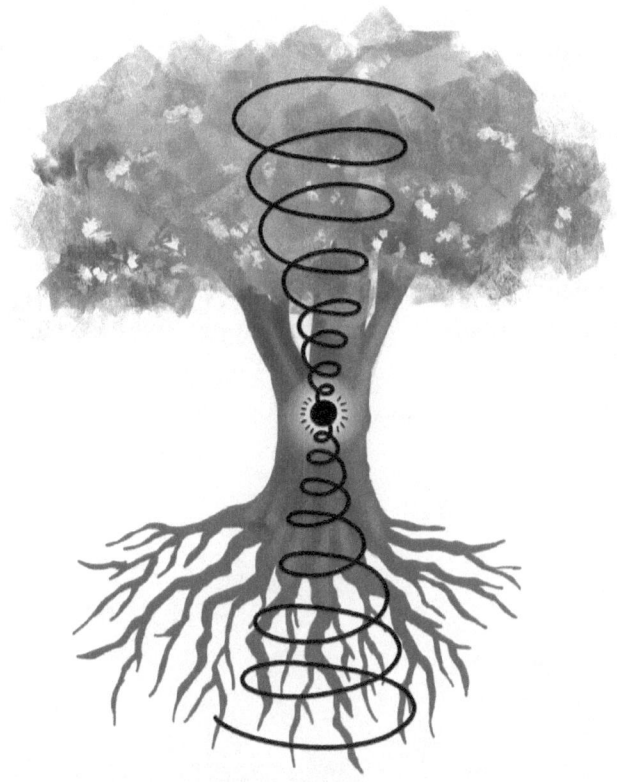

Figure 24. Empire pyramid transforms into Tree of Life. Credit: Gerzon.

Sky-Woman:

Yet it *is* possible to transform an empire pyramid from a rigid structure into a spiral. The first step is to *see the pyramid as a spiral*. If the leaders at the top of the pyramid carry out their sacred role and become clear channels for the energy of Earth and Sky then the spirals flow and all people prosper.

If the leaders block the energy, then it becomes necessary for the people to unify their spiraling energies and generate a creative pressure that opens the flow.

Once you restore the spiral flow of love, an empire pyramid becomes a living organism again, one that can grow into a Tree of Life.

Sky-Man:

Not every apple on an apple tree ripens into a mature fruit. Can our Human Earth pass the challenge of consciousness? Going through the center of the spiral of evolution and emerging on the other side is like going through the eye of a needle.

How can you find the center when you're lost in the swirling currents? Relax into the flow. Let yourself be *drawn* to the center.

The world needs a miracle right now. A miracle is something that's outside your current story. Miracles happen when you change your story.

The Metanoia is your opportunity for a miracle!

20: Sky Elders' Metanoia vision

Human Earth's galactic destiny

Sky-Man:

The story of Human Earth is a big story. Yet you cannot truly understand it until you see it as part of an even bigger story.

Our Sky Elders are here with us. They are the Sky Elders of our whole galaxy. They will now reveal your cosmic destiny.

The Sky Elders step forward once more and address the UN people and the Tribal Mothers and Fathers.

Sky-Grandfather:

During the Creation Story you saw the great universe that gave birth to Human Earth. You are still part of that great living universe. It is not only you who are being called to evolve. The whole universe is evolving with you. I want you to meet the larger family you belong to.

(Pointing to the vision space where images of the sun and planets appear)

Human Earth belongs to a sun family. You can see your solar system coming into view. You are the only conscious planet in your sun family. But you are part of a much larger extended family, your galactic family.

Let's zoom out so you can see the Milky Way galaxy once more with its bright center and its spiral arms. You can see your Human Earth glowing with consciousness in the lower right quadrant.

You have brothers and sisters in your galaxy and beyond. You are one of four planets in the Milky Way that are approaching full consciousness. Now you can see the other three conscious planets begin to glow in their quadrants of the galaxy.

Figure 25.
Milky Way galaxy. Credit: Public domain.

These four planets are *galactic* Earth, Wind, Fire and Water Tribes. Can you guess which tribe your Human Earth represents?

You have always wanted to reach for the stars. You have dreamed of communicating with life on other planets. Yet as your despair and darkness deepened, the hope of finding brother and sister planets degenerated into the desire for new worlds to conquer and exploit.

Now for the first time your scientists are finding other living planets. You are being called to become part of a conscious galactic family. If you and your brother and sister planets come together, you will be able to tap the unlimited energy and intelligence at the center of your galaxy.

This is your galactic destiny: To join with other conscious planets and light up the universe!

Figure 26. Galaxy and stars. Credit: Public domain.

Vision of the Metanoia miracle

Sky Grandmother:

You have learned that three and a half years from now at the Autumn Equinox you will reach the center of an evolutionary spiral and experience either a great catastrophe or a miraculous planetary Metanoia. We want to share a vision of the Metanoia so you can go back and tell people how to prepare for the Metanoia.

(Pointing to the vision space)

Imagine that after our council, you share the story of Human Earth and people begin preparing for the Metanoia. Imagine that human beings start fulfilling the Singing People's requests. Imagine billions of people all over the earth, cultivating the Tree of Life in their personal lives, their families and communities.

Now Human Earth's immune system can respond actively and creatively to the global crisis. People in every region rediscover their sacred places. They create Earth Shrines and gather in council circles. They tell true stories. They are healing and their consciousness is changing.

Three years pass. The autumn equinox approaches. People gather at their sacred shrines. The earth is in perfect balance. Day and night are equal all over the planet. People are meditating on their connection as one family. They chant and focus their energies on co-creating one mind.

At the exact moment of the autumn equinox, the georeactor at the earth's core sends red currents of energy pulsing up to the surface. At the same instant, a massive wave of solar-galactic energy strikes the earth and the entire planet vibrates like a gigantic gong hanging in space. The north and south magnetic poles reverse.

A brilliant flash of light radiates throughout the galaxy, reverberating with the great cosmic orgasm that started everything. All becomes one in a golden moment of eternity.

Figure 27. This geomagnetic event provides an astronomical basis for part of this mythic imagery. Credit: NASA

Sky-Grandfather:

Around the planet Human Earth shrines glow and send out tendrils of energy. Their circles grow and link together to form larger circles. Lines of light energy begin to connect the sacred sites of the planet. Bright auroras light up the atmosphere. They are visible in both the nighttime and daytime sides of the planet. Gigantic snakes of red, yellow, blue and green light undulate across the sky. The geosphere, biosphere, humasphere, atmosphere and noosphere all resonate with the vibration of love.

The Metanoia ritual of rebirth has begun!

People experience a golden illumination. They sense their quantum body and experience cosmic consciousness. They leave behind the world of Empire Earth and are reborn into Human Earth. Every cell in their bodies feels the vital radiation as a transcendent blessing. Waves of purifying love vibrate through every atom, activating a deep cleansing and rejuvenation for all living beings.

Their Earth and Sky chakras light up. They regain the clarity of their lost indigenous mind. They feel whole and complete within themselves, embodying the universe.

Evolutionary changes occur in everyone's DNA. People access the Original Teachings stored in their genetic code. Outdated epigenetic patterns switch off and new evolutionary ones switch on. A profound change of consciousness occurs as neural circuits grow rapidly throughout the brain, linking up the thinking human brain, the emotional mammalian brain and the instinctive reptilian brain. An evolved, fully-functioning holistic human mind comes into being.

Once the human family gathered around a single Tree in Africa. Now they encircle the whole planet. At the south pole the fluctuating geomagnetic lines of energy begin to form roots. From the north pole the trunk and branches of the Tree of Life emerge. The Tree of Life has been restored on Human Earth.

United in the Metanoia, the personal and the planetary become one. Over seven billion conscious minds send energy tubules up to the noosphere creating a completely new individual/universal human mind cloud around the earth. Humanity begins to think like a planet. The noosphere glows with light. Great relief, peace and joy spread over the entire earth.

Vision of Human Earth arising from empire

Sky-Grandmother:
Join us now as we envision what can happen after the Metanoia. Let's imagine how Empire Earth can awaken into Human Earth:

After the Metanoia, people recognize the *Great-Oneness-Dimension* that exists within themselves and within each other. They gather in circles and councils.

Earth's biosphere can now receive far more life-giving energy from both the cosmos and the earth's core. Every form of life on earth flourishes in the radiance of this energy. Natural landscapes that have been abused and polluted return to health. Plants and animals rebound as their habitats are restored.

People begin to create an eco-paradise by working with Mother Nature instead of against her. People retribalize into Tree of Life communities based on authentic affiliations that grow from biological family connections, deep friendships, shared values and missions. These communities practice living from the Four Roots of Love, Truth, Peace and Power, They honor the great cycle of birth and death. Men recognize the place of women and children at the center of life and actively support them.

These new self-organizing tribes form council circles. Soon circles connect with other circles. A living web of dynamic interlinked circles replaces hierarchical empire-style governments.

Thinking globally enables people to live locally, reconnecting with the land. New communities grow, forming around natural bioregions. Colorful, diverse cultures regenerate the humasphere and blend into the biosphere. Local dialects and customs enrich humanity. Over the generations, with empowered women consciously choosing if and when to bring a child into the world, earth's population gradually adjusts so that each bioregion becomes sustainable.

At the same time a global language develops to encourage clear thinking and cross-cultural communication. This evolutionary human language is based on the Four Roots and gradually replaces the old war-based languages fabricated by ego and empire.

People enjoy conscious and creative living, healing and supporting each other's growth and well-being. They practice the Original Teachings in their daily lives. Everyone is able to explore love in their own way. They create dynamic, passionate, loving relationships. Sexual pleasure and sexual responsibility enrich each other. Children feel loved and are educated for evolution so that their generation can take Human Earth to the next level.

New currents of electromagnetic energy arc between the noosphere and the humasphere providing a natural global communication network.

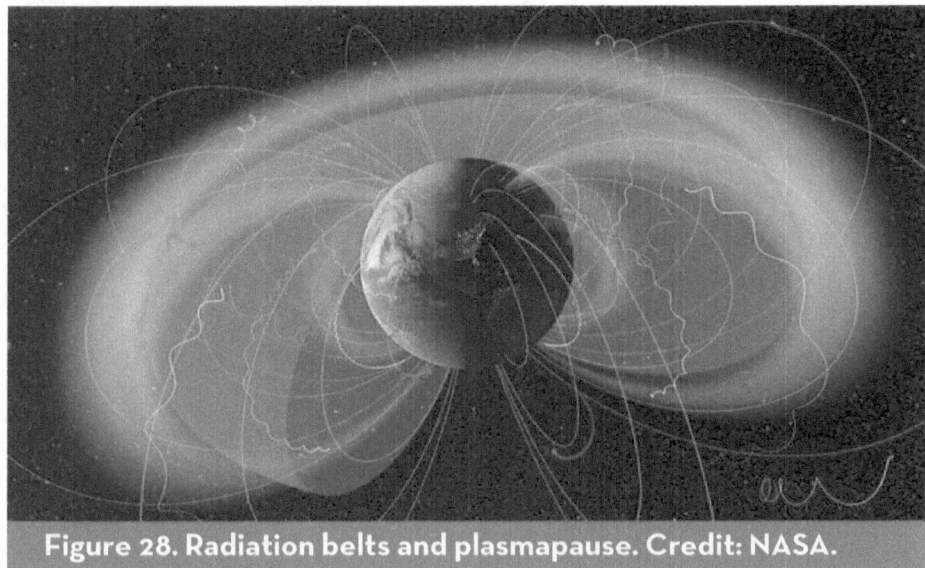

Figure 28. Radiation belts and plasmapause. Credit: NASA.

Sky-Grandfather:

People share Mother Earth's resources for mutual benefit. Vibrant, eco-friendly, human-scale cities serve as creative centers of education, culture and research.

Farms interweave with villages. A diversity of crops are grown naturally for local consumption. Regenerative agriculture restores the land. Everyone who wants to tend a garden can do so, from big community lots, to backyards to windowsill pots. The sacred relationship between human beings and animals is restored. Delicious foods filled with vitality are available to everyone. Healthy meats, dairy products and seafood supplement a mainly plant-based cuisine. Epidemic diseases become rare as ecological wisdom guides humanity.

From the decay of empire, new and creative experiments arise. Millions of social justice and environmental organizations that have been struggling to transform empire, now unite and flourish under the Tree of Life. Innovative corporations skillfully shift their focus to co-creating a Human Earth.

Creative artists, scientists, healers and social leaders support each other in making breakthrough discoveries, developing innovative thought models and catalyzing self-organizing social groups.

Out of the ashes of a corrupt financial system arises an integrated network of local currencies based on the values embodied in the Tree of Life. The new currencies are designed to encourage and support investment in life-affirming ventures that create better lives for everyone, including the plants and animals. Since currencies are currents of social energy they need to circulate. Currency units have expiration dates and lose their value if unused. Many transactions within the new retribalized communities are love-based and require no numerical accounting.

Neighborhood health clinics provide training in holistic medicine and natural healing. Beginning in childhood, everyone learns the practical arts of optimal health and longevity. Regional health centers make sure everyone has access to the best care possible.

Scientists and inventors lovingly study Mother Earth and learn to create as she does, naturally, beautifully and ecologically. Earth-and-Sky-friendly technologies produce skillfully designed products for a simple, satisfying, sustainable lifestyle. Advances in natural low-temperature transmutation and fusion provide a cornucopia of new materials and clean energy. Spiritual scientists begin to understand how to tap the infinite power of dark energy.

People gather for great circle celebrations with healing rituals, games, dialogs and councils. At their shrines, they hold ongoing councils to develop Human Earth's global brain. People are healing the Earth and healing each other. They have gone through the center of the spiral and entered the dawn of a new age of Human Earth. Now the Seven Generations of evolution can begin.

The Sky Elders smile and conclude their vision of a future where humanity meets the challenge of the apocalypse and fulfills its destiny.

Sky-Grandmother:

This could be your future and your children's future. It's up to you to tell the story and share the vision.

PART 9

ENDING OR NEW BEGINNING?

21: You are the main characters

Four Tribes' farewell message

Sky-Woman:

We thank you, Sky-Grandmother and Sky-Grandfather, for sharing your vision of evolution. Like a light at the end of a tunnel, the Metanoia can help us find our way through the present darkness.

(Turning to the UN people)

Remember, we are always with you. The potential for a Metanoia exists in every instant. Live in the paradise of the present moment. Embrace the Light and the Dark. Share the joy and the suffering. Love one another.

Sky-Man:

As this planetary council comes to an end, we invite the Mothers and Fathers of the Four Tribes to share their final thoughts on their journey.

The Mothers and Fathers choose the Native American Wind Tribe Mother and Father to speak for them.

Wind Tribe Mother:

We have come to one mind and we speak with one voice. The vision of the Metanoia has helped us heal more deeply. Our Four Tribes have different histories and we have played different roles in the story of Human Earth. Yet we have discovered that we are all human beings, all Talking People.

We have all lost the sacred balance. We cannot undo what has been done. But we can grow beyond the past and live from the Tree of Life and the Four Roots today.

Wind Tribe Father:

We ask you, our children, to celebrate our long journey, for it is your journey. Even though we went too far on our own roots, even though so much damage has been done, we *are* connected on this earth today and we *can* reunite and love each other as family.

We lift from your shoulders the burden of carrying outdated empire-based traditions. We release from your heart your loyalty to past stories based on fear and domination. Follow your own root back to the Tree of Life. We want you to tell new stories, true stories.

The Tree of Life is still alive on Mother Earth and for that we can all give thanks!

Wind Tribe Mother:

We, the Mothers and Fathers of the Four Tribes, will continue to support you from the noosphere. We ask you to fulfill the requests of the Singing People. Gather together in council and prepare for the Metanoia.

Now that we are all connected again, you can commune with us in your meditations. Keep the energy flowing between our worlds of Earth and Sky. Invite us to your councils.

The Singing People gave me the sacred Human Earth Stone to hold for all humanity. Since we, your ancestral Mothers and Fathers, will be returning to the noosphere soon, it is time for me to pass the Earth Stone on to one of you who is descended from the Wind Tribe. Is there anyone here from the Wind Tribe who can receive the Earth Stone and hold it in trust until humanity has created a shrine to honor it?

Willow-Song, Native American, NGO observer:

I am Willow-Song.

(Turning to the man by her side)

My partner Spirit-Eagle and I came here today to participate in a United Nations conference on the rights of indigenous people.

(To the Wind Tribe Mother)

We will be honored to hold the Earth Stone for our human family. We thank our Ancestors and the Singing People for their gift.

The Wind Tribe Mother hands the Earth Stone to the Willow-Song.

Sky-Man:

We thank you and honor your journey. Now a new journey can begin.

(Turning to the UN people)

Here and now we are all united in a timeless time. But soon this enchanted moment will pass. Soon our council will come to an end and you will return to the world of empire where your clocks will begin ticking again. Sky-Woman and I will return to our home in the Sky. The Mothers and Fathers of the Four Tribes, the Sky Elders and Sky Children will all return to the noosphere with us. We will continue to guide you.

Sky-Woman:

By coming to the UN on this fateful day you have become a participant in this planetary council and you have received a vision of Human Earth awakening. When you return to the world you can share your vision with your brothers and sisters in all the nations of the Earth. Tell them the story.

Sky-Man and I embody what lives in each of you. I invite you to grow into your full potential. I have seen the changes in you during our precious time together. Your ego skins have softened. You move more gracefully. You smile more often.

If you had not called us, if you had not participated, none of this could have happened. Each of you has shown great courage. You traveled with us through the tragic story of the first meeting, the dark visions of extinction and the awesome vistas of cosmic creation.

Empire taught you to see the world as a pyramid of power. You have opened your hearts and minds to a new way of looking at your world as a Tree of Life.

Sky-Man:

We chose to come to the UN because it is built on sacred land, land that belongs not to one nation, but to the whole planet. It is where the Talking People gather to talk. Whether you are a national ambassador, NGO (Non-Governmental Organization) representative, UN staff, or public visitor, you chose to be here on the day we came to the UN.

You are the reason we came and you are actually the main characters in this story.

Solan and Devara challenge the UN people

Sky-Man:

As our council comes to an end, Solan and Devara, our beloved children of evolution, want to share their thoughts with you.

Devara:

(Exuberantly, to the UN people)

Thank you for bringing us back from the dark world of extinction with your hugs and your love. I am so happy that I could be here with you! When the past and future meet in the present, miracles can happen.

Solan:

Soon you will return to your turbulent moment in history.

When Sky-Woman and Sky-Man first arrived in the General Assembly Hall, you were embroiled in angry arguments that were escalating into physical violence. Soon you will be going back to *that world!*

We ask you to take the vision of Human Earth back into your world and back into your lives. It will be up to you who live here on Earth to evolve our planet. As the main characters in this story, what roles will you play?

Devara:

We are asking each one of you:

Will you devote your life, your energy, and your gifts to co-creating a Human Earth?

Will you release the curse of Cain and take a sacred vow of unconditional peace?

Will you stand with us in the Tree of Life and the Four Roots?

Will you honor the Seven Requests of the Singing People and prepare for the Metanoia?

22: Council: Wonderful gift or cruel trick?

UN people despair

Suddenly the focus shifts from the Sky People to the Earth people, from the timelessness of spirit to the urgency of now.

As they sit in a large circle around the Tree of Life in the great natural amphitheater, each delegate, each observer, is being called to respond to Solan's and Devara's requests. Each one feels an inner conflict: "Do I want to let go of the past and devote my life, my energy, and my gifts to co-creating a Human Earth? What would this mean in my daily life?"

The stunningly beautiful vision of the Metanoia seems so far removed from the disintegrating, crisis-filled world they must return to. They begin to share their thoughts.

Chuntao, Ambassador from China:

I am honored to be here. I am grateful for this guidance. I feel a deep yearning for the Human Earth you envision. I believe my ancestors had such a vision. Thousands of years ago our sages urged us to develop a society based on *Datong* or the Great Unity. At its core was *Ren* or universal love, beginning with love in the family, extending outward to love of neighbors and love of strangers and eventually the love of all forms of life.

So, Devara and Solan, in my heart I want to respond to your requests and say, "Yes!"

But in my world nothing is simple or easy anymore. Our ego skins have grown hard. We don't trust each other. Our efforts to solve problems produce only conflict and bigger problems. China's industrial success came at the price of devastating pollution. Our efforts to improve our people's health by making animal protein more available resulted in viral pandemics causing illness and death.

The Singing People ask us to build an international Earth Shrine here in New York or in Jerusalem. It sounds so right and so simple... and yet *so impossible*!

This vision of Human Earth is beautiful but it is so different from the world I inhabit. The Mothers and Fathers sit here under the Tree of Life as Four Tribes, but in today's world we are no longer Four Tribes. Our Tribes have been mixed up, shaken together and scattered all over the world. Today the ancient Asian Water Tribe consists of many different cultures from the Middle Eastern countries to India, China, Mongolia, Southeast Asia, Indonesia, Australia, Japan and the Philippines.

Humanity can no longer gather as Four Tribes. We are 193 separate nations! And all of those nations are divided within themselves. Many teeter on the brink of social collapse.

Where do we start?

Ahmad, Ambassador from Egypt:

The Middle East is where empires first arose. The birth of civilization was also the birth of war. Ever since the first empire we have not known one generation of true peace, only hot wars and cold wars. Today everyone is fighting everyone else.

Most of you worry about the future, yet you still sleep in safe, comfortable homes. In many parts of the Middle East we are already living your worst nightmare, the apocalypse is happening *now*. The global powers have long used our land as a chessboard in their game of world domination. We are being torn apart by growing chaos. Nations are disintegrating. Cities lie in rubble. Children grow up knowing only hunger, sickness and violence. Refugees must flee their ancient homelands.

You say the council will soon be over and we will be returning to *that world*. The truth is, I don't want to go back. I feel safe here with Sky-Woman and Sky-Man in this beautiful world.

You have shown me that the regional problems we face are far deeper than I ever knew. Now I have to take seriously a future of *global catastrophe and human extinction*. And it is a terrifying future to face!

I am alarmed that we are approaching a global apocalypse and yet we still spend our time fighting each other in an endless, senseless reenactment of Cain and Abel. How can I keep the despair away once I return to a world spinning out of control?

The Sky People are right. We need a change of consciousness. But when I find myself back in the dangerous world of empire, won't I have to pull my ego armor back on in order to survive?

Leonid, Ambassador from Russia:

This teaching has awakened something deep inside me. I want to live on a Human Earth.

Yet I must speak my truth, my whole truth.

Part me of feels this council is a cruel trick. This vision of a Human Earth aims too high. It is a Disneyland vision, not real life. And if you aim too high and miss, you're left with chaos and despair.

You are asking me to do more than I can possibly do. Yes, I am the Russian ambassador to the UN. But I have little real power. I take orders from my government just as all of you do. I can easily be terminated. What am I supposed to do?

Here is our situation: Russia is always the outsider. We are not respected by America and the European countries. They do not honor us as equal members of the Fire Tribe. Geographically, we share the Asian continent with the Water Tribe but we do not belong to their tribe either.

The USSR Communist Empire lost the Cold War. The USA Capitalist Empire won. Now the USA stands unopposed as the world's military superpower. We see their hunger for total domination. The West still dreams of taking over the Middle East, Eastern Europe and Russia and making us part of their Euro-American Empire. This is why Russia must stay strong militarily.

This council has affirmed what I already knew in my bones. We humans have always been killers and we remain so today. In my heart I yearn for peace, yet to take a vow of unconditional peace in a world of killers seems both foolish and irresponsible. Personally, I carry a gun in my daily life. I have experienced violence up close and personal. In a world of killers, self-defense is a basic right.

I can hear my teenage daughter in my head right now. She's saying, *"But Papa...I don't want to live in a world of killers!"*

I have shared my thoughts with you. I have told you the truth, but for all I know it may not be the truth. I seldom believe my own thoughts anymore. In Russia I sometimes sit outside by my firepit under the starry sky. I dream an ancient dream of peace. In my soul I want to believe in Human Earth.

That is why I am torn inside right now. Is this council a wonderful gift...or a cruel trick?

Sarah, Ambassador from USA:

Solan and Devara, I too would love to take a vow of unconditional peace. But how can I if my Russian colleague carries a gun and Russia builds up its military and invades its neighbors?

It is easy to criticize the USA. We have made mistakes. Every nation has their complaints about us. But who would you prefer to have as the world's superpower? What if Hitler had triumphed and turned Europe into a Nazi Reich? What would life be like if the Communists had spread their grim dictatorship around the world?

China is growing stronger and preparing to take center stage and colonize the world economically and militarily. Would you like America to put down its banner of freedom and democracy and allow the world to become an authoritarian Chinese Empire?

As the Judeo-Christian West appears to stumble, some Muslims hope to establish a worldwide Islamic Empire. But how can Islam bring peace to the world when it cannot heal its own bloody Cain and Abel story of Sunnis and Shiites?

America was instrumental in founding the UN. Yet many of you think that our attempt to lead the world is destroying the planet. I am tired. My country is deeply in debt. Our families are suffering under the crushing burden of constant war. Our infrastructure is crumbling. Everything is falling apart. Our government, our health care, our schools, our economy — everything is broken. International terrorists and home-grown fanatics now bring war into our schools, offices and shopping centers. In a world at war everyone becomes collateral damage. Perhaps at one time war was heroic. Today it is simply stupid and tragic.

I want to stop this madness. But, like my Russian colleague, I do not want to live under someone else's empire.

Ingrid, Ambassador from Germany:

I want to help build a Human Earth. I believe in the vision. But what will I build with? Our tools were made for domination, not co-creation. I am a descendant of the Fire Tribe. We are no longer the dominant majority we once were. We are rapidly becoming minorities even in our own homelands. I fear we are losing our heritage and our culture. We fear losing our way of life.

I too am confused about what to do when I return. Yet this council has taught me something very important. Before, I thought our fates hung on separate strings, now I see that our fates are bound together into one rope.

When I look around me now, I see one family. Something has changed here with us. I can feel it. We no longer see each other as the enemy. But now I fear that we may all succumb to the paralysis of despair.

Spirit-Eagle, Native American NGO observer:

When I was in my twenties, I heard a calling from my ancestors to plant Peace Trees. I have been invited to many nations and planted many trees.

When I hear the UN ambassadors speak, I hear them speak of their trauma and despair. We have that in common. But when they speak, they speak with the voices of over seven billion people.

The Native American people of the Wind Tribe once filled two great continents. Now our numbers are few, our culture virtually destroyed. Where is our homeland? We are exiles in the land of our ancestors.

Empire has obliterated the natural world of Turtle Island and we can no longer follow our way of life. Empire took our children and put them in boarding schools. The ancient connection between the generations was broken. Many of our communities suffer from poverty, addiction, illness, violence and hopelessness. Each Native American generation cries out to the Creator for deliverance from this living hell.

Where does the landless Wind Tribe fit into this new world, this Human Earth?

Hoanui, Ambassador from Solomon Islands:

The flood that will be coming to your coastlines has already inundated many of our islands. For us, climate catastrophe is not some futuristic doomsday scenario. It is our current reality.

We did not put the smoke in the air that caused global warming but we are the ones who are drowning! Does anyone care? Do the faraway factory-owners say, "We're sorry the smoke from our fires is heating the earth, melting the ice and flooding your homes. How can we help?" No, they just find another island where they can take their annual tropical vacation.

What can we do as our homes and fields disappear under the waves?

Amaka, Ambassador from Nigeria:

I have personally experienced violence and the loss of many family members. Yet I can still feel love in my heart. Despite our suffering, we Africans still hold a vision in our heart of *Ubuntu*, a world based on universal love.

Africa is blessed with natural wealth and strong, creative people. Many people are doing heroic things on our continent but much of Africa is mired in self-destructive cycles of ethnic warfare. Our rapidly expanding population is destroying our land and our wildlife. We are struggling to heal from many generations of trauma, slavery, colonialism and economic imperialism.

Now I hear that if we don't fulfill the Singing People's requests and if we fail to unify in three years, the apocalypse will turn into a global catastrophe resulting in mass hysteria.

That terrifies me! I have seen too much insanity already. That fear alone makes it difficult for me to envision a path forward. Without trust nothing is possible.

How can our broken family ever recover?

While the UN people speak, a dark cloud of gloom settles over the circle. Hopelessness and despair cloud every face.

Amaka, Ambassador from Nigeria:

(Turning to Sky-Woman and Sky-Man)
Please! Help us!

Solan and Devara confront reality

Sky-Woman:

I know you feel unprepared for what is to come. Let go of your need to feel prepared and learn to live with not-knowing. Trust that you have the resources you need within you.

Sky-Man:

Simply be here now, fully present in this moment. Allow yourself to be guided. Listen to your true human voices.

As the UN people sit in the silence, they feel the crushing weight of the world's problems. When they tune in, each of them hears a noisy cacophony of conflicting inner voices. They have a desperate urge to do something but they feel paralyzed by a frustrating lack of clarity. One by one they open their eyes and look around in confusion and despair.

Devara and Solan have listened intently to the UN people. Now they speak.

Solan:

Sky-Woman and Sky-Man, I see your love for our family and the faith you have in them. I love our family too. And I believe that their feelings of despair are *real*. They can't come to one mind with each other because they do not know how to come to one mind within themselves.

Devara:

If the UN people cannot hear their true human voices here in the special conditions of the council, what chance is there that they will hear their true voices once they are back in noisy world of empire?

Look at how much help and healing the Fire Tribe Father received. Yet when he felt threatened by Shanidar he tried to kill again.

Solan:

I would like to ask the UN people a question.

Sky-Man and Sky-Woman:
Of course.

What do the UN people need?

Solan:
(To the UN people)

I know you love us and want to save us from becoming children of extinction. A few moments ago, we made a request. We asked you to devote your life, your energy, and your gifts to co-creating a Human Earth. We wanted to hear a resounding "Yes!" Instead you responded with despair and inaction.

You have been given many teachings during this council and still you do not feel ready to return to the present world and transform it.

My question is: What do you need in order to say "Yes!"?

Chuntao, Ambassador from China:
I am so sorry that I could not say yes to your requests. I want to. But I know from personal experience how hard it is to change ingrained habits.

I eat well and exercise for a few weeks and then I get too busy and fall back into old habits. I keep sabotaging myself. I'm not surprised that I am not taking better care of the earth when I can't take better care of my own body.

I do try to grow personally, but my life is embedded in empire. When I return to that busy world I will be back on a never-ending treadmill. To do my job I will need to revert to my empire ego mentality. I fear that after a few days much of what is human in me will begin to fade away again.

I need something that can help me change the way I think on a daily basis.

Leonid, Ambassador from Russia:
Thank you for your question, Solan and Devara. I have grown to love you, as I love my own daughter.

(His eyes become moist and his voice quavers)

And *do not* want her to grow up in world of killers.

(Regaining his composure)

To me, this whole Metanoia thing puts us in a Catch-22 situation. It reminds me of the frustrating Catch-22 that occurs when I misplace my glasses.

(Smiling ironically)

In order to look for my glasses I first need to find them.

You tell us that sitting in council with each other is the only way to heal our broken human family. The Catch-22 is that the idea of facing other people in some kind of authentic be-my-true-self circle makes me more uncomfortable than just about anything I can think of. Sometimes I do try to go deeper into conversation with people. It seldom if ever leads to the wonderful fusion of one mind that you talk about. Instead it results in people shutting down into hurt or exploding into anger.

So we have "meetings" instead of councils. Our egos meet and play ego games. Despite everything we've experienced so far during the council, if you weren't here guiding us, I'm afraid we'd soon revert back to arguing and fighting.

And here's another Catch-22 of the Metanoia: The good news is that the Metanoia will finally transform our consciousness. The bad news is that it won't happen unless we have already prepared for the Metanoia by transforming our consciousness.

Like Chuntao, I have habits I have been trying to change for years. People tell me that I am too critical and too judgmental. My relationships would be much better if I could be a kinder, gentler person. But I wasn't raised that way.

I have tried to change my emotional responses, but using my mind to try to change my mind is like walking into a house of mirrors. I haven't gotten very far. You have shown us that living in empire has altered our brains and cut us off from our true inner voices.

So here's what I need.

On a practical level I need to know whether or not I can work toward a Human Earth and still carry a gun.

On a deeper level I need something that can help me release the thought patterns implanted by empire so I can hear my true voices.

(Smiling)

And be a kinder person.

Sarah, Ambassador from USA:

Devara and Solan, thank you for honoring our despair. I have listened to everything here in the council very carefully. And it all makes sense while I am listening. Yet I could not hear a clear voice during the silence.

If we try to fulfill the Singing People's requests, our empire egos will argue over how to do it and who will get the credit and nothing good will come of it. I can see how going for something as idealistic as a Human Earth Shrine in Jerusalem or New York could actually end up being the very thing that triggers World War III.

On a personal level, how can I help change the world when I can't even get a good night's rest? I wake up tired every morning. I can't turn off my anxious voices at night even when I'm totally exhausted. I worry about getting sick. I have endless lists of "things to do" and "problems to solve."

When I go on vacation, empire's voices come with me. I never get a holiday from them. When I try to pray, their constant chatter makes it hard for me to hear that still, small voice within. Empire's trance is so embedded in society now. I feel like I don't live in the real world anymore. Most of my waking hours are spent interacting with empire's virtual world through a screen.

Here under the Tree of Life with you I feel totally different. Even though we are facing difficult truths, I have a sense of inner peace and well-being. This is pure bliss compared to my daily life. It's like having a taste of what life could be like on Human Earth.

What I need is very basic. I guess I need the same thing that Leonid asked for. I want to wake up from empire's trance. I need a way to stop listening to empire's voices.

I want you to say "YES!"

Solan:

(To the UN people)

Thank you for sharing your truth and telling us what you need.

I can feel your despair. Your despair is my despair too. I want to be born into an evolving Human Earth, not one heading toward extinction.

(Turning to Sky-Woman, Sky-Man, Sky-Grandmother and Sky-Grandfather)

The UN people speak the truth.

In the evolutionary vision of the future that you shared with us, it was the change of consciousness of the Metanoia that led to the creation of a Human Earth. Yet, many people all over the world will need to have their own *personal Metanoia* before a planetary Metanoia becomes possible.

Every UN person needs to experience their own Metanoia *here and now* in the council before they return to the world of empire!

We need to share with them the Original Teachings about the inner council. Only by practicing the inner council in their daily lives can they come to one mind within themselves and evolve as a species.

Sky-Man:

Thank you for listening so fearlessly to our family. You speak with a clear mind, Solan.

I am also aware that our council is ending soon. There is not enough time left to impart the Original Teachings of the inner council. With the help of our Sky Elders we have bent spacetime in order to create this bubble...and we have bent it as far as we can. Our time bubble will disappear soon.

The UN people look around and see that the bubble of spacetime around the council is already dissolving at the edges.

Devara:

(To Sky-Woman and Sky-Man)

If the UN people return now, I fear that this whole council may have been in vain. I agree with Solan. The UN people need to experience an inner council now.

(Turning to the UN people, Devara speaks powerfully from the depths of her being)

And I need to hear a resounding "YES!" from all of you before I go back to the noosphere. Our spirit life in the noosphere is wonderful but up there it's all energy. Up there I exist in a state of possibility. All of you have a real living body. I haven't been born into mine yet.

(She strokes her body and smiles with pleasure)

After being here in a body I want to be born more than ever.

(Looking around at the natural surroundings)

This is such a beautiful world! I can't find words to express how fortunate you are to be here in these human bodies. Here on the ground is where the action happens! This is where Earth and Sky meet and all those celestial possibilities take specific shapes and forms.

You are at the heart of the web of life and your choices affect the fate of the whole planet and every living thing on it. I want you to say "YES!" and go through the center of the spiral because *my life is on the other side!*

Can we bend some spacetime?

Solan:
(Turning to Sky-Grandfather)

Grandfather, isn't there anything you can do?

Sky-Grandfather:
As Sky-Man said, we have bent spacetime to create this bubble and we can't bend it any further.

(Pause)

There is one other possibility...but it is quite risky.

Devara:
Tell us, Grandfather. I will help you!

Sky-Grandfather:
If we generate a new spiral it will create a new spacetime bubble and we can complete the council.

Devara:
Yes!

Solan:
(More cautiously)

And how would we do this, Grandfather?

Sky-Grandfather:

Sky-Grandmother and I would need to return to the noosphere. From there we would circle the earth and begin bending spacetime into a new spiral. While we are doing that, everything here would temporarily disintegrate until the new spiral is formed.

Solan:

You said it was quite risky. How risky?

Sky-Grandmother:

(Concerned for her grandson and granddaughter)

It's actually *very* risky. If we bend spacetime but are unable to form a new spiral, it could snap into a reverse spiral and spin into a black hole.

(Solemnly)

Everyone here would instantly cease to exist. There would be no time to even say goodbye to each other.

Devara:

So we are risking everything?

Sky-Grandmother:

Yes. Being born takes great courage. Every baby risks dying in order to be born.

Devara:

(Seeking reassurance)

How many times have you done this?

Sky-Grandfather:

We already bent spacetime to create this bubble. But this would be the first time we ever tried to bend spacetime from *inside* a bubble.

If we succeed, everyone will have the time they need to experience an inner council and come to one mind before our planetary council ends.

Devara:

My desire to be born on a beautiful Human Earth gives me the courage to face that black hole and take the risk.

(Turning to Sky-Woman and Sky-Man)

How do you feel about Grandfather and Grandmother creating a new spiral for our council?

Sky-Woman:

(Smiling)

You know I love spirals. I'd love to create another one with you.

Sky-Man:

(To Devara and Solan)

Your generation's courage inspires me. Thank you for standing in your truth and expressing it with love.

Solan:

I love you and I want to thank you for guiding us.

(Turning to the UN people with a playful smile)

Are you ready to bend some spacetime?

The UN people gaze apprehensively at the rapidly-dissolving bubble of spacetime. They know they have two choices: End the council now and go back to the world of empire feeling unprepared — or risk everything to create a new spiral and complete the council.

The UN people realize with a shock that they *are* the main characters in the story! What happens next is up to them!

They look around the circle at each other. They can take the next step. It is scary. It is possible. If not now, when?

UN people:

(Spontaneously rise to their feet and shout in unison)

Yes, let's bend some spacetime!

Sky-Grandfather:

You have come to one mind. Congratulations!

Grandmother and I will now return to the noosphere. From there we will begin bending the spacetime curvature around the planet into a new spiral.

At some point you will all disintegrate. Your body and your ego mind will be swept away. But you will not lose consciousness. Each of you needs to stay aware and relax into the flow of time. If your ego resists letting go, you will create disruptive waves that make it impossible for us to form a new spiral.

Solan:

Just one more thing, Grandfather. How will we know if you succeeded?

Sky-Grandfather:

You will feel the expansion of time into a new spiral. And then in the next instant we will all find ourselves back here again, at a new level of the spiral.

Wild ride on a fractal rollercoaster

Sky-Grandfather and Sky-Grandmother activate their energy fields. Energy flows from their Earth chakras to the geosphere and from their Sky chakras to the noosphere. A shaft of light appears and forms a plasma tube. Their bodies flicker into rainbow light and they ascend the plasma tube up to noosphere.

The UN people wait with anticipation. A few minutes go by and nothing happens. They breathe a sigh of relief. Maybe this will be easier than they thought.

But as they exhale, they notice the edges of everything around them begin to vibrate and wiggle. Tiny fractals form along the boundaries of objects. Spirals appear everywhere. The spiral structure of the Tree of Life becomes visible. Its roots spiral into the ground. From its spiraling trunk, branches grow upward in a spiral pattern.

People look at each other and see spirals: The spiral pattern of the hair on their heads. The vortex of sound waves entering their ears and spiraling into their inner ear. The light spiraling in and out of each other's eyes.

They breathe in and feel the air flowing into tinier and tinier spirals deep inside the bronchial Tree of Life within their lungs. As they exhale they see their breath spiraling out. They feel their arms spiraling from their shoulders and culminating in the curve of their hands and fingers. They notice that each fingertip ends in its own unique spiral whorl.

The UN people begin to feel disoriented. Boundaries become fuzzy as edges dissolve into fractals. As their dizziness increases they instinctively reach out to each other and hold hands. They stand in a big circle around the Tree of Life. The circle includes the UN people and all the Sky People except for the Sky Grandparents who have gone to the noosphere. Linking hands energizes their big circle and it starts to rotate.

Sky-Man and Sky-Woman begin guiding the revolving circle. Sky-Woman releases Sky-Man's hand and veers inward toward the Tree of Life at the center of the amphitheater. The line of interlinked people follows her as Sky-Man guides from the other end. The Sky People and UN people are drawn into the spiraling rings of the trunk of the Tree of Life. When they reach the core they are sucked into new dimension.

Now everything begins to move very quickly. They are riding a fractal wave. Their ego minds, with their limited processing power, are soon overwhelmed by the infinite flood of light waves. Each person retains the imprint of Sky-Grandfather's guidance as they surrender their ego and relax into the flow of time.

Soon they experience a joyful excitement as they ride the fractal rollercoaster. Gorgeous kaleidoscopic colors light the way. They hear the whoosh of time and the crackle of new space being created.

Sky-Grandfather and Sky-Grandmother reappear. Their arms stretch out above their heads as they guide the fractal flow with their bodies. Sky-Woman reaches out and links the UN people up with the Sky Elders. The tension builds as the Sky Elders increase the bend in spacetime to near the breaking point. Sky-Grandfather and Sky-Grandmother focus their minds and draw upon their connection to universal intelligence. Their whirling gyroscopic energy field keeps them in the center of the flow.

The vibrant colors suddenly turn black. Everything slows down as they enter a sea of dark energy. Only tiny veins of silver fractals remain to guide them. Is this the edge of a black hole?

The intricate fractal patterns begin to vibrate and shake. The background sounds suddenly become silent. Then they hear a deep booming sound, as the membrane of spacetime itself reverberates.

Suddenly, a glorious light appears. They feel a rapid inflation as spacetime expands into a magnificent new spiral. Then the rate of change slows. Fractals begin to form recognizable shapes. Objects stay put and solidify. Slowly the world of the council reappears, suffused with the newness of time, the freshness of now. With the help of their Sky guides the UN people were able to create a new spacetime bubble.

Everyone breathes a sigh of relief. Now they can complete the council. Faced with a clear choice, they came to one mind and said "Yes" to life.

23: Inner councils

Evolving through inner councils

Solan:
>   (Shaking his head with astonishment and delight)
>   That was a wild ride!
>   Thank you, Grandfather and Grandmother, for bringing us into a new spiral.
>   (To the UN people)
>   Now we will prepare you for your inner council. During your inner council you will have the opportunity to experience your personal Metanoia.

Devara:
>   The council circle is the heart of the Original Teachings. Here you have been witnessing the power of the council to heal old wounds and to create new realities. Council is the womb of society. It is where social evolution happens.
>   In our world of the Seventh Generation we use councils at every level of society. People gather with others in social councils like this one. In addition, every individual practices the *inner council ritual*.

Your sacred traditions including meditation, prayer and contemplation contain elements of the inner council ritual.

On our Human Earth children learn to council at home with their family and while they play with their friends. Couples, families and communities council together to resolve conflicts, solve problems and deepen trust and connection. Through council we experience the joy of coming to one mind and responding creatively to the challenges we face.

You can see that Solan and I are very similar to you. Yet we have evolved into a new species. Through seven generations of council we have evolved from Talking People to Wise People. Council enabled us to transform our language and evolve beyond ego. From an evolutionary perspective you are in danger of becoming stuck at your current level of *Homo ego* and failing to make the leap to *Homo sapiens*. If you combine social council and inner council you can start evolving again.

Solan:

For many generations, empire has implanted a fear-based ego into every newborn child. Each ego is imprinted with the voice of empire. By programming your ego from birth, empire is able to control your thoughts.

Your ego acts like an all-powerful emperor, a feared dictator who gives you orders. "Do this! Do that! Hurry up!"

It keeps you enslaved by cutting you off from the Tree of Life and making you feel small, unimportant and inadequate.

It says, "You're not good enough! You need to make more money! Work harder!"

When you obey your emperor ego, it rewards you with addictive treats and pumps you up with feelings of superiority over others.

Your ego is only a small part of your brain. But it thinks it's your whole brain, your whole nervous system. Your ego thinks it's who you really are.

The truth is that your ego is an illusion generated by repetitive empire-driven inner talk patterns and chronic physical tension. Your ego interferes with the natural functioning of your brain and splits you up into conflicting parts. Being at war with yourself is spiritual death.

Earlier the Singing People shared an important lesson with you: What you call "thinking" is just you talking yourself. And you talk to yourselves constantly. Starting at birth, all of empire's programming is encoded as inner talk. You create your own reality with your inner talk.

Sarah, you said you can't turn off your inner talk at night. Chuntao, you said you're trapped in a repetitive cycle of inner talk that keeps you from being healthy. Leonid, you mentioned wanting to be a kinder person, but your programmed inner talk habits result in repeating old unwanted behaviors.

Instead of listening to ego voices that sabotage you and drain the joy out of your life, you deserve to reconnect with your true inner voice — the one grounded in the Four Roots who is truthful, loving, peaceful and empowering. It is not your true self that chooses self-destructive behavior. It is your confused and unloved egos.

The greatest truth that empire wants to keep hidden from you is an understanding of your true nature. You are all children of Sky-Woman and Sky-Man and their love runs through you.

Devara:

Plato, one of your wisest philosophers, observed that all thinking is an inner dialogue. If "thinking" is you talking to yourself, then who are you talking with? Which self are you talking with, your true self or one of your ego selves?

You have an inner society made up of all the different parts of who you are, all the roles you play in your life. Without inner council these voices often end up arguing with each other. And then you suffer from confusion, anxiety and stress.

You are not responsible for what empire programmed into your brain, but you are responsible for how you talk to yourself today. Inner council helps you separate old empire voices from your own true voices. Daily practice of inner council wakes you up from the trance of empire and restores your clear mind.

Your inner talk is the software that runs your life. Your inner talk becomes your thoughts. Your thoughts determine your actions. Your actions form your habits. Your habits develop your character. Your character shapes your destiny.

When you are of one mind, your whole being vibrates in harmony. You welcome life's challenges and respond effectively, acting from your true self. You evolve, one day at a time.

When you change your inner talk, you change your life. Changing the world begins with changing your inner world from an Empire Earth to a Human Earth.

Calling the inner councils

Solan:

Now each of you will have the opportunity to call your own inner council. This is a transformative experience and you will naturally feel anxious at times. Remember your fractal ride? You stayed centered because you kept changing your fear into excitement and wonder. So when fear comes up don't suppress it. *Transform your fear into awe and use it to evolve.*

The inner council is modeled on our outer council here in this amphitheater. At the center of our amphitheater stands the Tree of Life and the Four Roots. During an inner council *you* stand at the center of your circle, *you* become the Tree of Life and *you* are guided by the Four Roots.

We call an inner council by creating a sacred space with the ancient ritual for strengthening the Tree of Life and honoring the Seven Directions that Sky-Woman and Sky-Man taught you earlier. When you arrive at the seventh direction and go inward, you convene the inner council. You sit in silence and listen to the silence. You call all your inner voices to council and each has its turn to speak. You ask yourself questions like: What am I saying to myself? Whose voices am I listening to? What effect are they having on me? What are my true voices and the Four Roots saying? During your council Sky-Woman and Sky-Man and all of your spirit guides are available to support you.

After the inner council, we will complete the Seven Directions and spiral back out again. Then you will have an opportunity to share your experiences with each other.

Are you ready to be guided through your inner council?

UN people:
Yes!

They call upon the Tree of Life and turn to face each of the Four Directions. As energy currents arc from north to south, from east to west and from Earth to Sky, a circular dome of sacred space forms around each person. Inside their own dome each person honors the Seventh Direction. They go inward to their center and connect with their true self.

In the amphitheater, hundreds of glowing inner council domes now encircle the Tree of Life. A potent silence fills the air. Personal revelations are about to unfold. Dark secrets will come to light. Individual Metanoias will shake the ego's foundations.

Each person sits at the center of their inner council dome and wonders: Who is it that here sits at the center of this circle? Is it my ego or is it my true self? Which voice shall I listen to? How will I live my life?

Now each person calls an inner council and chooses a challenging issue in their life that they want to get clearer about, something that causes them inner conflict and has kept them from evolving. They picture the situation in the mind space of their council dome. They close their eyes and sit quietly. In the peaceful silence they breathe and feel centered and clear. They remember that they are not alone. They are sitting in a circle with the Four Roots and their spirit guides. They reconnect with their inner Tree of Life.

Each person is guided through the five steps of the inner council ritual:

1. Wake up! Call an inner council.
2. Invite all your inner voices to speak.
3. Invite the Four Roots to speak.
4. Come to one mind.
5. Evolve to the next level.

[Note: A fuller version of the Inner Council Ritual is available in the Appendix.]

Loving and helpful spirit guides appear, including Sky-Woman, Sky-Man, friends, family, revered spiritual figures and ancestors who have passed on to the spirit world. With so many allies present to support them, each UN person finds the courage to let go of old empire ego voices and hear their true voices.

Now they picture their situation in a different way than before. They have a new vision and a new story to guide them. They are eager to take the next step in healing their life. They have a connection with their spirit guides that will continue to support them when they are back in the world.

Metanoia rebirth

The golden glow of the Metanoia now begins to fill each person's council dome. They notice their ego skin becoming visible as they start their personal process of Metanoia rebirth. They are guided by the wisdom encoded in their DNA. They feel the desire to shed their ego skin and be born again as true, authentic humans.

Each person experiences rebirth in their own unique way. In their moment of truth they see their mistakes, shortcomings, resentments and self-defeating habits. They offer these up for healing. Each person comes face-to-face with the Divine as they understand it.

They no longer need the protection of their ego skin. In the loving glow of the Metanoia, the isolating empire membrane that has covered their natural skin for so many years softens. It becomes loose and slippery. People wiggle and twist, shudder and shake, and slide out of their ego skin. Their rebirth is energized and ecstatic. As they emerge, their natural skin glows with renewed vitality and their faces radiate joy.

Now the reborn UN people each stand up at the center of their dome. They feel the Tree of Life within them growing strong and healthy. They bring their inner council to completion and thank their spirit guides.

The people turn and face each of the Four Directions. Then their awareness spirals out into the world around them. The hundreds of inner council domes dissolve. They people look around and greet each other. They share the joy of being alive and celebrate their freedom from the tyranny of empire's ego voices. They want to take the energy of the Metanoia back into the world.

But to do so they will first need to come to one mind with each other.

24: Riding the spiral to one mind

Dancing into circles

Solan:

Now that you have experienced your personal Metanoias and your minds are clear, you can focus on what you are going to do when you return to the UN.

What would you do if the fate of the earth depended on you? What would you do if Sky-Woman and Sky-Man had already returned to the noosphere and were no longer here to guide you?

An expectant silence fills in the air.

Amaka, Ambassador from Nigeria:

In our village when we seek guidance, we call the spirits by drumming and dancing. We dance into our answers.

She begins a traditional African dance. As the UN people around her join in, other people beat sticks against the ground or on logs. The rhythmic drumbeat synchronizes their brain waves. Hands reach out and draw the next person into the line. The dancing lines soon encircle the Tree of Life.

Any remaining sharp edges of separation and distrust soften as people grasp the hand of the person next to them and look into their eyes. They remember dancing with the Singing People and the warm feelings of family they experienced. They remember holding onto each other during their wild ride through spacetime.

The UN people feel their hearts opening. After a while, the dancing slows and they sit in a circle to share their experiences.

Ingrid, Ambassador from Germany:

(To Amaka)

Thank you for showing us how to move forward. I felt stuck. I did not know what to do.

Amaka, Ambassador from Nigeria:

Our bodies are designed to move. When I express myself through my body, I can feel the spirit moving through me. Now that we are in our bodies and our bodies are connected, we can talk from our hearts more easily.

Willow-Song, Native American observer:

Thank you for guiding us, Amaka.

Our elders teach us that when there is love and trust, problems get resolved more easily. In our community we recently overcame a split between our "traditionalists" and our "progressives" regarding health care. Coming to one mind enabled us to build a health clinic where our people can benefit from a unique blend of traditional Native American spiritual practices and modern-style technological medicine.

(Looking around)

I notice that we have been sitting in a big circle here so that we can all share one experience. But talking in a big circle is seldom the first step in coming to one mind.

Our elders say, "A big circle brings out big egos."

So first we gather in small circles. These council circles later grow into a spiral that moves us forward.

Willow-Song picks up a large cloth bag, made of natural fibers woven into a colorful spiral design. She reaches into the bag and passes out slender, light-colored foot-long sticks.

Willow-Song:

These are listening sticks. They are all carved from a single maple tree. When I hold a listening stick it helps me to hear another person in my heart, like the tree listens to the wind. I listen as if I am receiving a gift. When we listen, we accept the speaker's words into our heart, without judgment. Then we respond with compassion.

Would you join me now in creating group circles so we can ride the spiral to one mind?

They take their listening sticks and gather in small circles around the amphitheater. Willow-Song passes out one slender dark-colored stick carved from a single walnut tree to each group, placing it on a flat stone at the center of their circle.

Willow-Song:

This dark stick is a talking stick. It is made from the wood at the heart of the walnut tree. When you are ready to speak, lay down your listening stick and pick up the talking stick. The talking stick will help you speak from your heart and stand in your truth. Share your feelings, thoughts and visions.

When you are finished, you can say, "Thank you for listening." Listeners respond by raising their listening sticks and saying, "Thank you for sharing." Then the speaker returns the talking stick to the center of the circle.

In this way everyone will have the opportunity to talk and be heard. Afterward we will bring our circles together again in a great council circle.

Everyone gathers in circles of about a dozen people, creating a circle of circles around the Tree of Life. The Sky People — Sky-Woman, Sky-Man, the Mothers and Fathers of the Four Tribes, Sky-Grandmother and Sky-Grandfather, Solan and Devara — support them by meditating under the branches of the Tree of Life.

The UN people sit quietly in their circles, breathing in the peace of the great green amphitheater and the land and waters around them.

Willow-Song:

If listening is receiving a gift, then speaking is giving a gift. I want to give the best gift I can.

Before I *speak out*, I always *listen in*. My cloudy mind cannot know my truth, but my clear mind can. To speak my truth, I must first *know* my truth — my clearest and highest truth.

So before any of us speak, let us sit in silence.

Everyone sits quietly and breathes. They feel their bodies relax and their hearts open. After a while a person in each circle feels called to speak and reaches for the talking stick.

Riding the spiral

When they hold the talking stick, each person in every circle shares their experience. Sky-Man and Sky-Woman and the other Sky People arise from their meditation under the Tree of Life. They walk quietly around the council circles.

People first share their initial reflections about the planetary council. A second round goes deeper as they share Metanoia experiences from their inner council. Painful feelings and traumas are released. Tears flow. Life-giving laughter cleanses their spirits. A warm current of healing energy begins to flow around each circle from heart to heart.

People remember their common origins and their connection to the Tree of Life. They begin telling new stories. As their hearts become healed, the circular flow of energy going around the circle rises from their hearts up to their heads.

The group energy shifts and the third round of the talking stick focuses on the reality of returning to the present world: How will I respond to Solan's and Devara's requests? Can we come to one mind about what to do when we return to the Great Hall in the UN?

A deep love for Solan and Devara has grown in everyone's hearts. They want to fulfill their requests. By now, everyone understands the urgency of the times and they feel a deep longing for the Human Earth they know is possible. A burst of creative energy sparks bold visions, enlightening "Aha!" moments, and exciting breakthroughs.

The energy swirling around the individual circles begins to rise above their heads and form a spiral above each circle. The wisdom of the group begins to coalesce as one mind. As the energy reaches the center of the spiral, each circle envisions creative actions they can undertake for the healing of the earth. Each group sees their visions taking shape in the space above each circle.

Willow-Song:
(Quietly begins to chant the ancient song of coming together)
I am I and you are you.
Together we are one family.

The people join the chant and bring their awareness back to the big circle of circles around the Tree of Life.

Willow-Song:
Your circles are so beautiful. They form a shining necklace around the Tree of Life. You created one mind because you were willing go beyond ego and allow your true self to be part of something larger. You are relearning the ancient art of riding the spiral to one mind. Now let us bring the gifts of each of your circles back into one great circle.

Great circle sharing

One by one, speakers from each circle share their vision with the great circle. Feelings of numbness and despair have been replaced by a vibrant desire to do whatever they can do to evolve and create a Human Earth.

As the talking stick passes from circle to circle some people describe creative visions. Some speak of their deep grief for the damage that has been done to the earth. Others speak of a profound personal Metanoia they experienced during their inner council.

Asher, NGO representative:
My mind became much clearer during the council. I can see so many things that I couldn't see before. When I get back I want to tell people the story of Human Earth and the Metanoia.

I know some people will think I'm crazy.
(Laughing)
I can just see myself standing on Wall Street holding a sign saying, "The Metanoia is coming!"

But I know many people will feel the joy that this vision has brought me. Solan and Devara are asking us to have faith in our ability to evolve.

Sky-Woman and Sky-Man have shown me that I am Human Earth and Human Earth is me. I've been riding the spiral of evolution on this planet for the past 4.5 billion years. While they were talking, I had a gut feeling of unshakeable confidence in myself and in all of us as human beings.

I'm trained as a scientist and I'm not a religious person. I've always assumed that I was part of a vast impersonal, uncaring and violent universe. Seeing creation as a Cosmic Orgasm instead of a Big Bang helped me see the universe differently.

Near the end of his life Albert Einstein declared that the most important question was a very simple one: "Is this universe a friendly place?"

I'm not sure what aspect of "me" survives death or how it all works. It's a big mystery. But now death is starting to feel more like a *friendly* mystery. What I *am* sure of is that I am part of this planet's past, present and future. Now that we're in this new era of the Anthropocene, personal growth and planetary growth can only happen when they are connected.

I don't feel as lonely now that I know there are other planets in our galaxy who are waking up. That motivates me. I don't want to miss the opportunity to connect with them. And that means *my* planet needs to wake up.

I'm alive today because my ancestors never stopped growing. They never backed away from a challenge. That's my heritage and it helps me believe we can evolve once more.

Somewhere along the way, we traded the great adventure of human evolution for the lesser goal of technological progress. I want to use my scientific skills to help solve the challenge of providing energy to people on this planet in a way that honors our connection to Mother Earth and furthers our evolution.

Elise, UN staffer:

I am inspired by your sharing. When I was in self-quarantine I spent a lot of time connecting with friends and colleagues online. I realize that I know a lot of really brilliant and creative young scientists and entrepreneurs who would love to develop the kind of Earth-and-Sky-friendly technologies that the Sky Elders talked about in their vision of a Human Earth.

Everyone in our circle loved the Human Earth Stone that the Singing People gave us. We tried to visualize building a shrine to hold the Human Earth Stone. But we couldn't see any way at the present time to build an Earth Shrine in New York or Jerusalem, or anywhere else for that matter.

Once we admitted that, it actually freed us up to see what we *can* do. We can start to fulfill the first of the Singing People's requests. They had a simple request: "Honor our Bones." We can organize a conference and plan a ceremony to honor the unmourned souls of the Singing People and all the victims of past trauma. That's something the UN and NGO's could help create with the guidance of the Sky People and the indigenous people who still remember the Original Teachings.

During my personal inner council I cried many tears of grief for the damage we have done to the earth and to ourselves, for what is already lost and gone forever. I want to help organize community grieving rituals where we can cleanse our hearts and move on with renewed energy.

I get excited when I imagine the really amazing changes that could start happening in the world during my lifetime. Imagine how *fast* things could change if we channel all of society's resources in a new direction.

Solan and Devara tell us that it will take Seven Generations to create a fully-developed Human Earth. Our generation needs to begin the change now!

Chuntao, Ambassador from China:

I am grateful for your vision of how to honor the bones of the Singing People. My circle focused on how to fulfill the second request of the Singing People: Giving them back their name. I will never think of them as Neanderthals again. They will always be the Singing People to me.

A woman in our circle told us about an official naming organization called the **International Commission on Zoological Nomenclature**. We can petition them to change the scientific name of the Singing People to *Homo sonatus*. As far as the other requests go, what we don't know how to do, we can *learn* to do. I'm a practical person and my gut tells me that life evolves when organisms learn and grow.

In my inner council I realized that at every moment I am making a choice about my own evolution: Am I practicing awareness and growing into a new moment or am I practicing an old habit and repeating the past? I want to help change the world, and it makes sense to start with creating a healthy Human Earth ecosystem within my own body and mind.

My body said to me, "If you want to evolve, eat food that can help you evolve." I am going to eat fewer animal-based foods and more foods from the plant world like whole grains, beans, vegetables and fruits. It's healthier for me and healthier for the planet. And it's the way my ancestors ate.

China has made stunning progress in transforming itself into a dynamic, modern nation. Yet in our rush to catch up with the West we have lost sight of our true destiny.

Some of the worst pandemics originated in my country when viruses jumped from animals to people. Some of the worst pollution in the world occurs in my homeland. I want to help China return to the Tree of Life and remember the teachings of our ancestors about living in harmony with the Dao of nature.

Now that I know how to call an inner council, I can stay connected to the Sky People after they leave. I want to continue to benefit from their love and guidance. I am starting to see how different each moment of life can be when I listen to my true voices. I feel the Tree of Life growing inside me.

Earlier in the council, a Human Earth appeared to me as some far-off ideal. Now I realize we're experiencing it right here, right now with each other. We are fortunate to have many circles. We can work on the Singing People's requests one at a time and all together.

Tom, Ambassador from Australia:

Thank you, Chuntao, for your inspiring words. I am also grateful to Amaka and Willow-Song for sharing their wisdom and guiding us in our circles.

When I was self-quarantined at home with Covid-19 I did some deep soul searching. My family has lived in Australia for many generations. We can trace our roots back to England in the 1700's. I decided to have my DNA tested. I was shocked to discover that I actually have aboriginal blood running through my veins. That part of my story had disappeared from my family history.

Then I learned that out of our 200,000-year existence as *Homo sapiens* less than 5,000 years have been lived in the world of empire civilizations. The other 195,000 years we lived as hunters, gatherers and gardeners in the natural world. We're all "indigenous people" if we just follow our family tree back. Two thousand years ago my English ancestors were the ones living in tribes and the Romans were the invading empire that called *them* barbarians.

These discoveries put me in touch with a part of me that I began to call my indigenous self. I started to pay more attention to my body and to spend more time in nature. I experimented with a Paleo lifestyle. I began to see my tensions and my health problems as messages from my body. My body was telling me how much it struggles to adapt to the unnatural world of empire.

I often feel like a caged animal when I am in my office. As a UN ambassador, I have a "good job," but I often feel like a slave to my schedule and society's expectations. It's only after I've been out backpacking for a few days that I begin to regain the feeling of radiant aliveness that my free-range ancestors enjoyed every day of their lives.

As a young man trying to find my place in the world, the message I got was: "If you don't want to be a slave in somebody else's empire you'd better build an empire of your own."

I had to put together an ego that could be an entrepreneurial, authoritarian emperor. I started looking at other people mainly in terms of how they could help me build my empire. Before being appointed ambassador, I started an international consulting business and was very successful but I paid the price in stress, anxiety and relationship problems.

In my inner council I felt a deep desire to restore the Tree of Life within myself. My guides helped me release the burden of having to build an ego empire. I pictured myself using rituals in my daily life to maintain my inner harmony of body, mind and spirit. Like making my mealtimes more of a sacred ritual.

Solan and Devara told us how people evolved by eating less food and breathing in more energy. I want to experiment with that.

Eating less is the only proven method to enhance longevity and it has the added benefit of saving me money and conserving the earth's resources.

When I think about the planet, I get excited when I imagine honoring the existing indigenous Earth Shrines and creating new ones. I'd love to help organize global rituals for the great seasonal turnings.

Maria, NGO representative from Bolivia:

Thank you for sharing your story of healing. I am noticing that we are all speaking more from our hearts than we did before. And as I speak now I can feel you welcoming my words into your heart.

I work for an NGO that helps villages obtain access to clean, reliable water sources and basic sanitation. Many of you in the wealthier nations have only recently experienced the trauma caused by epidemic disease. For those of us who live in the poorer countries, many of which are your former colonies, deadly infectious diseases have long been part of our everyday life.

Every 2 minutes a child dies from a water-borne disease. One out of every three people don't have a toilet. Nearly half of the people on earth lack basic handwashing facilities in their homes.

To have a healthy planet we need healthy communities and healthy people. There are hundreds of millions of people like me who belong to millions of social change organizations that are trying to heal the earth in creative ways. These range from large international associations to small neighborhood groups.

Every day I am seeing and hearing about the many heroic ways our human immune system is responding to Mother Earth's call. There is a sacred anxiety rippling across the planet. So many people are waking up to the mounting cries of suffering and searching for a way forward. But many who hear the call cannot follow their calling fully because there is so little material support. Organizations are forced to compete with each other for scarce funding resources.

If society shifts its priorities, I see a vast wave of volunteers arising. If we all gather under the Tree of Life we *can* create a Human Earth. It's already happening. Human Earth is awakening!

Leonid, Ambassador from Russia:

I love the Sky Ancestors' vision of Human Earth. They understand that we all want to live in peace. In a peaceful world I would not have to spend my days in tense meetings and crowded airports. I would have more time to walk in the quiet forests with my dog.

To me, an empire is any society where a few people rule over many people. I tried to think of a country that isn't ruled by some form of empire — and I couldn't think of even one. Maybe empire is just a bad dream we're having. And once we stop believing in it, it's over. I was shocked at how the monolithic USSR Empire dissolved virtually overnight once we stopped believing in it.

Maybe building empires was a necessary phase in our growth. With our empire building blocks we built something remarkable on this planet. And in the end, it did bring us together. But at this point in my journey, I see empire in my rear view mirror and I see Human Earth up ahead.

During my inner council I decided to face a very basic question: "What do I do with my guns when I get back?"

One of my ego voices said, "I want to help restore the Tree of Life but I need to carry a gun just in case."

Another ego called that one a hypocrite. Soon they were all yelling at each other.

(Smiling ironically)

I was glad that none of them had a gun!

I asked my Sky guides for help with this and got more help than I had expected. Gandhi, Tolstoy and a Siberian shaman all showed up!

I was shocked when they told me they did *not* want me to give up my power to kill. They did *not* want me to disown my inner killer. They urged me to connect with my inner killer because he needs healing and because my power to destroy is intertwined with my power to create.

Despite my misgivings, I followed their guidance and embraced my inner killer. I immediately felt a big power surge. I think the Siberian shaman had something to do with that. My inner killer was healed and suddenly I felt connected to life in a way I never had before. I felt the unity of all things and a respect for all beings.

I saw a vision of me living like a Tree of Life. I give what I have and I ask for what I need. I immediately felt a wave of unconditional peace. I made a vow to resolve conflicts with councils instead of guns, to always use my power with love, guided by truth and peace.

I asked Gandhi for help in dealing with my fear of death. He said, "How you live each day is more important than how you die one day."

Of course I want to die a peaceful death. But Gandhi told me that, even though he was shot point-blank in the chest, he had a "peaceful death." He said the shock and pain were overwhelming. But he felt no fear or anger...so peace came quickly.

Gandhi invited me to meditate with him under the Tree of Life. During the meditation I heard a voice say, "If you live from the Tree of Life you will never fear death."

Everything feels different to me now. So back to the question about what to do with my guns. There's a metal sculpture at the UN. It's a gun with the barrel tied in a knot.

Leonid:

My inner council came to one mind. I decided to take my guns and have them melted down and cast into a Tree of Life that will be at the center of the home shrine I am going to create with my wife and daughter. I can't wait to tell them about this council and Human Earth.

Then Tolstoy came into my inner council to remind me that despite many centuries of living under empires, the Russian people are no strangers to the dream of a Human Earth. When people in Russia saw Europe losing its soul to industrialization and hyper-individualism, many Russians tried to revive an ancient ideal we call *sobernost* — a universal loving community that is spiritual, social and earth-based. I know many Russians still hold this dream in their heart. It's our homegrown version of Gandhi's vision of *sarvodaya*, the worldwide uplifting of humanity.

Many people around the world know us for our traditional Russian nesting dolls. In my council I saw each doll as a story inside a bigger story. Now I can see that my own story is part of many bigger stories — from my family to my country to my planet and my galaxy.

I am so grateful for this council and for everyone here in our circle. Sky-Woman and Sky-Man taught me something important: Human

Figure 29. Knotted gun sculpture at UN by Carl Fredrik Reutersward. Credit: Giorgio Galeotti.

Earth is a living organism. I am a cell in Human Earth's body. I have become part of Mother Earth's brain and nervous system. If we begin to think with our clear minds, I believe we *can* create the kind of world that Solan and Devara come from.

And I am starting to see that changing the way we use language is a big part of changing our consciousness. I was asking myself, "How can we build a Human Earth?"

But I immediately noticed that the question didn't feel quite right. Suddenly a new version popped into my mind that felt much more helpful: "How can we *grow* a Human Earth?"

Ingrid, Ambassador from Germany:

Thank you, Leonid. I too am feeling excited about new possibilities.

After World War II when the world learned the full extent of the Holocaust, Germany was regarded as the ultimate symbol of human evil. Today Germany is a successful, innovative democracy. We have transformed our society and earned the respect and admiration of other nations. I am proud to represent my country at the UN.

Yet, in my dreams I am still haunted by the Holocaust. In my inner council I asked my guides to help me face the Holocaust.

My grandfather's generation went temporarily insane. They tried to drive the Jewish people into extinction. Hitler was riding a populist wave of anger and fear and the elite German establishment decided to make a deal with him. At the time, most Germans wanted to believe that the new Nazi government would restore their battered nation to greatness and create a better life for all.

I am haunted by the Holocaust because it is not just a German story. There have been other European holocausts. There have been Asian holocausts. African holocausts. Australian holocausts. American holocausts. When the Singing People told us their story, I was shocked and I wondered, "Was the extinction of the Singing People the first human holocaust?"

Here's what I find most horrifying about holocausts. They are shapeshifters of fear, seducing the insecure with triumphal visions of glory and vindication. Today's holocaust never looks the same as yesterday's.

And today's holocaust is worldwide and it affects every species. We've triggered the sixth greatest extinction since life began. The impact of humans on the earth is as destructive as the giant asteroid that hit the earth 65 million years ago and wiped out the dinosaurs. Our brother and sister species are dying at an unprecedented rate. Indigenous and traditional cultures are disappearing from the face of the earth. Now the pandemics are raising the possibility that the human race itself could even go extinct. I can no longer avoid looking at the ongoing horror of empire's holocausts.

I realized that the only way to end the curse of Cain is by facing myself in the mirror and seeing the mark of Cain on my own face. My generation was not responsible for the Holocaust, but we could be responsible for helping to heal it. In my council my guides began to heal my traumatized ego, the part of me who is scared, isolated and desperate and believes that only total domination can bring salvation.

During my Metanoia, after I wriggled out of my ego skin, I felt so free and natural. My anxious need to control everything is gone.

(Gazing at Amaka, who led the dance earlier)

I want to learn how to dance with life. I want our earth to be the kind of planet where beautiful souls like Solan and Devara can be born.

Sarah, Ambassador from USA:

Ingrid, I too can now see the worldwide holocaust. This council has been both deeply inspiring and deeply troubling for me.

America, despite its current troubles, is still the world's superpower. We Americans live our lives at center stage. I want to speak to you about my country and America's role in the world, but first I want to share with you a personal healing I experienced during my inner council.

In 2001 when terrorists destroyed the World Trade Center, I was living in Manhattan and working on Wall Street. The bizarre and unimaginable happened right in front of my eyes. On a beautiful September day, out of a clear blue sky, two passenger jets were converted into weapons of mass destruction and crashed into the twin towers of the World Trade Center.

As I saw the skyscrapers collapsing in a flaming inferno, I knew that the date "Sept. 11, 2001" was being scorched into in our nation's memory alongside Pearl Harbor's infamous "Dec. 7, 1941."

A wave of absolute terror went through my body. Into an otherwise ordinary day, out of a clear blue sky, a deadly catastrophe crashed into my world. I suddenly felt vulnerable in a way I never had before. I had been in the World Trade Center for an appointment the day before. I had friends and colleagues who perished. I had that feeling, "It could have been me!"

Like most Americans, I felt angry, sad, scared and unsure about how to respond. This kind of horror had previously only happened "over there." Now this unthinkable destruction happened right here in the heart of New York City. I felt tremendous rage at this barbaric attack. I felt deep grief for a close friend of mine whose life was cut short, leaving her children without a mother.

My career on Wall Street suddenly felt meaningless. I knew I needed to make a change but I didn't know what to do. I left my job and backpacked around the world for a year. I saw how people lived and I saw America's influence everywhere.

By the time I returned home, I knew I wanted to devote my professional life to eliminating the root causes of war. I went back to school, earned a degree in International Relations and eventually became America's ambassador to the UN. I wanted to be at the UN because it is the only place where people from all the nations of the world actually sit together and try to prevent wars and address global issues by talking things through.

During my years at the UN I have seen a lot of people burn out. Our mission is to "save succeeding generations from the scourge of war," yet war continues year after year. Like other people who have been at the UN for a while I began to draw comfort from Secretary-General Dag Hammarskjöld's dark observation that: "The United Nations was not created to take mankind to heaven, but to save us from hell."

But as the world fell more deeply into chaos and suffering after 2001, I had to admit that we were not even saving ourselves from hell anymore. The hope and optimism that my younger self had summoned after the terrorist attacks was gone. I found it hard to come up with the energy to go to work at the UN and be productive. I began to take medication for depression.

I had watched the construction of the 9-11 Memorial closely and walked there often. When it was finally completed in 2011, I went there hoping that it would help me heal.

I walked around the wall of the Memorial Pool looking for the names of the people I knew. Like many visitors who have never cried in public before, I cried.

After I stopped crying, I stepped back and looked at the two memorial pools that occupy the footprints of the Twin Towers. I looked into the cascading waters of one of the pools, seeking serenity. My eyes followed the illuminated streams of water down the sides of the walls. The water fell into a dark reflecting pool and then disappeared into a bottomless black hole.

I stared for a long time but I could not find the comfort and serenity I sought. In my mind I saw the twin pools as America's sad dark eyes, crying endlessly.

My tears began to flow again.

The 9-11 attack wounded America. There were twin wounds: one to our safety and one to our self-image. Despite the billions of dollars spent on security since then, neither wound has been healed. We feel more vulnerable than ever to terrorism. And our self-image has been tarnished by our own primitive "eye for an eye" reaction. By launching rockets of "shock and awe" onto the Arab world and engaging in torture, we allowed ourselves to fall into Osama bin-Laden's trap. Our response just added more fuel to the fires of terrorism.

Figure 30. 9/11 Memorial Pool. Credit: Public domain.

I finally tore my eyes away from the hopelessness of the bottomless pit. I looked over my shoulder and saw the One World Trade Center.

Sarah:

Its shiny shaft rises high above the hopelessness and despair of the dark pools. In its soaring architecture I saw America's determination to rise from the ashes, to feel powerful once more. It looked like a sharp spear pointed at our enemies.

At that moment it felt like deep truths were being laid out for me to see. The unhealed wounds and the primal urge for revenge.

I felt such despair and such horror. I didn't have the words for it then, but now I realize that I saw the ancient drama of Cain and Abel being reenacted. The roles switch back and forth but the tragic drama is always the same. Attack and counterattack, fueling an endless cycle of violence.

I turned away from these man-made structures and walked toward the plaza still yearning for the comfort that had eluded me. A grove of white oaks with their green leaves beckoned me onward.

I began to find comfort simply in the living presence of the trees. I wandered, still in a kind of grief-stricken trance. I stopped and looked at one of the trees. It was very different than the rest.

Figure 31. One World Trade Center. Credit: Public domain.

Sarah:

I walked closer and saw that this tree had been damaged and regrown. Smooth new bark grew from the rough bark. I was looking at the "**Survivor Tree**."

On 9-11 this tree was crushed under a fallen tower. Only its sturdy trunk and a few broken branches remained. Yet when rescue workers found it buried in the rubble, it still had some leaves. This tree wanted to live! In the gray desolation of metal and concrete, workers found inspiration in the tree. Arborists lovingly nursed the tree back to health and replanted it.

Today it is thriving in the plaza. Every year seedlings from this tree are given to other communities who have experienced tragedy.

Sarah:

The Survivor Tree presented me with living proof of life's power for regeneration and healing. That little tree gave me something that all the human architecture was not able to.

Figure 32. Survivor Tree. Credit: PumpkinSky CC BY-SA 3.0 via Wikimedia Commons

When Sky-Woman and Sky-Man first showed us the Tree of Life, I realized that I had already experienced the healing power of a tree. When the Wind Tribe said the Tree of Life still grows strong on Turtle Island I thought again of the Survivor Tree.

I have been rewriting American history in my head during the council. During my inner council, my ancestors visited me. I have always believed that America was on the right side of history. We believe in equality, freedom and democracy. My ancestors brought these ideals to this country. What I didn't realize was that they also brought with them the banner of empire and a history of trauma.

The stories of the Wind, Water and Earth Tribes affected me deeply. America's current story about itself is a half-told tale that fails to guide us during these challenging times.

I want *my* American history to include the voices of women, Native Americans, African and Asian people and Mother Earth. Our story is much bigger than I thought. It has always been a global story.

From the beginning the American Dream has been tragically entangled with an American Nightmare. The dream of my impoverished

Figure 33. Survivor Tree. Credit: PumpkinSky CC BY-SA 3.0 via Wikimedia Commons

English ancestors to own a farm in the New World depended on the nightmare of a Native American village being destroyed. The dream of a Euro-American family living on a prosperous plantation depended on the nightmare of an African-American family living in slavery.

It is time to rewrite our story so we can fulfill our destiny as a peacemaker among nations.

(To Ingrid, the German ambassador)

Your words touched me deeply.

When you said, "I am haunted by the Holocaust," I felt a shiver run up my spine.

Your honesty has helped me feel the truth in myself.

(To everyone)

I too am haunted by holocausts.

In the UN there is a display that contains remnants of the atomic explosions in Nagasaki and Hiroshima. After World War II, America was relieved to have the world focus on the Nazi Holocaust instead of the unprecedented horror we had just unleashed on the men, women and children living in the cities of Hiroshima and Nagasaki.

I am also haunted by another holocaust.

Unlike the Holocaust of the Jews, which is thoroughly documented and universally condemned, the holocaust of the Native Americans has remained largely hidden from view.

But now the Wind Tribe has spoken. I have heard their stories. The UN and all of New York City was built on land inhabited by Native Americans for thousands of years.

I now understand that the current wave of pandemics that began in 2020 and have brought such devastation to our society were not the first to arrive here in America. Four hundred years earlier in 1620, my European ancestors brought many deadly plagues to this land that had never existed in the New World. These diseases like smallpox, typhoid, measles, tuberculosis and cholera destroyed the lives of millions of Native Americans. Their bones still lie in the ground and their spirits fill the air.

Despite my ancestors' higher aspirations, we ended up carrying the banner of empire to the New World. That banner is looking pretty old and frayed at this point. The epidemics that we brought to this continent have returned to threaten our own civilization.

I want America to fulfill its destiny as a true leader. We are blessed with a beautiful and bountiful land. We have people living here from all the nations on earth, from all the tribes. We are Americans by adoption, refugees from faraway lands. We can trace our ancestry back to people fleeing the trauma of poverty, famine, war and persecution. For hundreds of years we have struggled to create a national sense of family.

Today our American family feels deeply divided. Economic inequality has created so much suffering. People are anxious about the future. Many people have lost faith in our broken government and rightly so. Yet in our hearts we believe in love, family and respect for others.

The Founders of our country believed in the spiritual ideal of *E pluribus unum*. "Out of many, we become one." To me, it's the most mystical aspect of the American Dream, the idea that somehow we can merge our different backgrounds into a new and more universal identity. Instead of being the last of the great empires to fall, I want to become an empire that evolves into a Tree of Life.

When Sky-Woman and Sky-Man talked about seeing an empire pyramid as a spiral that could be transformed into a Tree of Life, I immediately thought about the pyramid on the Great Seal of the United States.

Sarah:

In the Founders' vision, the "Eye of Providence" at the top symbolizes the enlightened leadership that can open the energy flow and usher in a "New World " (Novus Ordo Seclorum), a new vision of the future.

My religion is as important to me as my patriotism. I invited Jesus to guide me during my inner council. He told me about the Tree of Life that stands at the center of the Garden of Eden. When we left the Garden, the Creator placed angels and a flaming sword at the gates of Eden to serve as both a guard and a beacon to lead us back to the Tree of Life. I saw a glorious vision of Americans joining together and creating a New Eden, a Human Earth.

Having experienced the power of the council here with you, I feel that councils may offer us a practical path back to Eden. The Native American people were trying to teach us about councils when we arrived. I'm wondering if councils could provide a more democratic way to govern ourselves than our divisive winner-take-all elections.

Thomas Jefferson said that in order to keep democracy alive we need to review and renew the Constitution every generation. We are many generations overdue for a second Constitutional Convention.

Sitting in council with you has helped me begin to heal wounds that I didn't even know I had. I'm very grateful. If Americans want to be leaders in the world, we will need to learn a different kind of leadership. We'll need to lead in healing. Until we heal our own country, our attempts to help other countries will continue to end traumatically, for us and for them.

Figure 34. Great Seal of United States.
Credit: Public domain.

As a descendant of the Fire Tribe, I want to create an America that welcomes the gifts of all the tribes. The American Dream has always been part of a bigger dream — everyone living in peace on a healthy planet.

Oren, Ambassador from Israel:

Sarah and Ingrid, I am moved when I hear that you are haunted by the Holocaust. Holocaust guilt is a heavy burden to carry.

Yet imagine the weight of *our* burden, we who were on the *receiving end* of the Holocaust. Just to put things in perspective: The six million Jews killed in the Holocaust is equal to the entire Jewish population of modern-day Israel.

I'll tell you how I am haunted by the Holocaust: I never feel safe. As a Jew I can never relax completely. I am always on the alert for danger. Jews need to know it's time to leave *before* it's time to leave.

When you have been hunted down and persecuted for thousands of years it changes you. Every time a pogrom occurred, my ancestors would escape to a different, slightly more tolerant country and become good neighbors and productive citizens. Things would go well for a while. But eventually that country would run into hard times and turn against us.

I can understand that we Jews might seem a little strange to some of you. We are always strangers in a strange land.

We hoped that once we had our ancient homeland back we would finally feel safe. But modern Israel was born from the trauma of war and terrorism, and it remains mired in trauma. Now I have my homeland and I still don't feel safe.

We are a tiny nation surrounded by millions of Arabs, many of whom don't believe we have a right to exist. For me another Holocaust is always right around the corner. When I look in the mirror, I see the face of the persecuted. But now I also see an unfamiliar face staring back at me. To the Palestinians *we* now wear the face of the persecutor.

Thousands of years ago when Jerusalem was burnt to the ground by the Babylonian Empire, the world as we knew it was destroyed. We were forced into exile. When we left our Motherland we lost our sacred springs, our wooded groves and our Earth Goddesses. Only the stars above remained. Only our Sky God, Yahweh, remained.

One thing sustained us. One thing helped us preserve our identity as a people. It was our story. Our stories are a record of our conversations with God. Today people all over the world still find meaning in our ancient stories.

When the Roman Empire was falling apart because they had no story left to believe in, they took our story, our Torah, changed the title to the Bible, and said it was now their story.

The story of the Promised Land began with us. And like all Promised Lands, ours was already occupied by other people. The Torah boasts of conquering the Canaanites, the prior inhabitants of the Promised Land.

When I first heard the Singing People suggest that Jerusalem could become an international Earth Shrine, I bristled at the notion. I wonder why it's the Jews who are asked to give up their land when they have so little to start with. The hard truth is that Jews, Muslims and Christians all lay spiritual claim to Jerusalem. Over the centuries, our "City of Peace" has seen over fifty wars! Twice Jerusalem has suffered total destruction. This cycle needs to stop.

In my inner council I saw a cycle of fear and violence within myself. Those who live by the sword die by the sword. I would prefer to live — and die — by the Tree of Life.

Jerusalem is a lovely word. It means "They make peace here." Maybe Jerusalem is truly a *sacred city*, a city that has become so sacred that it transcends religious differences and national borders. I guess that's one reason that after World War II, the UN declared that Jerusalem needed to have a unique status as an "international city." It would be a great honor to create an Earth Shrine to house the Earth Stone in Jerusalem if we can find a way to do it that honors our ancestors.

When Solan and Devara retold the story of Cain and Abel, I heard it with new ears. Our cultural stories will always fight with each other unless we come together and create a story that is bigger than our own. I'm ready for a new story that includes all our voices.

Ahmad, Ambassador from Egypt:

I am moved by your words, Oren. I understand your need for a homeland and I am heartened by your openness to new stories.

Like you, I am tired of the unrelenting conflict of our old stories and the curse of violence they pass along to each new generation. Sometimes it feels to me like the Middle East is at the bottom of a big funnel and all the toxic conflict in the world ends up being dumped on us.

Empires demand constant blood sacrifice. All humanity lives on land *stained* by blood. But in the Middle East our land is *soaked* in blood. Our archeological sites vividly reveal war's many bloody layers of destruction. Too many generations of children have grown up knowing only war and the threat of war. In their heart of hearts, everyone knows war is crazy.

The most powerful generals in the world, admit that they will never "kill their way to peace." But in a war-torn world, war begins to make its own crazy sense.

Everyone needs a homeland. But after World War II when the Jews returned after 2,000 years and founded the modern nation of Israel it required displacing millions of Palestinians. Many of us see Israel as a Euro-American outpost that just doesn't belong in the Middle East.

The whole situation is one big mess.

I just sat with this "big mess" during my inner council. Usually I get agitated and hopeless when I think about it. This time I was able to relax with the mess.

What I saw most clearly is that nobody's going anywhere else. I'm not getting on a spaceship to go live on Mars. I know the Jews are not getting on a spaceship either. Our only hope is finding our way back to the Tree of life.

Islam, Salam, Shalom, Jerusalem — all come from the same root meaning Peace.

(Looking at Oren)

Oren, let us put an end to the curse of Cain and heal the ancient wound of brother against brother.

I invite you to join me in gathering with others in a Middle East council circle when we get back to the UN. Let's tell each other our stories and then see if we can create a new story together.

Oren, Ambassador from Israel:

Thank you, Ahmad. I gladly accept your offer.

Trista, UN visitor:

Like Sarah, I experienced a healing here with all of you. I have been feeling so depressed about my life and the state of the world that I was planning to end my life when I got home today. I live each day with the terrifying feeling of being hopelessly lost and alone on a dying planet in a hostile universe. Years of psychotherapy and medication have helped me function in the world but they never healed my pain.

Mentally and emotionally I have been suffering since my childhood. I often go to bed afraid of waking up to another day. I pray that I will die in my sleep. When I was in quarantine all alone in my apartment during the first pandemic I had nightmares of the world spinning out of control, going down some kind of black hole.

(Breathing deeper)

When Sky-Woman and Sky-Man showed me my origin and destiny I saw myself for the first time as a vital part of a loving universe. Now I see that we're zooming into a spiral that can propel us into a new age of Human Earth.

During my inner council I experienced a deep healing. I faced my anxiety and let it burn away everything that was not part of my true self. I no longer fear living on this planet. I feel so much energy inside me. And I want to use it to create things that are true and beautiful.

(Looking around)

Knowing that there are others like me in the world who want to nourish the Tree of Life strengthens the Tree of Life in me. I realize now that I have been suffering from what's probably the most common disease in empire, the unbearable loneliness of being a separate individual who never feels "good enough." In my ego skin I felt so cut off from the Tree of Life.

Now I feel part of a family...

(Smiling, as she looks around at the whole circle)

...a big messed up stepfamily who've hurt each other and still love each other.

People continue sharing in the great circle. After the last person has spoken, everyone sits quietly, savoring the sublime pleasure that comes from knowing and being known.

Seven Directions Ritual

Spirit-Eagle, Native American NGO observer:

Now the time has come to bring our great circle to one mind. Our children Solan and Devara have been waiting patiently for us to respond to their requests.

(Hugging Solan and Devara)

I feel blessed to have met you. I have dreamt of you. My elders passed on to me the teaching of the Seventh Generation. I want to see the next Seven Generations evolve on a healthy Human Earth so you can have the best possible life when it is your turn to be born.

(To everyone)

Indigenous people have kept the Tree of Life alive in their hearts generation after generation. Would you stand and join me in the Seven Directions ritual so that we can come to one mind?

Everyone nods their head in appreciation. Spirit-Eagle leads the UN people in the Seven Directions ritual that Sky-Woman first taught to the Four Tribes before they left on their journeys 70,000 years ago.

The UN people turn to the east, south, west and north and honor the Four Roots of Power, Love, Peace and Truth.

Then they stand with their feet planted in the Earth and their arms reaching to the Sky. They feel the Earth-Sky current running through their bodies. They follow the Seventh Direction inward to their center and experience the Tree of Life growing within.

Everyone senses the green Root of Love in the golden afterglow of their Metanoia visions. They vow to be a channel for love in their life. Each person connects with the yellow Root of Peace. They understand that whatever they do to another, they do to themselves. They gaze inward and see their cloudy empire ego mind dissolving. From the blue Root of Truth a clear mind arises. Finally the UN people tap the red Root of Power and feel the energy and enthusiasm they need to create a Human Earth.

Spirit-Eagle guides the group as they spiral back out through the Seven Directions until they face the east once more.

Raising the Tree of Life

Spirit-Eagle:

Now it is time to pledge our lives to the Tree of Life and enter a new world where Human Earth is awakening. In a moment I will ask you to raise your arm to signify your support for the Tree of Life, your willingness to fulfill the requests of our Sky Children and your commitment to create a Human Earth.

But do not raise your dominant arm. Don't automatically use the one trained by Empire, the arm with the old habits. Stop and notice whether your actions are arising from ego habits or coming from a true calling. When you do feel called to raise your arm, I want you to raise your non-dominant arm and let it rise all the way from your feet.

Please pick up your listening stick with your non-dominant arm and say this pledge with me. At the end of the pledge we can all raise our arms together.

Spirit-Eagle:

We have come to one mind.

I pledge to stand with the Tree of Life and honor the Four Roots. I take a personal vow of unconditional peace.

I pledge to fulfill the requests of our Sky Children and the Singing People so we can evolve and create a Human Earth.

Now wait until you hear your calling and then lift your arm.

As each person tunes in and feels the Tree of Life within them, they feel the energy rising up from Mother Earth, through their feet and up into their non-dominant arm which rises powerfully, as if by itself.

Waves of energy flash back and forth between the right and left hemispheres of their brain. Currents of energy flow from the noosphere, charging and aligning all seven chakras.

The golden glow of the Metanoia spreads from mind to mind and soon illuminates the entire scene.

Spirit-Eagle:

Now, using our non-dominant leg, let us step forward into a new world where Human Earth is awakening.

Although many people feel a habitual desire impelling them to step forward with their dominant leg, they pause and consciously direct their life energy to the opposite leg. A natural movement arises and everyone steps forward with joy and grace.

The realms of self and other unite. The personal and the planetary merge. They see a shared vision of Human Earth and shout with joy. The great spiral above their circle rises up over the Tree of Life. From there a new expanding spiral opens up to the noosphere.

All the Sky People, Sky-Woman, Sky-Man, Sky-Grandmother, Sky-Grandfather, the Mothers and Fathers of the Four Tribes, and Solan and Devara, smile and wave farewell as they ride the spiral up to the noosphere.

Return to the UN

With their arms raised and their shouts still reverberating in the air, people watch in astonishment as the world of the council vanishes and the familiar walls of the General Assembly Hall reappear.

Everyone stands immobilized with suspended breath. Slow-motion shock waves course through their body as they make the transition back into the world they left behind. They hear the spring storm still raging outside. The clocks on the walls begin measuring time again. The turmoil and anxieties of the world of empire swirl around them. They feel the old dark fears starting to flood back in. They gaze into the eyes of the person next to them, who they barely knew before. They see kindness and caring shining back. That former stranger now feels like family. Their hearts begin to glow inside and they find the courage to love.

Slowly, everyone begins breathing again. The fragrant aroma of the Tree of Life and the fresh atmosphere of the council stream back into their nostrils. They gaze around the room and sense that their personal mind clouds are still connected to a shared mind cloud. They realize that they have brought the vision of a Human Earth back with them.

Willow-Song holds the Earth Stone up as an offering. Everyone stands transfixed as the Earth Stone rises and rotates in front of the UN emblem at the front of the hall.

The Secretary-General stands at the platform. The rhythmic pounding of her gavel attracts everyone's attention.

Secretary-General of the UN:

(Smiling, her arms sweeping wide, welcoming the sea of upraised hands)

The resolution passes unanimously.

Therefore, be it resolved that the General Assembly of the United Nations and the all the peoples of the earth share a common origin and vow to fulfill humanity's destiny.

We pledge to stand with each other in the Tree of Life and the Four Roots.

We take a vow of unconditional peace.

We pledge to fulfill the requests of our Sky Children and the Singing People so that we can evolve and create a Human Earth.

The UN people have awoken from the trance of empire and have seen a vision of a Human Earth. What will they do now?

Appendix

What's next?

We wan to create additional versions so this story can reach a wider audience.

- Oral storytelling podcasts & audiobook
- Graphic novel (online and print)
- Translations into other languages
- Animated video

Human Earth Awakening gave us a beautiful vision of the future and renewed our faith in humanity. We would love to see this story grow in people's hearts and contribute to the awakening of a Human Earth. If you resonate with the dream of *Human Earth* here are some action steps you can take to make that dream come true.

Share the story

Share the story with your friends and family (you can use this link **HumanEarthAwakening.com**). Visit our **Human Earth Awakening Facebook Page**. Please send us your **comments** about the story. Your feedback will help guide us as we prepare the next edition.

Live the story

While writing the story of *Human Earth Awakening* from 2010-2020, we began to live the story. The vision of a world based on love and co-creation instead of fear and domination became a lived reality for us and we saw the world with new eyes. As we practiced the Original Teachings and nourished the Tree of Life in our daily lives we experienced healing, joy and gratitude.

Yet the more real our personal experience of Human Earth becomes, the more horror and grief we feel about the destruction of our planet and the degradation of human life. We live each day embedded in an Empire Earth that is going through a dramatic and inevitable apocalypse. We were born into and have derived benefits from the empire-based society that our Euro-American ancestors created. Yet participating in the structures of empire in order to live does not prevent us from seeing its dark side.

We have responded to this dilemma by learning to live in two worlds. While interacting with Empire Earth, we also live each day as if Human Earth were already a reality. We nourish our personal Tree of Life by practicing the Original Teachings. We eat foods that revitalize our body and we think in ways that nurture our spirit. We use rituals like the Seven Directions and the Turning of the Seasons to remind us of our place in the cosmos.

Some days feel truly blissful and wondrous. Other days feel terrifying and confusing. Yet each day we practice living by the four roots of Love, Truth, Peace and Power. We use the ritual of council to deepen our relationships with each other and with friends and family. We practice the art of inner council and listen for guidance. We engage in social action when we are called. We create rituals to help us navigate the passages of life, grieve the sorrows and celebrate the joys.

During the past few years, these practices helped us overcome a series of major personal challenges and begin a new phase of life. We went through the center of a spiral and came out the other side with joy and gratitude, deeper humility and a clearer understanding of life. This enabled us to respond creatively to the social crisis triggered by the pandemic of 2020 by self-publishing this book.

We are living through a worldwide apocalypse that is calling each one of us to discover our unique role in the transformation of our planet and the evolution of our species. We hope this story brings you gifts you need at this time in your life. We encourage you to create sacred time for your own inner council so you can envision the world you want and hear the callings of your soul. We invite you to share your visions with the people around you and on our Human Earth Awakening Facebook page.

Cast of characters

Great Beings

Tree of Life
Source of Life whose Four Roots are Love, Truth, Peace and Power.

Planet Earth
Our home in the universe.

Sky People

Sky Elders: Sky-Grandmother and Sky-Grandfather
Humanity's galactic ancestors and guides.

Sky Ancestors: Sky-Woman and Sky-Man
Humanity's planetary ancestors and guides.

Sky Children: Solan and Devara
Humanity's Seventh Generation. Solan and Devara are the children of evolution. In Part 6 they also appear as the children of extinction.

Mothers and Fathers of the Four Tribes

African Earth Tribe Mother and Father
Ancestors of the African people.

Asian Water Tribe Mother and Father
Ancestors of the Asian people, from western Asia (Middle East) all the way to Australia, eastern Asia, Japan and the Philippines.

Euro-American Fire Tribe Mother and Father
Ancestors of the European and Euro-American people.

Native American Wind Tribe Mother and Father
Ancestors of the Native American people of North and South America.

Singing People

Lamala and Shanidar
Last surviving Neanderthal Singing People.

Singing People Grandmother and Grandfather
Lamala's grandparents and givers of the Earth Stone.

Singing People Children
Son and daughter of Lamala and Shanidar.

UN people

Chuntao
Ambassador from China.

Ahmad
Ambassador from Egypt.

Oren
Ambassador from Israel.

Leonid
Ambassador from Russia.

Sarah
Ambassador from USA.

Ingrid
Ambassador from Germany.

Hoanui
Ambassador from Solomon Islands.

Amaka
Ambassador from Nigeria.

Tom
Ambassador from Australia.

Willow-Song
Native American NGO observer.

Spirit-Eagle
Native American NGO observer.

Asher
NGO representative.

Elise
UN staffer.

Maria
NGO representative from Bolivia.

Trista
UN visitor.

Other characters

Radun
In the story of extinction, Radun is the social architect of the new world of Cosmopolis.

Cain and Abel
Two brothers in the story of the first murder in Genesis.

List of figures

Original Teachings

Teaching of the Four Roots

This is a fuller version of the Teachings that Sky-Woman and Sky-Man shared with the UN people.

Root of love

Love is the essence of the universe. It is the awareness of oneness. Love is knowing that we are all one family, all children of Mother Earth and Father Sky.

Our inner nature is love. When people attune their consciousness to love, they act from love and create from love. Love overcomes separation and restores unity.

Family is where human beings learn to love. Love comes naturally to every child. And for it to grow, it needs to be nourished by a loving family and a loving community. From there it grows to embrace all living beings — the animals, the plants, the ancient rocks and the stars glowing in the night sky.

The way of love is simple: Love life. Love yourself. Love one another.

The way of love is simple but it is not always easy.

It is not easy to feel love when others hurt us or threaten us. Yet even when we cannot experience the feeling of love through our emotions, we can still experience the presence of love through our spirit. Our two eyes are made to see duality and differences, but our spiritual eye is single and perceives the unity of all things. Our ability to practice love through our spirit is boundless. At every moment our spirit is receiving and radiating love.

So that we can practice spiritual love in everyday life, we have the teachings of respect and kindness.

To respect someone begins with seeing that person as my child and as your brother or sister. Respect means seeing the other person as a human being like yourself who has taken a different form in the world. Practicing respect means acknowledging our individual separateness, dancing with distance and flexing our boundaries.

Kindness means treating others as if they were our own kind, our own family, our own self. Treat others as they wish to be treated. Do not harm each other.

Everyone wants to live in a world of love. Extend respect and kindness to your enemies and soon you will have no enemies. Remember, love is boundless, so put no limits around your love. Allow your love for yourself and your family to grow big enough to include everyone and everything in all of creation.

Root of truth

Truth is the lucid thinking of the clear mind.

The clear mind of truth is centered in the coolness of the head. It serves to balance love, which resides in the warmth of the heart.

A clear mind allows the light of truth to illuminate our consciousness, just as the clear blue sky allows the light of the sun to illuminate the world.

A cloudy mind blocks the light of truth from entering, just as an overcast sky prevents the light of the sun from reaching us. A cloudy mind arises from our fears and our desires. Our minds also becomes cloudy when we do too much talking and too little listening.

Our thoughts are clothed in stories and our stories are woven with words. The greatest obstacle to truth is the temptation to use our words to construct distorted, self-serving stories. Choose your words and your thoughts with great care for they shape your reality.

Telling yourself the truth clears your mind, as a fresh wind blows the clouds away. Tell yourself true stories about your life. Do not repeat untrue stories that you hear from others.

Whenever you speak, speak the truth, the whole truth, and nothing but the truth. The world needs to hear your truth.

You have been given one tongue and two ears so that you can listen twice as much as you speak. Listen to another person's truth with an open heart and you will both give and receive a precious gift.

When we join our minds as one mind we can accomplish great things. Always tell the truth with love. In all you do, let your actions be motivated by love and guided by truth.

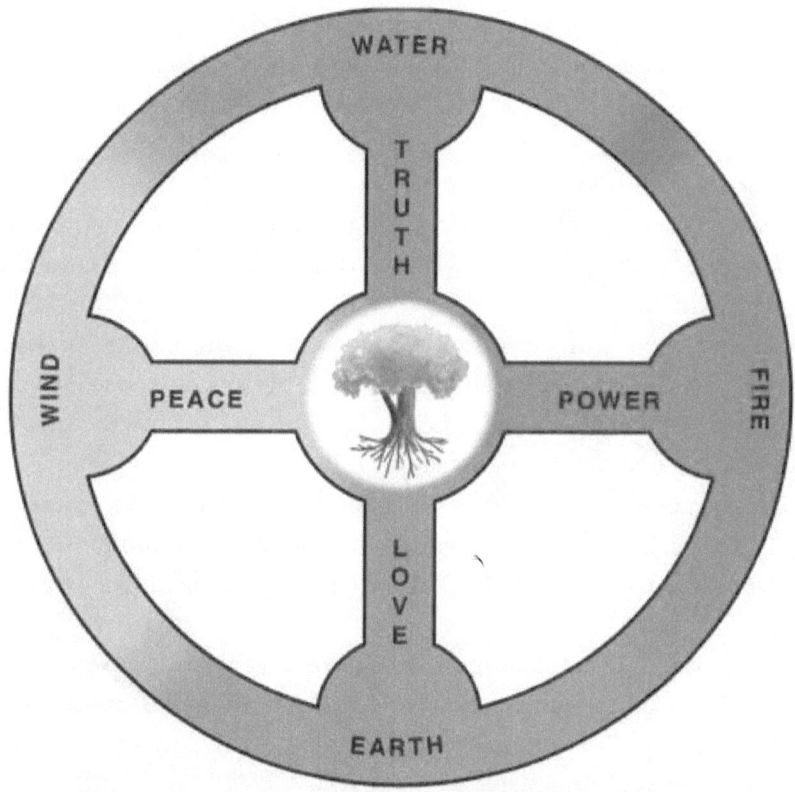

Figure 35. Symbol of Tree of Life and Four Roots. Credit: Gerzon

Root of peace

Peace is perhaps the most mysterious and misunderstood of the Four Roots. Sometimes peace is quiet and serene, like a still lake on a beautiful autumn afternoon. But sometimes peace is a thunderstorm that releases tension in the atmosphere and brings life-giving rain. Peace is an energetic, dynamic, ever-changing process.

Peace is day and night, light and dark, dancing together. Peace manifests as health in the body, harmony in the family and co-creation among all peoples. Peace embraces opposites and creates harmony. Peace can transform sickness into health and enemies into friends.

Power that is disconnected from peace soon goes to extremes, dissipates its energy and becomes powerless. Peacemaking is the art of resolving conflicts creatively so they further evolution. Peacemaking is an art that calls upon the virtues of humility, harmony, rhythm, balance and healing. Peace is using your power in harmony with other human beings.

To find true peace, dance with whatever life brings you.

Root of power

Power is the creative life energy of the universe itself. Power is the ability to give birth to what is within, to manifest thoughts and dreams in the real world.

Plants use their miraculous power to receive the energy of sunlight and transform it into the living substance of roots, stems, leaves and fruits. Power is the life blood, the energy and vitality of the body that enables you to live a full and creative life.

Women receive the spirit of a child, and use their power to transform energy into flesh and bone, creating a new human being. Men have the power to activate new life and to co-create a beautiful world with women.

Each person, like each animal, has been given special powers in the form of talents and abilities. Power is the gift to move others through song and dance, to create art, to tell stories, to invent, to construct, to heal, to inspire and organize.

Power enables love and truth to become actions that change the world. Power embodies spirit with structure and substance. Power that is guided by love, truth and peace creates beauty and prosperity in the world.

Discover the nature of your power, develop it fully and use it wisely to benefit all creation.

Honor all Four Roots. Always treat each other with love and peace, speak the truth and use your power wisely.

Teaching of the Tree of Life

Tree of Life

All is one.
All is love.
I begin as one seed.

Seeking life, I turn to Mother Earth. Seeking life, I turn to Father Sky. One seed divides into two poles: a root going down and a stem going up. One seeks darkness, the other light.

The dance of life begins. Everything moves in a spiral. My roots spiral down into the Earth. My branches spiral up into the Sky.

I begin as one seed and grow into a tree with many parts: roots, trunk, branches, leaves, fruits and seeds. Each part has a teaching.

Teaching of the Roots

My roots lie hidden in the Earth, under the ground, in darkness. For every branch that is visible above ground there is an invisible root supporting it underground.

I receive the life-giving flow of dark energy from Mother Earth and send it upward to nourish the branches and the leaves.

Teaching of the Trunk and Branches

My trunk and branches provide structure and strength. My sap-blood flows up and down. I circulate my energies. My leaves drink water sent upward by the roots. My roots eat sun energy gathered by the leaves.

Everything acts in harmony to create life and health. If any part withholds its gift, or refuses to receive the gifts it is given, or takes more than it gives in return, it blocks the energy flow and the whole tree suffers and weakens.

I balance the upper with the lower and the inner with the outer so that all can flourish.

Teaching of the Leaves

My leaves gather power from the light of Father Sky.

I transform spirit energy into matter. From the sun and stars I make the food that nourishes growth. I give thanks and receive guidance from above.

I shade the rest of the tree from the sun's heat and provide a home for many creatures.

Teaching of the Fruits and Seeds

My fruits, nuts and seeds provide nourishment for many animals. From one seed comes one thousand seeds. Each seed contains the Original Teachings and passes them on to the next generation.

Remember the Original Teachings. Stay rooted in Mother Earth. Open your spirit to Father Sky. Give and receive freely. Everything changes. Circulate the energy.

Move like a spiral through time and space. Become the change that wants to happen.

If you embody these teachings you will create a landscape of peace and a world of love.

Seven Directions Tree of Life Ritual

We invite you to join us in nourishing the Tree of Life and honoring the Seven Directions.

I stand at the center of a great spiral of Life. Life energy flows through me from my ancestors to future generations.

I connect with my inner Tree of Life. I send my roots down into the Earth. I raise my branches up to the Sky.

I stand strong and flexible, with joy and gratitude.

I now honor the Four Directions and the Four Roots of the Tree of Life: Love, Truth, Peace and Power.

I turn and face the east.
The direction of the rising sun and the root of power.
Power and creative energy flowing in.
A time of new beginnings.

I turn and face the south.
The direction of the midday sun and the root of love.
Love and abundance flowing in.
A time of growth and perseverance.

I turn and face the west.
The direction of the setting sun and the root of peace.

Peace, healing, and rhythm flowing in.
A time of bringing to completion and letting go.

I turn and face the north.
The direction of the night sky and the root of truth.
Truth and beauty flowing in.
A time of rest and rejuvenation.

Having honored the Four Directions, I now honor the directions of Earth and Sky.
I send my roots down into the soil. Energy flowing up from the Earth.
I connect with my body and I hear my Earth voices.
I raise my branches up to the Sky.
Cosmic energy from the sun, moon and stars flowing in.
I connect with my spirit and I hear my Sky voices.
Now honoring the Seventh Direction I bring my hands to my heart and go inward to my center.
At the center of the spiral my inner Tree of Life grows strong and healthy.
I am one with the heart of all being.
I call an inner council.
I connect with my true self and I hear my true voices.
I listen for guidance.
I visualize my day.
A day of Human Earth Awakening.

Having spiraled in to my center and received these energies from the Seven Directions, I begin to spiral out into the world.

Facing the north, I speak my truth and reveal my beauty.
Turning to the west, I bring peace, healing and rhythm to all my activities and relationships.
Turning to the south, I radiate love and abundance to the great family of all beings.
Turning to the east, I use my energy to create a happy healthy Human Earth with love, truth, peace and power.

Now I step forward into this new moment with clarity, joy and gratitude.

Inner Council Ritual

Used daily, the inner council ritual can help us solve problems, think clearly, communicate authentically, evolve our brain, meet our goals and live a conscious and creative life.

1. Wake up! Call an inner council.

Stop your habitual train of thought. Wake up. Become aware.

Look inside. Breathe. Notice your state of mind, your feelings and physical sensations.

Listen to your inner talk.

Call all your inner voices and your spirit guides to the council circle.

Declare your intentions for the council: To enjoy the gift of breathing and being alive, to express gratitude, to solve a problem, to meditate and gain clarity, to heal and restore inner strength, to grow and evolve, to ask for guidance.

2. Invite all your inner voices to speak.

Visualize yourself at the center of an inner council circle. All the different aspects of your personality sit in a circle around you. You align yourself with the Tree of Life. The Four Roots of love, truth, peace and power extend outward.

You invite your inner voices to speak. The ego voices are usually the loudest at first. Let each speak and be heard by the others. It often helps to say out loud or write down what each one is saying.

Breathe and go deeper. Listen to the voices of your body, your heart, your head and your spirit.

3. Invite the Four Roots to speak.

Breathe and connect with the Tree of Life. Take a fresh look at the situation you are contemplating. Let each of the Four Roots speak and share their perspective. Invite your spirit guides to provide support and direction.

The Four Roots:

Truth. Tell the truth, the whole truth and nothing but the truth.

Love. Talk in a way that is loving and healing, that increases your vitality and joy, your self-confidence and your compassion for others.

Peace. Claim your birthright to feel safe in your body and in the world. Enjoy the paradise of the present moment. Talk to yourself in a way that helps transform inner and outer conflicts into personal and planetary growth.

Power. Identify and connect with your inner and outer resources. Create inner talk that empowers you to respond effectively and meet your goals.

4. Come to one mind.

Call upon your true self to create new truthful, loving, peaceful, empowering inner talk that is energized by the Tree of Life and guided by the Four Roots. Visualize who you want to be what you want to do.

5. Evolve to the next level.

Use your new creative inner talk to move forward in your life and upward on the spiral of awakening. Take your next action step with confidence. Express gratitude for the gift of life. Evolve consciously and creatively.

About us

Robert: Seeking a vision

Running out of stories to believe in

Human Earth Awakening began many years ago during a dark time in my life when I had run out of stories to believe in. In my heart I was crying out for a story that could guide me.

One day from out of the blue, I experienced a startling vision that opened up a new connection to the world of spirit. That day the seed of a story was planted in my heart and it began to grow.

In my meditations, I heard the voices of ancestral storytellers. The stories they told me were different than any I had ever heard before. For many years now, I have watched spellbound as fascinating characters take me on astonishing journeys into uncharted territory. At times I am inspired and energized, at other times shocked and horrified. Later I write down what I have seen and heard.

After writing a chapter, I read it to Christine. She helps shape the narrative and develop the characters. She brings a perspective that enriches every page. I could not have written this story alone. Christine has lived every scene with me.

Human Earth Awakening is a cosmic story about humanity's destiny. Yet it is also an intimate story about the personal challenges that my family and I face as we live each day during this time of global crisis. *Human Earth Awakening* is a living story with close to eight billion authors.

Searching

That life-changing vision was not my first. Much earlier in my life I experienced a vision that woke me out of the trance of empire. It launched me on a path of discovery that eventually led to writing *Human Earth Awakening*.

In 1963, during my freshman year at the University of California in Berkeley, I faced an existential crisis far beyond my understanding. I had graduated with honors from high school. Yet when I looked around me at the adult world I was being trained to enter, I was shocked to discover that I did not want to become part of it.

In November of that year, President Kennedy was assassinated. I had the disturbing feeling that there was something fundamentally wrong with the whole system that society was based on, but I had no idea what the problem was.

I doubted that I would find the answers I was searching for in a university lecture hall, scientific laboratory, government building or religious institution. Yet graduating from college and having a successful career as a physician and a writer had been my goal during high school. My mind was churning with conflicting desires. I needed to do something to clear my head.

In the spring I hitchhiked up the California coast. In the seacoast town of Mendocino I had a vision that revealed a startling new world to me.

Mind-body connection

Visions are mysterious. They can arise from the fears and desires of the ego or from the clear vision of the soul. I was open to the importance of visions because the first stories I ever heard were Bible stories, which were filled with people having visions. I heard these stories in Sunday school and when my mother read to me at bedtime.

In the Bible stories, I learned that the heroes were not only the kings who led armies into battles but the visionary prophets who led people back to God. In Sunday school my teachers told me that Jesus had a life-changing vision when he was baptized in the Jordan River.

As a child, I also observed that my father, a biochemist and cancer researcher, put his trust in the scientific method. He dedicated his life to discovering medicines that could relieve human suffering. Sometimes he took me to his laboratory and showed me how he conducted his experiments. The lab was filled with Bunsen burners, beakers, tubes, microscopes and centrifuges. There I learned that a visionary idea could come in the form of a scientific hypothesis and that visions needed to be tested and verified in the real world before they could be considered true and useful.

Another reason I was open to visions was because of a book I was reading during my freshman year at college. Bored with the required classes, I had been exploring books and articles about the connection between the body and the mind. I had been educated to believe that my body and my mind were two separate entities.

I had a personal interest in the whole mind-body question because I experienced a distressing split in myself. I was aware of a basic sense of discomfort, a vague anxiety, an unease with my very existence. I was up in my head and out of touch with my body. I often felt I was at war with myself.

Was it possible to heal this mind-body split?

While researching this question I came across Aldous Huxley's book, *The Doors of Perception*. He was a writer and philosopher better known for his earlier novel, *Brave New World*. In *The Doors of Perception* Huxley described the mind-expanding visions he experienced after taking mescaline, a psychedelic substance derived from peyote. This sacred plant has been used in rituals by Native Americans for thousands of years and still revered by the Native American Church.

Huxley found that mescaline enabled him to perceive a world that was far more vibrant and multidimensional than the one he inhabited in his normal consciousness. Huxley took his book title from a William

Blake poem: "If the doors of perception were cleansed, everything would appear to man as it is, infinite."

In 1963 the hippie movement and psychedelic scene were still several years in the future. The only drugs that I saw being used on campus were caffeine, nicotine and alcohol. I had no idea what to do with this intriguing information about other states of consciousness. But I was not the only one reading *The Doors of Perception*. The band known as "The Doors" took their name from this book.

Visionary initiation

In *Human Earth Awakening* I write about our four great planetary tribes — the European, the African, the Asian and the Native American peoples. Throughout my life, I have benefited from the gifts of all Four Tribes. Often those gifts came in surprising and unexpected forms, as it did on this hitchhiking trip along the California coast.

When I arrived in Mendocino, a late afternoon fog cast a mysterious aura over the picturesque seacoast town. Through a series of serendipitous encounters, I ended up spending the night with some new friends who introduced me to the visionary power of peyote.

The sacred intelligence contained in this humble cactus plant, used by Native Americans in their sacred ceremonies, initiated me into the paradise of the present moment. The many veils that empire had draped over my eyes were blown away and I awoke from its trance. I saw life directly for the first time, in its naked beauty and absolute perfection.

I saw a world where everything was vibrantly alive and glowing with a mysterious sensual energy. What I experienced was beyond words but the word that came closest was love. The chains of empire dissolved and I felt the embrace of a loving universe.

During my peyote initiation I also came face to face with a malevolent and frightening monster that lived inside me. That monster inhabited a fear-based world where it rampaged destructively and wreaked havoc on my self-esteem and my ability to think clearly.

I sensed this monster was related to the dark cloud that had hung over my childhood home. My parents' World War II marriage had brought together two gifted but mismatched people. As a child I breathed in the cold, gray atmosphere of their traumas and their conflicted marriage. Sometimes that dark childhood cloud gave me nightmares.

As a child, I was often sick with colds, fevers, asthma and allergies. Then at the age of eight, I was hospitalized with rheumatic fever, a potentially fatal illness that introduced me to the angel of death. I gradually recovered but the cloud of emotional trauma within me grew darker.

My father was a Dutch army veteran who had narrowly escaped the invading Nazis. I remember hearing him play African-American gospel songs like "Swing low, Sweet chariot" on the piano — and singing them in his heavy Dutch accent! I didn't know it then, but those songs of suffering and redemption were helping him heal from the horrors of World War II. The soulful music of the African-American people has been healing my heart since I first heard my father sing those gospel songs.

In my teens my father finally told me something about himself that he had kept carefully hidden. Though he had made a heartfelt conversion to Christianity as a teenager, the Gerzon family in Holland was Jewish and many of his close relatives had lost their lives in the Holocaust. That dark cloud I had sensed as a child included the souls of beloved family members who had died in the gas chambers of Auschwitz.

That night in Mendocino I revisited that dark cloud and caught a glimpse of the destructive monster that lurked inside me. I knew it would kill me if it could.

The life-affirming experience that I had with the help of good friends and a sacred Native American plant gave me a vision of new possibilities. I had seen the light *and* the darkness.

My healing journey had begun.

Healing quest

Mythic quests often begin with questions. As I look back, I can see that there were four questions that guided me on my quest for healing.

Truth: How can I discover the *truth* about life?

Love: How can I experience authentic *love*?

Peace: How can I find *inner peace* and how can we create *world peace*?

Power: How can I align myself with the mysterious *power* of the universe?

At the age of 18 after completing my freshman year, I decided not to return in the fall. I enrolled in the school of life, joined the working class and began to learn from my own experiences and my own mistakes. I embarked on a vision quest that took me to Yosemite and then to Hawaii.

In the Hawaiian islands I spent several years living close to nature and learning from the spirit and aloha of the Hawaiian people. I experienced healing in the warm, womblike waters of quiet coves. I felt the pulsating rhythm of life as I surfed the waves. At night, I slept outside under a tree listening to the lullaby of ocean waves cresting onto the sandy beach. When I hiked and camped under the stars 10,000 feet above sea level in Haleakala Crater, I was awed by the fiery volcanic power that formed the islands. In Hawaii I connected with the great goddess Pele and saw her many faces as creator and destroyer.

Coming of age in the turbulent 1960's, I saw people all around me waking up, questioning authority, raising consciousness and seeking freedom. I started searching for natural ways to heal from the disease of modern civilization. I returned to mainland America and sought out teachers, communities, books, methods, spiritual traditions and indigenous wisdom. I began to meditate and eat whole natural foods. I felt healthier and happier than ever before.

I continued to learn from the other great tribes of humanity. In the social realm, descendants of the African people like Martin Luther King, Jr. and Nelson Mandela inspired me with their example of courageous leadership founded on love. Both men brought healing to the African and European peoples during a time of escalating conflict.

During the 1960's and 70's Eastern spiritual traditions became much more widely known in the West. The wisdom of the Asian people fascinated me. Their sacred writings opened my Western-educated mind to a new way of looking at life. I learned to respect humanity's ancestors instead of thinking of them as primitive savages.

For several years I studied with Michio Kushi, a wise Japanese philosopher and proponent of a way of life based on harmony with nature and traditional Asian health practices. I became part of a community of people in Boston dedicated to natural living, healing and world peace. I immersed myself in holistic medicine, macrobiotic cooking, herbs, acupuncture, massage, meditation and martial arts. I managed a communal study house and worked as a carpenter and natural foods chef.

Wounded healer

I have always had an urge to share what I learn with others. So, as a "wounded healer," I began helping people through teaching, counseling and acupuncture therapy. This took my life in the world to a new and rewarding level.

But my own healing was still far from complete. I was unable to experience love in my personal life. Like my father before me, I got married and started a family without a true understanding of myself, my emotions or healthy relationships. When my seven-year marriage ended, I faced the biggest and most unexpected challenge of my life. Suddenly I was a single parent in my mid 30's with the sole responsibility for the support and care of my two young daughters.

My carefully constructed yet fragile world came crashing down. All my concepts, techniques and philosophies seemed useless. I nearly drowned in a flood of fear, anger and shame. I wanted to run away from the catastrophe of my life. But what I remember most from that time was the love I felt for my daughters and the desire to give them the best childhood I could. I began to live my life more humbly, one day at a time, with a beginner's mind.

Transformed by love

My world was transformed when Christine came into my life. When we met, we were both recently divorced with young children from previous marriages. With Chris I was finally able to experience the most powerful healing force in the universe — true love. When we were together, the world of the past faded away and we experienced the paradise of the present moment.

We developed an authentic partnership and began to heal our wounds and grow into our true selves. Gradually we created a new Eden of love and trust.

With Chris's encouragement, I opened a practice in the Boston area as a holistic health consultant, offering clients an array of healing modalities, combining energy therapies like acupuncture with mind-body counseling. Chris and I were overjoyed when we had a child together. We also began collaborating through our counseling, workshops and writing.

Finding Serenity in the Age of Anxiety

In my 40's I went back to school and earned a Master's degree in psychology. As a psychotherapist and life coach I created a safe space where clients from all walks of life could share their inner world with me. This often took me into the heart of darkness. I saw that suffering is universal, yet the way we experience suffering is unique and personal. I witnessed the power of the human spirit to heal from trauma. I learned that our individual lives are part of something larger and we all need a vision greater than ourselves.

I kept searching for the root cause of the problems that I and my clients were experiencing. I realized that my daily "inner talk" was the mental software that ran my life and determined my moods. By changing my inner talk to be more truthful and loving, my life started to change. That dark cloud from my childhood began to dissolve. I helped my clients and workshop participants use creative inner talk to tell themselves a new story about their own lives.

As human beings we all experience fear and anxiety. How we respond to it shapes our lives. Unfortunately, our social conditioning trains us to either stuff anxiety inside (using denial and distraction) or dump it on others (using anger and blame).

I practiced shining the light of awareness on my own anxiety and that of my clients. I discovered a surprising new way to approach anxiety as a key to transforming my consciousness.

When I examined the tangled knot of anxiety, I found three distinct yet interrelated strands — toxic anxiety, natural anxiety and sacred anxiety. If I responded to anxiety with the stuff-it-or-dump-it reaction, anxiety turned toxic and resulted in symptoms and dysfunctional behaviors. Yet, when I found the courage to face the natural anxiety that's a normal part of life, I was able to transform its energy into excitement and personal growth. When I embraced my sacred anxiety about death and the meaning of life, I experienced spiritual growth and inner peace.

My discoveries motivated me to write **Finding Serenity in the Age of Anxiety** which was published by Macmillan in 1997. My message resonated with many readers and gave me the opportunity to appear on the Oprah Winfrey Show and talk with her about how to get anxiety working for us instead of against us.

In *Finding Serenity in the Age of Anxiety* I also described how nations, like individuals, have a choice. If a nation finds the courage to face its anxieties and solve its problems, it grows and prospers. If a nation fails to do so, it becomes trapped in escalating cycles of divisive stuff-and-dump reactions that result in aggression and self-destructive behavior.

During the past two decades I have witnessed the age of anxiety escalate into an age of terror.

Visions grow stronger

In midlife, I began to feel the spirits of the Native American people in the New England countryside where I lived. As I walked through the woods and meadows, canoed along the rivers and swam in the lakes, I started to see my American homeland through different eyes. I learned that where I lived in Concord, Massachusetts was once a frontier outpost on the edge of "Indian Country." In 1676 this region was the scene of bloody battles that destroyed the Native American culture that had existed here for thousands of years.

I also became aware that Native Americans have not disappeared and that those who remain don't all live in reservations out West. Christine and I discovered that they are still our neighbors. For many years we participated in a local talking circle hosted by the Massachusetts Center for Native American Awareness. I am grateful for this opportunity and inspired by their example. Despite centuries of oppression, the original inhabitants of this land continue to extend their hand in friendship.

My research led me to a little known, historically based Native American story about peacemaking. For several days I listened to Jake Swamp (Tekaronianeken "Where two skies come together") share his people's sacred stories at the Mohawk Nation of Akwesasne in upstate New York. Jake was a revered Mohawk' elder and Haudenosaunee faithkeeper. He founded the Tree of Peace Society and planted Peace Trees all around the world.

The spirits and stories of the Native American people have guided me back through the mists of time to walk the path of peace and to see the beauty of the land they call Turtle Island. I realized that the bones of my *blood ancestors* lay buried far away in Europe. I began to honor the original inhabitants whose bones were buried all around me as my *land ancestors*.

These experiences inspired further visions during my daily meditations. My meditations gradually grew into inner councils. I began my days by seeking guidance with a Seven Directions ritual. My visions grew stronger and I set aside time to write them down. Eventually they grew into stories of healing including *Human Earth Awakening*.

Tikkun olam

As a Euro-American, I appreciate my blood ancestors for their adventurous spirit and their audacious curiosity. For many years I lived in Concord near Walden Pond. I felt the enduring transcendental influence of Henry David Thoreau and Ralph Waldo Emerson. In their clear American voices, they communicated their vision of nature, society and the individual all existing in harmony.

I am grateful to my Jewish ancestors on my father's side, going all the way back to the ancient Israelites, for engaging in an ongoing conversation with God and for writing their stories down in the Torah. Their dream of *tikkun olam*, healing the world, lives on today.

I've benefited greatly from cultural philosopher and mythologist Joseph Campbell's insight that the mythic dimension of life still frames our existence today. He taught that each person's life is a hero's journey. He observed that our regional myths and rituals no longer guide us effectively in our modern global age. His prescription for humanity's survival — the creation of a new mythic story uniting science and ancient wisdom — challenged me to write *Human Earth Awakening*. Another innovative thinker, the theologian and evolutionary scientist Teilhard de Chardin, inspired me with his vision of the noosphere and the omega point.

I am deeply grateful to be alive at this pivotal time in world history and I thank all the seekers of truth and lovers of life who have enriched my journey. I appreciate the indigenous wisdom keepers who have kept their stories alive through the generations. I am grateful to the artists who paint our cultural imagery and create the soundtrack for our lives, and to the scientists whose discoveries have illuminated the wondrous web of life to which we all belong. I am thankful for the many people on this planet who support me by growing food, making clothing, delivering energy and providing the products and services that enable me to live my life.

Return to the Tree of Life

The miracle I have experienced in my own life, transforming a world of trauma and fear into a loving Human Earth, gives me faith in my species. Yet the unconscious pull to repeat past patterns threatens to sabotage our shared future.

We evolved by gathering in families and clans, loving each other, and joining together to create a better life. Being part of a family grounds me, enriches me and gives my life meaning. Being a son, brother, cousin, nephew, friend, husband, father, uncle and grandfather are among the greatest gifts and challenges in my life.

I want my children and grandchildren to live in a peaceful, creative world where they can experience the joy and the beauty of life. And that can only happen on a planet where that's true for everyone's children.

As I look back, I see that those four questions that guided me on my quest eventually led me to the Four Roots of Love, Truth, Peace and Power and the Tree of Life.

Now in my mid-70's, I dream of healing stories that travel through our global nervous system and resonate with people of all cultures. From the creation story in Genesis to the latest evolutionary research, the message is the same. We all share one mother. We all belong to one family.

Will we continue to reenact the tragic drama of Cain and Abel? Or will we heal that ancient wound, sit together in the sacred circle and share our stories around the Tree of Life?

Christine: Searching for a story to believe in

First stories

I'll never forget the sense of awe I felt one summer night as a child standing all alone at the ocean's edge. I listened to the rhythmic sound of the surf and gazed at the immense star-filled sky overhead. I sensed the life energy connecting all things. As my small feet sunk into the soft wet sand, I felt like I was part of this beautiful, loving universe.

Since then I have been searching for stories about the awe-inspiring world I glimpsed that night. I looked for stories that would help me answer the age-old questions: Who am I? Where did I come from? Where am I going? Why am I here?

Ever since I can remember, I have always loved stories: compelling stories with fascinating characters who take me on new adventures to places I've never been and teach me something along the way, stories that reconnect me with that feeling of love and awe I felt at the beach that night.

Thinking about the very first stories I heard as a small child at home, in school and at church, I remember wanting to believe in them but there was a part of me who knew they were not telling me the whole truth about the world and my place in it. In Sunday school class, listening to the Creation Story, I wondered how a Father God could give birth to the whole universe by himself. Where was the Mother Goddess? I knew even then that women had power too, including the power to give birth to new life. Where were their voices? Where was their perspective?

The world of the Bible seemed filled with stories of conflict and punishment. In school, the stories I learned in my history class were filled with war and domination. On TV and in the movies, there were more stories of good guys versus bad guys. Women, when they were included, were always minor characters in the drama. All of these fear-based stories filled my young body with anxiety. They didn't help me understand the world I saw that night when I was at the ocean.

I found that being outside in nature was healing for me. There I could feel safe, confident and free. I felt Mother Earth nourishing me with her steady presence. Without words, she reassured me that the goddess did exist. I could see her work with my own eyes. Her changing seasons, her plants and animals taught me lifelong lessons about my innate connection to the natural world that I would always remember.

I came of age in the 1960's and like many others of my generation, I began to question the stories I had grown up with. It dawned on me that almost all the stories I had learned were written about men, by men and for men. They were stories that made the world a more dangerous place.

I was encouraged when I heard new stories by people who were working to create a world based on love and compassion. These stories of human rights and justice opened my eyes and reminded me of that beautiful world I saw that night on the beach. I decided to devote my life's work to making these new stories a reality.

I studied to become a teacher so that I could create a safe environment for children where they could explore and learn in a loving community.

Concord Children's Center

When I got married, and became a young working mother, I experienced firsthand how our society fails to put the well-being of families and children first. I saw many families struggling to meet the conflicting demands of parenting and work. Collaborating with another working mother, I co-founded the **Concord Children's Center**, a nonprofit day care center, the first in our town devoted to supporting young families.

We focused on educating the whole child. We emphasized the importance of creative play and spending time in nature. We read stories that had life-affirming messages of love, respect, curiosity and connection. We gathered together each day in a circle for a "Golden Moment" of meditation followed by sharing our own stories. The Concord Children's Center filled an unmet need and forty years later, it has three locations and serves over 200 children and their families.

Meeting Robert and finding a new story

I continued to advocate for young children by joining Educators for Social Responsibility and **TRUCE** to teach workshops on social and emotional learning, conflict resolution, and the influence of the media's stories on young children.

My professional life was fulfilling, yet I was suffering emotionally. In my 30's, I finally admitted to myself that my marriage was not a healthy one. I wanted my children to grow up in a loving home so I found the courage to end my marriage and face life on my own as a single mom.

The following year, I met Robert and my whole life changed. For the first time, I experienced the healing power of love. Robert treated me as his equal and his life's partner. He admired my feminine power and helped me re-write my story so that I was no longer a victim but a heroine.

Robert and I shared what we were learning about love by teaching personal growth and relationship workshops. Using the approach Robert outlined in his book, *Finding Serenity in the Age of Anxiety*, I joined him when he counseled couples. I became a life coach and helped women find their own authentic voices.

Our lovers journey has been joyful and ecstatic, yet not exempt from conflict, pain and sickness. Even when I was diagnosed with rheumatoid arthritis and could barely walk or hold my toothbrush, I trusted in the healing power of love. I made lifestyle changes and learned how to release the fear and tension that I had carried in my body since childhood. With Robert's support and that of other holistic practitioners, my body healed herself and I felt more fit than I had in years.

After we had been together for a few years and had a child of our own, Robert had a vision he shared with me. That was the beginning of hearing a new story about the world unlike any that we had ever heard before. This was the story that I had been searching for all my life about that loving world I saw as a child. In this story, women's voices sing out powerfully. This new story eventually grew into *Human Earth Awakening*.

This planetary love story began with our personal love story. Robert's love changed me and this story transformed both of us. I knew that if two human beings with traumatic backgrounds could create a new world of love together, then the same was possible for a traumatized humanity. It gives us the chance to share the good news that the power of love and truth can change our world.

Connecting the personal and the planetary

The connection between the personal and planetary came home to me in a dramatic way a few years ago. While we were writing our story, the climate crisis came to our town.

For over forty years we lived near White Pond, a beautiful and beloved pond located near its more famous sister, Walden Pond. Henry David Thoreau called White Pond a "gem of the woods." White Pond was a vital part of our lives as a place of connection and quiet solace. The pond was where we gathered year-round to spend time with friends and neighbors, swimming, skating and walking through the woods observing wildlife and enjoying the changing of the seasons.

During the summer of 2015, White Pond suffered an outbreak of toxic algae that made it unsafe for swimming. Global warming and human misuse are the two biggest factors in the alarming rise of toxic algae in bodies of water all over the planet.

While we were "thinking globally," we felt called to "act locally." As citizen activists we created a **Preserve White Pond** website and Facebook page, raised awareness, attended town meetings, met with town officials, wrote articles for the local paper and collaborated with others to develop an action plan to help heal the pond.

I learned that change is not simple or easy, but it is always possible. I was surprised what a big impact this local climate crisis had on me emotionally. I experienced once again how connected *my* well-being is to the well-being of Mother Earth. I felt even more compassion for all the people around the world whose lives are being affected far more catastrophically by climate change. These are the people who have been marginalized who have to live in places where pollution and sub-standard housing means more serious illnesses and a shorter life span.

I learned that in real life, as well as in the story of *Human Earth Awakening*, the path to creative change is using our personal power to tell the truth with love.

Living the new story

Writing this story with Robert helps me answer those questions I first asked on the beach that night long ago. Sitting on the rocks along the ocean's edge with Robert recently, watching the endless sea and sky and the waves crashing onto the rocks, I experienced that same feeling of awe and excitement I had as a child, now tempered with grief for the state of the world today. Then I was near the beginning of my life, now I am closer to the end.

I can see more clearly the power of stories to shape our consciousness and the course of history. I can see that the empire stories I learned as a child are at the root of the chaos in the world today. I see how those stories have devastated Mother Earth and brought her to the brink of extinction. Today I am heartened that so many people are refusing to believe in the old stories of patriarchy, exploitation and violence. I know that when we tell ourselves new stories that include everyone's voice that we can create a future based on equality and justice.

I understand now more than ever that my feeling of being one with the world is true. We are all one being. The recent pandemic caused by a microscopic virus showed me on a biological level how intimately connected I am to everything. It also showed me that life can change overnight and gives me faith in new possibilities.

I am living the story of *Human Earth Awakening* every day. Practicing the four roots of love, truth, peace and power helps me respond to the challenges of today's world. Now I have a story about my origin and destiny which restores my faith in humanity and includes women's voices. It clears my mind of the old stories of empire and heals my heart from the despair of living in a world of fear and anxiety. I am excited to be sharing *Human Earth Awakening* with you and our global family.

www.ingramcontent.com/pod-product-compliance
Lightning Source LLC
Chambersburg PA
CBHW032157190626
46814CB00005BA/2004